Jamie Mollart runs his own advertising company, and has won awards for marketing.

Over the years he has been widely published in magazines, been a guest on some well respected podcasts and blogs, and Patrick Neate called him 'quite a writer' on the Book Slam podcast. He is married and lives in Leicestershire with his wife and cat.

THE ZOO

Jamie Mollart

SANDSTONEPRESS
HIGHLAND | SCOTLAND

First published in Great Britain
And the United States of America
Sandstone Press Ltd
Dochcarty Road
Dingwall
Ross-shire
IV15 9UG
Scotland.

www.sandstonepress.com

Editor: Moira Forsyth

The publisher acknowledges support from
Creative Scotland towards publication of this volume.

ISBN: 978-1-910124-24-6
ISBNe: 978-1-910124-25-3

Jacket design by Jason Anscomb
Typeset by Iolaire Typesetting, Newtonmore.
Printed and bound by Totem, Poland

For my family.

Acknowledgements

To my wife, Sam, for putting up with me in every sense of the word.

To my parents for instilling an unshakable love of the written word and making it impossible for me to leave the house without a book in my bag.

To Mr Braddick, my English teacher. Teachers don't get enough credit for the work they do and when they inspire someone that deserves even more credit.

To Peter Cox, for teaching me that while writing is an art it is also a commercial concern, for seeing something in me and for pushing me on when I was near giving up.

To Henderson Mullin for picking up the phone when he did, for believing in me and for opening some doors.

To Tim Clare for his advice and wisdom, for showing me that less is more and many other clever and useful things.

To Dom White for inspirational reading material and literary curries.

To my agent Leslie, for taking a risk when others wouldn't.

To my editor Moira, for just getting it.

Whoever fights monsters should see to it that in the process he does not become a monster. And if you gaze long enough into an abyss, the abyss will gaze back into you.

Friedrich Nietzsche

1.

In the dark I can sense The Zoo.

I can't see it, but I know it is there. In the black it's blacker and I imagine the outlines of The Figurines and The Animals: all spikes and claws and weapons and sharp edges.

I can hear it too.

A buzzing. Like electricity in the air. A noise that lifts the hairs on your arms. As if it has to remind me at all times that it's there and active. I hear it over the noise of a shriek in the corridor outside my room; it may be laughter, or tears, I can't tell. Over the noise of bare feet slapping on the tiles. Over the click and whirr of the heating.

Over it all I can hear The Zoo.

It's the sound of blood in my veins and heartbeat in my ears and throat, of my fingers scratching on the coarse bedcover as I pull it over my head and the panic in my breathing.

When it becomes too much I force myself out of bed and try to confront it. But I stand impotent and wordless and it knows I am weak.

Time passes before I dredge up the words from my stomach. I question myself, I force my name out between bleeding gums.

It doesn't even sound like my name anymore. It's abstract and once removed.

'What do you want?' I scream and get only a fist banged on the wall from the room next door in reply.

The Zoo is mute and judgemental; it doesn't need to

justify itself to me, never has. It's the wires behind the TV, hopelessly knotted. It's a foreign dialect, impossible to translate.

It's been here as long as I have. I've asked them to take it away from me three times, but each time I sank into a despair that was physical and begged for it, so they returned it. We are tied together.

I face it off and it doesn't blink.

Of late it comes in the day. Fearsome explosions of noise and aggression that cause the world to shake until I collapse on my knees and the teeth rattle in my head, my eyes cry blood and every sinew tenses until I think they are going to rip. This continues until I plead for death and then it is silent.

'What do you want?' I ask in the darkness.

In the strip light day I try to ignore it. Stay in the day room, pace the corridors.

Eventually though, I return to my room to get my cigarettes and it is there in its place. Glowering.

So I have to break it down. Reduce it to its core components. Only then can I begin to unravel it.

This is how it goes.

At the very top sits The Cowboy.

He is crafted from metal, although his base is plastic. This seems to be the wrong way round. The metal is heavier and yet it's the plastic that does the supporting. In the past this has bothered me and I have tried to understand why he would be crafted this way, when the opposite is more logical, but the train of thought leads nowhere so I've buried it.

I used to believe he was made of lead, but I've absent-mindedly chewed at his body many times and, despite the obvious difficulties associated with my present location, I'm in rare health.

The brim of his Stetson is wide and elliptical, casting a shadow across his immovable face. One cannot help but be impressed by the firm set of his jaw and the steely determination of his chiselled bone structure. He is a formidable opponent.

The Cowboy has two Colts he knows as The Equalisers cocooned in patterned holsters on his belt and, in his right hand, a Winchester rifle. This is the Gun that won the West and it is this weapon that places him on top. He holds it with a knowing pride. He is aware of the power it gives him over the rest of The Zoo and I can see him lying by a campfire, head balanced on rolled-up bedding, hat tipped over his eyes, but always watchful, the rifle resting on his chest, rising and falling with his breathing, a gloved hand brushing the trigger. It is an image of self-awareness and danger and an acceptance of the unknown and it pleases me.

He means many things. He is the pushing of boundaries, the suppression of cultures. Colonial. He is the wide plains and the romance of adventure. He is the wild frontier. He is the contrast between the beige of the desert and the stark black silhouette of clapboard buildings. But he is also line dancing, and fat Americans, Boss Hog and the Marlboro Man who died of cancer.

The Cowboy is about the relationship of man with his surroundings, dwarfed and yet somehow integral. The unbalanced, but symbiotic, equation of human being within a landscape. A shape in a doorway, black against the dusty foreground, mountains poised in the distance, the possibilities of white clouds in a dome of perfect blue.

He is Eastwood and Jesse James. The neon sign waving over a temple to gambling. He is Shane and, at the same time, the Milky Bar Kid.

He is at the top. He is the principal and takes his place as a leader of men with a stoic acceptance I respect. He knows this is his position, he expects it, but doesn't seek it, and this is why it is his.

2.

It's a Friday afternoon. About three or four months ago I think, but time means less to me now than it did then, so this could be wildly inaccurate. We're in a Russian themed vodka bar, but they are running an Italian promotion. I'm sitting behind an uneven screen of Peronis. I look at the world through the green glass of the bottles and their gassy contents.

The bar is all black tiles and shine and chrome and glass and people drinking in the afternoon when they should be working.

It is as slick and shallow as spilled oil.

We've won a substantial pitch, so this counts as work and I am smug and drunk.

Outside, the sky hurls grey rain into the faces of the people who lean into it, heads pivoted sideways, the world slapping them on the cheek. Someone has spray-painted "What kills a skunk is the publicity it gives itself" onto the hoarding which skirts the scar of a building site. The letters are tall and tense, scrawled in haste.

'We fucking rock,' says Baxter, his face rouged by drink, hoisting his bottle in a toast. The others clink it and beer spills onto the polished glass tabletop.

I shoot him a glare.

'You fucking rock,' he corrects. I look at his jaw, which seems skew-whiff and clenched and I idly wonder whether he's had some coke and what I would do to him if he had.

'I do,' I confirm, 'I fucking rock.'

Later, in the toilets, Baxter collars me and slurs about how he respects me and it is an honour to work with me and he feels he has learned so much already, but if he could work on this account he would give it his all, and all I can think is his breath stinks of garlic and beer and it makes me feel bilious. Washing my hands, I scour his objectionable face in the mirror, really look at it, this backwards face. The other way round, and yet what he sees every day. I think half a thought about self-image, then it's gone, like the water down the plughole, and I stalk back to the bar.

Collins is talking to the group. He looks like an aftershave advert: chiselled and tanned, crisp white shirt under pinstripe suit. But I know his suit is from Marks and Spencer's. The female clients love him, some of the male clients too.

The barmaid catches my eye, her walk telling me stories. I could sell to her, she has ideas.

'The place where I used to work, the Creative Director, he was a real asshole,' says Collins, looking at me as if to point out that I'm not an asshole, 'I'll call him Mr Chips, because if I say his name you'll all know who he is, and I may need him as a reference one day.'

He grins at us all, milks the pause.

'Well, his wife phoned into the office one morning, really early, like 7.30 or something. It rang for a bit and then a newbie account exec picked it up and just answered "hello." This really fucked Mrs Chips off and she screamed down the phone, "That's not how you answer the phone, young man." The kid goes, "Fuck you" and this made Mrs Chips even angrier. ' "Do you know who this is?" she said. "No" says the kid. "This is Mrs Chips, your boss's wife," and she's getting madder and madder by the second. She's really fucking spewing by now. "Okay," says the kid, "do you know who this is?" "No," says Mrs Chips. "Good, then fuck you."'

Collins roars with laughter and the others join in. He has two silver fillings on his bottom teeth and a grey tongue. I peel the label off my beer and wait for them to calm down.

'That's not a true story, is it Collins?' I say, loud enough so he can hear, quiet enough to be threatening.

'What do you mean it's not true?'

'I mean, I've heard that story before, about a different Creative Director, somewhere else. But same story.'

'I'm not sure what you mean?'

'It's an urban myth. A legend. It didn't really happen. It's like the pencil up the nose in the exam, or the hook in the car door. It's made up. It's a funny story, but it didn't happen. You should know the difference, Collins. This is what we do. We make up stories.'

I peer over his sagging head at the barmaid. She is glasses and cleavage and pouting lips. She makes me want to drink. I go to the bar and order a round of shots. One little capful of clear, burning liquid for everyone. She flirts with me and I look down her top. The edge of a black bra. It looks like home.

In the early hours, as we weave out into the night, I put my arm around Collins and whisper in his ear.

'I was only fucking with you, Collins. That story was true, but it was about me. I was the account exec. Now I'm the Creative Director. Go figure.'

3.

My room is about the size of a broom cupboard. The walls are steely grey and as soft to the touch as sea-smoothed bone. The ceiling is covered by chip paper. In the light of the uncovered bulb the bumps cast the shadows of insects and my skin crawls. I often stand on tiptoes on the bed, muscles in my thighs straining to keep me steady on the sagging mattress and surrendering springs, trying to flatten the chips into the ceiling. My under-exercised legs scream and I inevitably slump back onto the bed, frustrated.

Out in the corridor I see Beaker. This isn't his name. I don't know his name, or if I do I have forgotten it. But he looks like the Muppet. His head is long and cylindrical, his top lip doesn't move when he talks and his eyes panic behind thick glasses.

He mutters something I can't quite catch, but I think I hear the words 'Amateur Photography Magazine'. He holds an imaginary camera to his face and mimes pulling focus on me. I smile, a lopsided affair that hides my teeth, and pose. The tourist at the edge of the precipice uncaring of the fatal drop behind. In the muted quiet I hear the click of the shutter.

In the day room we slouch around a large scratched table with smoothed-off corners and try to be creative. Creativity is the core element of our recovery. This is ironic considering it was one of the core components in my fall.

Plastic scissors and Pritt Stick and paper.

7

I watch a heavily bearded man suck his moustache in and out of his mouth, fascinated by the pinkness of the tip of his tongue, but after a while it begins to make me feel wrong. He starts an argument about the volume of the television with a microscopic Asian lady, who always cuddles an old radio. 'We're trying to concentrate', he is screaming at her, spit flying from his mouth and landing in the hair of a catatonic next to him.

'Fuck you,' she shouts back, 'Fuck you, fuck you, fuck you, fuck you, fuck you . . .' Tailing off until she is just standing there whispering it. I try to read her lips. Across the table the Beard is riled, I can see it in him; he is tensed and unable to let it go even though she has turned the volume down. He storms over to her and she is still mouthing 'fuck you, fuck you,' just a whisper, and he puts his Beardy face really close to her peanut of a head and roars 'CUNT', throwing a hand full of coloured paper into her face. All hell breaks loose and I skulk away to the outside smoking area.

This from my childhood: crossing fields with my jeans soaking up dew. The sun on a window, highlighting the fingerprints of a child, one, two, three, more, a lattice-work of little hands.

I think this now as I breathe my smoke into the cold air and gaze in through the glass at the Beard being dragged down the corridor, the soles of his shoes drawing a rubber eleven on the tiles.

It's like watching a silent movie.

In the night I think of her and when we were first together. I hold her hand under the covers, the most lingering of touches. She grips my index finger, instinctively, gently. A newborn. Her body is warm next to mine, comforting. Although we aren't touching, apart from the so slender

8

contact of her fingers, I'm aware of where she is, where every contour of her body is. She rolls towards me, her breathing a whisper which moves the hairs on my arms. Each movement is laden with potential, unspoken futures, and I move away, release my finger from her grasp. Immediately I regret it, the distance cold and prohibitive. I understand the shading on this moment will make up the background for others in the future, so I roll close to her again, my lips pressed against her neck. She smells of promises and of sharing. She moans and I wrap my arms around her, feel her chest rise against the inside of my forearms and now I remember her by the beat of her heart.

I freeze this, am just left with brittle sheets against my face and the orange of streetlights invading my room in slats, highlighting the shapes of The Zoo and mocking my restlessness.

In the morning the world is the colour of old chewing gum and I'm faced with a wall of depression that hems me in. I try to pass around it, but it envelops me completely until there is nothing else. I sit in the courtyard, smoke endless cigarettes and watch the hexagon of dull sky above me. A seagull flies across my view, far up. I think of its perception of the horizon and feel momentarily dizzy. I rest my face against the rough bricks and run it backwards and forwards. The texture against my skin, the noise of my stubble scratching against it, my nail under a piece of gum squashed onto the bench, the beaten down grey wood I sit on: these things are everything.

4.

Managing Director looks at me, expectant and eager. He's waiting for me to say something, like he asked me a question, but I don't recall him asking one. It's hot in the presentation room, the floor to ceiling glass wall acting like a greenhouse. I can feel the warmth on my cheek and it is not altogether unpleasant, and I can't help but think of car journeys with my parents and a summer English lesson.

Managing Director peers at me over his glasses, his steely eyes seem to have sunk deeper into his wrinkled face. He's small. A wave of salt and pepper hair drooping over one eye. Stack heels. A handkerchief in a blazer pocket. A mouth puckered from years of smoking.

'Well?' he asks, 'What have you got for us?'

'Dutch bank. Tenth biggest bank in the world. Recently re-located here, in London. Weren't touched too badly by the downturn in the world finances.'

I pause and look around the table at the supposed cream of our agency. They are gawping at me open-mouthed and empty-headed.

Through the plate glass windows of the meeting room I watch a plane cross a blue sky, a powder puff trail spreading behind it. Opposite I count the windows on a tower block, become annoyed that there are more on the left side than the right, that they don't line up properly. A magpie lands on the roof of the office block. One for sorrow.

I realise I've been talking, and they've been taking notes,

only when someone closes a pad and they begin to leave the table.

The magpie explodes into the sky.

Sometime later I'm sitting in the worn corner of our local. Managing Director is half soaked, his head rolling a bit. He's muttering and his voice is all echoes and slurs in his pint glass. I would love to ram it in his face. Or smash it on the table and stick the jagged edge into his throat. I don't even think he would bleed, cunt is so dried up. If you cut him, his insides would have the texture of a mushroom.

We have one meeting and the reward is to come and sit here for the afternoon, in the dozy womb of a half empty pub.

I need to piss again.

It splashes on my feet as I focus on the yellow river lapping back and forth in the metal tray of the urinal. As I dry my hands I read the condom machine. Rooting around in my pocket I find a pound coin and choose ribbed for extra pleasure. For him and for her. When I get back to the table I slip the packet into the pocket of Managing Director's overcoat, for his wife to find later. It makes the next pint taste that little bit sweeter.

'This could be the making of you,' he says to me, but it sounds like one long, gloopy word, the syllables running all over each other.

'What?' I ask.

'The bank, this could be the making of you.'

'I wasn't aware that I needed making?'

He's fumbling with a packet of crisps. Gives up. Throws them down onto the table.

'We all need making. Every single one of us. Write your own history, son. This could be your Sergeant Pepper or Rattle and Hum.'

I squint at him as I drain the last of my pint, his face

distorted and rolling in the liquid. I'm unable to compre-
hend the juxtaposition of those two albums. In the car park
back at work he fumbles with his car keys and drops them
underneath the wheel. I pick them up, hand them to him,
then lean against the wall and watch him trying to start it.

5.

The ward is quiet. Angel ladders fall through the skylights and kiss the floor at intervals. I dip my hand into one, expecting heat, but there is none.

In the day room I sit opposite Mark. He's drawing something, concentrating real hard, I can see it in his brow. He cocks his head from side to side like a bird. I look at the top of his head for a long time. His shoulder-length hair is tied back in a scraggly ponytail, starting from the middle of his head. I've never really noticed this before.

'What are you drawing mate?'

He glances up from his work, then pushes a finger hard onto the paper and pivots the drawing round it. I try to move it closer, but he holds it firm. The drawing is childlike and shows little talent, but I've asked so I look. It's of him, I can tell from the hair. But it's a disproportionate him, viewed from the back. He is at a doorway and above the door is an exit sign.

'What is it?' I ask him.

'The doorway to wellbeing,' he replies, his voice drowsy.

I study his face for irony, but there's none. One of his eyes is closing, as if his face is wrinkled in a smile, but it's not. A giggly eye – full of medication.

'Do you fancy a fag?' I ask, putting the packet on top of his drawing.

'Go on then,' he says, sliding the cigarettes back to me, then, picking up the drawing, he folds it very deliberately into four, going over each crease again and again, and then pushes it into the pocket of his tight jeans.

Outside I perch on the back of the bench, my feet on the seat. Mark circles the yard. On the other side of the wall someone shouts something I can't decipher. I'm not even sure it is English.

'Did you hear that? Mark? Did you hear that?'

He either hasn't heard me or chooses not to reply. I tap my feet on the bench and little puffs of dust rise about them.

Somewhere in the past she puts her arm around my neck as I am sketching at my desk and I breathe in the vanilla perfume on her wrists.

'I love it when you draw,' she says.

'I don't get to do it so much anymore,' I reply.

'I know. Bloody computers.'

She snorts with laughter.

'You're such a fucking Luddite,' I say, craning my face back to try and kiss her, but she pulls away.

'You're working.'

'You've distracted me now.'

'I'll just sit here and watch.'

'It's too late. You've broken the spell. You're supposed to be my muse. Not distract me.'

'Don't sulk. You look like a petulant child when you pull that face. It's not attractive.'

She sits down on the sofa at the back of my office, crosses one leg over the other and rests her hands palm down on her knee. Like the teacher she is.

'Go on. Carry on. I like watching you.'

I raise an eyebrow at her then turn my attention back to the paper. It's a campaign for a pest control company. I've run this over and over in my head for a couple of days now, but am no closer to a solution. I'm struggling to decide between two approaches. Either balls out declarations of

14

being able to kill everything or softly-softly, makes your garden a nicer environment. I pop the lid off a marker pen and take an illicit sniff of it. I half-heartedly sketch out a facsimile of an ant, but the moment has gone.

'It's no good,' I say, spinning in my chair, 'You've ruined my concentration. Now you're going to have to make up for it.'

She laughs, a rich, clean, melodic sound that resonates about the office, and then she stands to meet me halfway across the room.

Mark is hunched down over the work surface, waiting for the kettle to boil. Something is kicking off in the day room. The sound of a chair being kicked over. A scuffle. Then nothing. I roll my eyes at Mark and he smirks and rolls his back. The kettle clicks off, filling the small kitchen with steam. I take two stained mugs out of the cupboard and drop in a couple of tea bags. I run my finger around the rim of one.

'This one's chipped.' I tell him. 'Not very hygienic. I'll have this one.'

'Cheers,' he replies.

On the fridge someone has written "suck my balls" with the magnetic letters. I push my hand through, scattering them out over the surface. Taking the milk out, I sniff, pour it into one mug, then the other.

'Say when.'

'When.'

He holds his tea between his hands, blows into the top of it, then drinks it with a slurp. We go back through to the day room. It's quieter now, everyone has left, the TV is on but silent, showing the local sports news. I look about for the remote control, but can't find it. Mark comes up behind me.

'They're shit. City. They're shit. I don't know why I bother with them. They only ever piss me off. I swear I can count the times I've come out of that ground with a smile on my face on one hand.'

I settle into one of the armchairs and balance my tea on a wooden arm. We sit in silence for a while, watching the TV screen, people mouthing words at us. There is something hypnotic about it. After a while I give up attempting to work out what they are saying and just gawp at the shapes their mouths make. Oval, circle, pout, oval, teeth, smile.

'Mark?'

'Uh-huh?'

'You from round here? Your accent's not a Leicester accent is it?'

'No, I'm from Derby originally.'

He says it Darbeh. He's lying back in the chair, his feet crossed in his hightop trainers with their scuffed toes and lolling tongues.

'How did you end up here?'

'What, in here?'

'No, Leicester.'

'We moved over here when I was a kid. Me Dad got work in a hosiery factory down Frog Island. Course, they've all gone. It's a shithole down there now.'

'Not for long. They want to turn all the old factories into apartments.'

'Like we need more apartments. How many ponces do they think live in one city?'

He's grinning at me with a gap-tooth grin and I know I should have laughed so I squeeze one out for him. I hold my mug up to my face, push my chin into it and enjoy the heat rising against my skin. I don't really know what else to say to him and after a bit he gets up and starts to leave.

'I think I'm going to get an early night,' he says.

16

'Okay, 'night then.'

He walks across the room, his slippers slapping on the tiles. When he reaches the door I call out to him 'Mark?'.

'Yes?' he replies, but I realise I haven't got a reason to stop him.

'Nothing. 'Night.'

''Night.'

I sit on my own until my tea is cold. I imagine that it's a cool, illicit pint, sizzling on my tongue and insinuating its way down, and my psyche reaches out over the walls clamouring for it. I wait as long as I can before returning to my room. I pause outside it and put the palm of my hand flat against the door. I can feel The Zoo hum through the wood and know that it won't let me be, so I turn away and attempt to delay it a bit longer.

6.

It always starts like this. Cramp in my calves.

I try to massage it out, hoping it's only cramp, but it's not and I know it isn't. This hope, that there is a natural explanation for all this, never really goes away, I cling onto it, even as I should dismiss it.

I'm talking to the night porter when it starts. He's behind the desk, telling me about his kids, two of them, a boy and a girl. Then the sound goes funny, like a wah wah pedal, and I know it's on the way.

Not now, not now, I silently plead, please not now.

It doesn't listen to me. It never listens.

I bite my bottom lip as it tightens on my legs. I'm squeezing my fists, forcing nails into my palms, straining to keep a smile on my face, looking for a break in his speech so I can leave, but now he's taken out photos and is holding them out to me. I know I'm supposed to take them, but my hands are shaking and there's blood in my palm, so instead I smile and nod.

Make it stop, make it stop, make it stop.

I concentrate on my breathing. Focus on it. Count it. In. Out. In. Out. The Zoo is shouting louder, drowning out the counting. Louder, always louder, so I try and concentrate on the porter, his face rippling like a reflection in a pond after someone has thrown a stone into it. Concentric circles across his face and onto the wall, the ceiling, then up over my head. I blink hard, shake my head, causing the ripples

18

to change direction and I feel nausea rising, a warmth in my throat, try to focus on him, pick a point on his face and really drill into it. He's talking about his children's mother and how he loves her and the pain is so intense my vision is spotted with stars, explosions across each eye so I can hardly make out his features. Somewhere he's asked me if I've got any children.

'A son,' I force the words out, a croak in a voice that doesn't belong to me.

Another wave of nausea hits me and my stomach tightens. I mumble something about having to go and he's asking me 'everything alright mate?' as I back away from him, cannon into a wall, nodding, saying 'I'm fine, I'm fine'. I double over and he puts a hand on my shoulder, but I shrug it off, saying 'stomach cramps'.

I'm away down the corridor, the walls curling in over me, the door to my room moving further away, perspective shrinking. My hand is big on the handle and the metal hot and heavy to my touch, then I'm inside, sliding down the door.

The sensation grips my legs and I try and stretch my toes out. It feels as if a vice is being tightened on me so I scream out and roll myself up in the foetal position. It's on my back now, pressing into my spine, I can feel it rattle off the vertebrae, one by one, slowly at first, then quicker, quicker, until I feel it throughout my body, my teeth against each other, clacking, and my vision is blurred by the movement. I squeeze my eyes shut, behind the lids there is an explosion of colours and I become dizzy. The weight of it presses me down into the bed and the material of the bedspread is in my mouth, choking me, forcing down my throat. I'm struggling to breathe, nose squashed against the bed, the material blocking my airway. I try to push back against the weight, enraging it further, and it pushes me harder. I can feel my bones creak, my skull feels like it is going to crack, my eyes bulging. The blood rushes to my head, pumping in my temple, my face burning red. I attempt to scream for help, my face in the bed, the words gone, muffled, useless, and this is happening to me and me on my own.

When I think I can take no more, when I think I am actually going to die, the weight is off me and I can breathe again. It lets me take a few breaths, I'm reaching for them, snatching at them and then the noise starts.

First the sound of waves on a shore, pebbles against pebbles, the clack of stones, the water itself, rolling over and over. This grows in intensity, tinnitus filling my head. Then a clanging: the clanging of bells, not church bells, not tuneful, more the sound of a ball being kicked against a garage door, a dull metallic ringing, discordant.

In one ear, then through my head to the other ear. I press my palms onto my head, try to block the sound, but it is in me now, it is of me and it is too late.

All the air is sucked out of the room and I exist momentarily in a vacuum. I panic and flail about. I always do this, even though I know it is temporary. My fingers scrape into the wallpaper, ripping it beneath my nails. It bunches up in furrows as I plough it.

Then the air comes rushing back in and it smells of sulphur and burning and it is close and hot, scalding me as I breathe it in. I can taste it, feel it singeing the hair in my nostrils, prickling my eyelashes. I gasp.

Then on top of that the noises return, the sound of static electricity in the air and in it are words I can't make out, like a choir or the murmur of a discontented crowd. I can feel myself lifted, buoyed by it and I fight, struggling to keep myself grounded, my feet dangling, and I bob for a second on it, then it is a rough sea and I am thrown against one wall, then the other, each time with a thud that winds me, I try to stop myself with an outstretched hand but the

20

force of it snaps my wrist back and I cry out in pain. Then my face is pressed against the ceiling, the chipboard cutting into my cheek, my legs thrashing about for purchase where there is none. The noise of it fills everything. I can't tell whether it is in my head or outside, or both. I can't hear my own voice but know I am screaming out. The Zoo is speaking to me and it is a vengeful God.

I wake on top of the sheets, half on the bed, half off. I run my hands over my body and look for injury. I find none, so I roll my body and test the floor with my feet.

The Zoo is still.

In the half-light of early morning it is safe. The outside is trying to force its way through the blinds in silver-blue slivers. I get up and cautiously avoiding making eye contact with The Zoo. I split the blinds with my fingers and find a world that is two-dimensional. In the trees above the chain mail fence a rook barks at me. From the main road I can hear the thrum of cars. They seem miles away. The sky is threatening morning, wisps of cloud light with the hint of day.

I can feel the presence beneath me, so I kneel, let the blinds snap back into place and now I am eye level with The Zoo. I know I can do this now; it never comes for me twice in such quick succession. There is always a break, as if it has to recharge itself or regroup, or let me recover before it takes from me again.

I look right at it.

'What are you?' I ask it.

It says nothing. Why would it? It doesn't need to say a thing.

I clamber back into bed and doze fitfully.

I wake again to the sound of screaming and a commotion in the hall. It takes a second to register this as real and, when it does, I jump upright, rush out of my room and into chaos. There are people everywhere, jostling and running about. A nurse passes me, head in hands, muttering to herself, 'I can't believe it, I can't believe it'.

I attempt to halt an orderly. He brushes me aside and heads into the depths of the ward. Beaker comes out of the day room. I stop him with hands on his shoulders.

'What's going on?'

'Wrong, wrong, wrong, wrong,' he replies, spittle on his lips, wild in his eyes.

In the day room there are a crowd of people, inmates and orderlies, huddled about one of the armchairs. I try to force myself through, but the group is too tight and I can't. Then I see the wall and I know who they are encircling and why. I slump down at the table. Everything is knocked from me. I slam my forehead on the table again, the vibration passing up through my body.

Then I force myself to look.

In the centre of the wall is Mark's picture. The one he folded. Above the picture is his ponytail, severed at the root and stuck to the plaster with Sellotape. About it, speckled with glitter and star shapes are words written in shit, big and ragged and from hell. Then around this, lumps of shit have been lobbed at the wall. Beneath the picture and the hair is drawn a smiley face, like the Acid badge from 90s rave culture. I look at the words and I moan.

There is no way out.
There is no way back.
This is all there is.
This is it.

7.

We're in one of the glass pods that line the main office space. The blinds are lowered, lights off. It's warm in here. We're all squinting at a projection on the far wall. Collins is fucking about with the MacBook Pro, trying to get what's on the screen onto the wall.

'I hate these things,' he whines, 'every time I try and use them, this happens.'

'It's got to be something you're doing then,' Client Services Director, to my right.

'I don't know, I swear it does it to make me look stupid.'

'If it does, then it's doing a bang-on job.' The others laugh at my joke. Probably through politeness.

Collins glowers at me from over the top of the laptop screen. His face lit from underneath like a Halloween pumpkin.

'Turn it off and turn it back on again,' I say.

Baxter, to my left, sniggers into the back of his hand. I dip the tip of my finger into my glass of water, allow it to drip off onto the tabletop and try and stretch the droplets out into my name. I only get the J and the A done before Collins guffaws in triumph and the company logo appears on the wall behind him.

'I'll skip through the creds, you know what's in them. Blah blah. Right.'

He pauses here. Points at the screen.

'The Big Idea. Transparency.'

He enunciates it with a flourish. Teases out each syllable. Tran-spa-ren-cy.

'We need to have absolute transparency. You have been allowed to hide behind the old institutions for too long. Old boys' networks and funny handshakes. Our money spent doing God knows what.'

A second of darkness as the slide changes, then a picture of a baying mob, black and white, grainy, Baader-Meinhof maybe.

'We need to get from here. To here,' says Collins and clicks through to the next slide.

A 50s style picture of a classroom, robotic kids in a row, eyes front, attention on the teacher, blond hair and the whitest of teeth.

The warmth of the room is making me tired. There is a weight in my eyelids. I begin to drift away from what he is saying. I need to do something to snap myself out of this torpor.

'Wait. Collins. Go back. Go back to the beardy-weirdy revolutionaries. Yes there. Stop.'

I look at the picture for a while. Everyone is waiting for me to say something.

'What the fuck are we trying to say here? The population of England is so pissed off that they are likely to turn into hairy fucking German terrorists? And that what we really want is to turn them back into the Stepford fucking children?'

'They're just pictures?' offers Collins.

'Just pictures? Just fucking pictures. Fuck me. How long have you worked here? Just fucking pictures. There's no such thing as just fucking pictures.'

'Visual metaphors?'

'For what? What the fuck are you trying to say? Who put this together? Collins, sort those two slides out. Next time I see it I want to have something in place of those two, not just some pictures we used because some teenage art-worker liked the look of them. Jesus.'

The room is quiet now. I can hear the fan of the laptop. Client Services Director raises an eyebrow at me. I sneer back at him and suck my teeth.

'Get on with it,' I say. 'And go straight to the campaign visuals.'

Pictures of an obvious banker type, pinstripe suit, red tie, arms outstretched, being searched by what looks like airport security. The headline reads 'We've got nothing to hide' and the rejoining text 'so you know your money is safe with us.'

'Good,' I say, 'show me more.'

Later in the corridor Managing Director stops me with a hand on my shoulder. He is all smiles, Stepford too, but with a weariness to his face.

'The Bank looks good,' he says.

'Thanks. You okay? You look tired.'

'Yes. Fine. Don't worry, trouble at mill, you know, the bread knife. Stroppy old bitch. Nothing I can't handle. When do you present?'

'Next Wednesday. At three.'

'Excellent. Let me know how it goes.'

'Will do.'

The following morning and I'm stuck in traffic. My car smells of winter meadows. The speedo is white with black Times New Roman numerals and I've been watching the needle as it points at zero for what seems like half an hour. The stereo is on. The seats are tan leather and they creak as I shift my weight.

We are next to the glass monstrosity of the new shopping centre. Above our heads a bridge acts as an umbilical cord between the womb of the car park and the shopping centre. I can see a flock of feet clattering across it and I giggle a little, thinking of Billy Goat Gruff. Collins is next to me. He has been spitting hyperbole forever.

'I mean. There's no proposition. There's no fucking brief. How can we put anything together without a brief? I mean. Come on. She's supposed to be a marketing director and she's totally fucking clueless.'

I look across at him and he's all smirking smugness.

'I mean, she must know that without a good brief you can't do fuck all. We may as well be in the sixties.'

I've no idea what he means by this and I don't think he does either. There is a spot of blood on his white collar.

'We are the music makers and we are the dreamers of dream,' I say to him.

He nods enthusiastically, thinking me profound. The blood on his collar seems to be spreading. The traffic starts moving again. We pull level with a truck and I realise it belongs to one of our clients. 'Call now' it says in a big, crass starburst on the side. I jump the red lights and burst away from it and when I think about the van again later I can't be sure that the number on it wasn't mine.

8.

Beaker peers at me. His eyes are narrow and they dart about so it takes me a second to realise he is addressing me.

'It's not right.'

'It's not,' I reply.

'It's not right,' he says again, this time with a little more force.

'I know. It's not.'

This time he leans right into me. His breath smells of mint and whistles down his nose. It reminds me of cocaine and my brain stretches out for it. This is how the white lady works. Even when it's out of your system and your body has long since forgotten all about it, your brain remembers and reminds you.

'It's not right.'

'I fucking know. I said it's not. What else do you want me to say?'

He sighs and repeats it once more, then spins on his heels, his shoes squeaking as he walks away.

Since the ponytail incident I'm sure the dosage of the meds has been increased. I'm in a funk. The drugs dull me. I don't really know what they are. They reduce everything to the static of an un-tuned TV. Like when I was a child and the transmissions stopped with a pop, the image contracting on itself and then for hours there was nothing but the dancing of the fuzz. Hypnotic. Empty. They questioned everybody, but no-one knew anything. No-one said anything.

The ward is an uncomfortable place to be, so I go back to my room. I look at The Zoo. Using only my peripheral vision I consider The Knight, get thinking about him and where he sits.

Secondary to The Cowboy is The Knight. I suspect he is from the Round Table, but am unsure so wouldn't presume to name him Gawain or Lancelot or Percival. He is just The Knight. He too is cast from metal, but the painting is a little more slapdash, as if it is done by machine or a less skilled hand than that of The Cowboy. This is one of the reasons that he is second, as well as the lack of a Winchester.

The Knight has a long sword as his peacemaker and he leans nonchalantly on it as he looks off into the distance, the wind whipping his dark shoulder-length hair up around his face. It is this alertness that makes him The Cowboy's lieutenant; he is surveying the horizon, protecting The Cowboy's domain. But I have to wonder whether he is happy with this position, whether that alertness alludes to something more sinister.

The Knight wears a full suit of armour, has spurs as sharp as razors and a red cloak with a dragon painted on it in gold. He has a scarlet plume on his helmet that curls down the back of it, proud as a rooster. He faces out at the world from behind a shield with a spike in the centre. His armour is broken down into panels – shin pads, knee pads, box over his groin, breastplate, upper arm and lower arm, metal gauntlets. His weak spots are between them. I want to dig at the space behind his knees with my fingernails.

He is Morte D'Arthur and I think of its author locked in a cell, collating myths. He is greedy empires and attacks on a Holy City. He is about honour and dignity and chivalry, and the contradiction behind killing in the name of God.

He is the chess piece that moves forward two, left one or forward one, left two or forward one and right two.

He is about fighting for an ideal, for belief even if that means committing wrong in the process. He is the muscle behind a cause. The horrific violence that only unthinking loyalty can deliver.

He is a Knight before his title was given to benevolent pop stars and retired football players.

He is the Templars and the White Knight, but also a perma-tan eighties actor in a black car with a moving red light.

He looks up at one and down at many, me included.

9.

Another day. A Thursday in November of blue ice and low sun that chops your windscreen in two and makes it impossible to drive. I leave the car on a terraced street and cross a road as snow hangs in the air, in my mouth, in my eyelashes.

A bar. A line of what I think is coke but probably isn't. Fear is at the edge of everything. I buy a gram of actual chop to clear my head. Just the one to sort me out. But it's never one, and there's a bottle of vodka in the middle of the table.

Walking home, listening to Led Zeppelin on my iPod, as I slip on ice and land on my elbow, half in the road, half out, asking the sky, 'How many more times?'

When I get in the house is dark and I stumble over loose shoes in the hall. In the kitchen I fill a glass with tap water and gulp it down, pouring it over my chin and shirt. I drink another. Have to close one eye to judge the distance of the glass to the tap, still can't stop myself from clanking the rim against the metal.

The stairs creak. I stumble. See the nightlight under my boy's door, want to go in and sit with him, to watch him sleep. I don't.

She's turned away from me, but I can tell she's not asleep.

I undress, clothes in a pile. The air's cold. So is the duvet as I climb under it.

I whisper, 'I'm sorry.'

'Fuck you,' she replies.

'Meeting ran over.'

She snorts and turns further away.

'Sally?' I touch her shoulder, feel her tense, take my hand away.

I try to sleep but can't, instead run over things in my mind, over and over. Work and us. Us. Mostly us. I want to roll over, spoon her, press myself against her. It's just because of the coke I say to myself, just the coke, making you think like this, she's annoyed because you're late, that's all.

I watch the slice in the curtains change colour.

I sweat.

When she gets up to go to work I pretend to be asleep. I listen to her get him ready for school. Imagine her helping with his shoes and his gloves, putting the sandwiches in his Sponge Bob box. Hear their conversation in the kitchen.

She comes back into the bedroom to get her handbag. As she leaves the room she turns back and looks at me, I snap my eyes shut too late and she notices.

When she leaves I pad into the kitchen and collect a selection of cutlery. Hold a spare duvet over the window and use the cold knives and spoons to wedge it under the curtain rail. The room is pitch black. Turning my phone off I collapse back into bed and sleep in shallow bursts, dreams filled with faceless figures in autumnal parks.

The morning of the pitch, a week later, smoking a cigarette in my car. The rain plays a solo on the roof, sobs down the windscreen. Collins taps along on the top of the laptop case.

'Will you fucking stop that?' I ask.

'Sorry,' he says.

I watch my smoke hit the inside of the windscreen and

31

spread out across it. Collins starts tapping again. I lay my hand on top of his. He stops. I leave my hand there for a second, squeeze his fingers and when he looks at me I can see the nerves in his eyes so I smile.

'We've got this,' I say and he nods.

I take another drag of the cigarette. Paper crackles. Opening the door I let it drop onto the wet tarmac where it fizzes and dies.

'Okay.' I take a packet of Extra Strong mints from the glove compartment, put two in my mouth and pass them to Collins.

I step out into the rain, closing the door with my knee. Water runs down my face, drips from the end of my nose, where I catch it with my tongue and taste metal. We cross the car park, aquaplaning. Through the automatic revolving doors, Collins missing the gap, stepping into the next, his face is stretched by the glass, ugly, contorted, then we are in the foyer, met by a wall of warmth, stifling, and for a second I gasp for air, loosen my scarf, gulp. Then we're through it, at a huge curved desk, the mahogany cold on palms and I'm looking into the smiling face and cold eyes of a beautiful girl who is saying 'Can I help you?'

I tell her my name, then Collins' and she gesticulates at a visitors' book. I sign us in, with a signature that doesn't look like mine. She's on the phone, saying my name, and then she's smiling at me again, asking me to take a seat, pointing at a sofa.

We sit. And wait.

Music in the air.

Smell of perfume.

Collins' breathing.

Through this I struggle to identify the music. No vocals, just guitar and I can't place it.

A man comes in, leans over the desk, kisses the receptionist on the cheek, only his toes touching the floor. They laugh and my mind is full of Sally.

Then another man is standing in front of me.

'Berkshire,' he says and holds out his hand. I shake it and as we follow him I catch a glimpse of my game face in the window of an office and feel a surge of confidence.

10.

Delicate hands against a porcelain face. Round tears in black eyes that dart about, but are cloudy and half blind under cataracts of medication. Beneath the blur and the weeping and the panicked search for words is a smudge of intelligence and with it a warmth, the first I've seen in here. It makes me want to listen to her. I turn my chair from the TV, try to drown out the chunter of Beard.

'It's about dignity,' she's saying.

I reach back, search for the object of her sentence. But I'm foggy too and can't find it.

'Dignity,' she says again.

She's talking to an old man. He's nodding. I move my chair closer to them. She smiles at me, a gap between her teeth. I mouth 'Hi'.

Drugged boy meets drugged girl.

Hear the music in the background of the advert, feel the words scrolling under my chin and wonder what I'm selling. Hope it's something good.

She's staring at me.

'Beth,' she says and from her voice I know it is hand cream or shampoo or perfume.

'James,' I say and hold out a weak hand. She takes it, her fingers like toys amongst mine, her skin cool and soft.

As she takes her hand back the sleeve of her hoodie rides up over the white of a bandage. Her body folds in on itself. I watch her shrivel. I raise my left hand and when

34

she sees the bandage over my thumb and around my palm she unwinds, fills her body again, says 'Snap' and gifts me a wan smile.

I'm unsure what to say, so we fall silent. Just the chatter of the TV, where Jeremy Kyle is launching into somebody, saying, 'You've got to take responsibility for yourself, you've got a child now, you can't be out there running around with your boys, you've got to be a man, you've made a life and now you're responsible for it, don't smirk, look at you sitting there smirking, it's not funny, my friend, this isn't a joke, let me make something very clear for you, you can't . . .' and then an orderly is speaking quietly to Beth and leading her away. As she passes me I hold my breath and she whispers something that sounds like 'damaged'.

I look about the day room. Mark is sitting in an armchair, a magazine on his lap. I walk over, lift the cover of the magazine, try not to notice his flinch and ask, 'What you reading?' He doesn't reply. It's a copy of Hello magazine with the Beckhams on the cover. At least three years old.

'Not a lot to be learned from that, mate,' I say.

He shrugs.

I pat my pockets for cigarettes, find them empty, so return to my room. I pause at the door and count to ten. Nothing, so I push the door open and tense in readiness. Light streams into the room. The window is open and it smells cold and fresh and safe. I pull the window shut and as I do my elbow catches The Pirate and sends him tumbling from the shelf, bouncing off the radiator and skidding across the floor.

I freeze.

I swallow my heartbeats.

Outside a siren rips the day in two.

Nothing happens.

I pick The Pirate up.

Still nothing happens.

I put him back in place in The Zoo.

The adrenalin surges through me like mercury. I run to the bathroom, fall to my knees in front of the toilet and vomit stomach lining into the bowl. When it stops I wipe my eyes, fill a plastic cup with water and swill my mouth out. Fetching my cigarettes out of my bedside table I study The Zoo.

'I don't understand,' I say to it and get the impression that it doesn't want me to.

Later I look about for Beth. When I catch Mark's eye he hurriedly looks back into his magazine.

Outside in the courtyard I spark up my fag and squat on the bench. In the corridor I catch a glimpse of blond hair and there's Sally again. The night we met. Student halls. The first Friday. I'm young, drunk, cocky and stupid. She's a couple of years older. Wiser. Sexy. Distant. She holds everyone off. It means we all want her.

The whole hall goes into town. A grey Nottingham. Stumbling into pubs, unsure of which are student friendly. I'm laughing at the way they talk. The northern-ness of it all. A barman calls me 'duck' and I dive into Stella laughter. Later, a club, a Ritzy or a Park Lane or Dazzle or Razzle or Glitzy or fuck knows. She passes a pill from her mouth to mine, electric shocks as our tongues touch and I fall in love.

Following day we're all coming down and the reality of the world frays the edges. I knock on her door and she tells me to come in. It's cold. I get under the duvet with her. She's naked. She's so tiny and skinny. My heart bounces off every one of her ribs.

She says, 'You've caught me on a come down, it's not fair, I'm horny as hell,' and pulls me in for a kiss that tastes of cigarettes and last night.

She teaches me how to go down on her properly with tuts and guiding hands.

I fall in love again.

Inside the ward a door slams and I look at the cigarette, which is just a filter between burned fingers.

11.

When the call comes I'm talking to Baxter in the kitchen. He's hungover and trying to hide it so I'm forcing him to explain the complexities of a direct mail campaign he's organising for a local university.

'How can you be so targeted?' I ask.

'Because there's only 100 targets.'

'What do you mean there's only 100 targets? Surely what they offer can apply to everyone who wants to go to university?'

He gets a cup out of the cupboard and drops it hard onto the work surface, where it bounces and rights itself. He looks at me with startled deer eyes.

'No, no. It's not the students. It's businesses. Didn't I explain this?' he asks.

My phone rings. I recognise the number.

'Need to take this, Baxter,' I say, and watch the relief wash across his face in a tide.

I step out into the corridor, take a couple of deep breaths and when I answer the phone I am calmness and professionalism and nonchalance.

'Mr Berkshire,' I say.

There's a pause. He's making me sweat. This can be good or bad. Like the judge of some cheap talent show on Saturday night TV, the audience waiting for him with bated breath. Then he tells me we've got the work, asks me when I can come in to sign the contract and begin the creative process. He calls it this: the creative process. I pretend to consult a diary, tell him next Wednesday and that I'll get my PA to confirm with his, but really I'll cancel anything that's already booked for that time. He tells me he's looking forward to it. I thank him and hang up. Shout 'Fuck yeah' in an echoing corridor.

I manage to keep a straight face as I walk back through the office and knock on Managing Director's door. There's a muffled response through thick wood, so I open it and peer round, 'Hilary?'.

'Yes?' he looks up from the pink pages of the FT.

'You got a moment?' I ask.

'Of course.' He folds the paper and puts it aside. I close the door behind me.

'Bank?' He asks. I nod. 'Well?'

I don't say anything, make a show of not meeting his eye.

'Don't be a prick, son. Come on, spit it out.'

'How much do you love me?'

'More than Mrs Perkins herself, although Lord knows she doesn't love me too much right now. Now, stop being a bloody Prima Donna and tell me. Did we get it? I assume that's why you're in here?'

'We got it,' I say, 'We got it. Got to go in next week for immersion.'

He gets up from behind his desk and gives me an awkward, bony hug. I keep my arms by my side. Can taste his aftershave.

'Good work. Good work. You told the others?'

'Not yet. Came straight in here.'

'You told Collins?'

I shake my head.

'You're the first.'

As he sits back in his chair it welcomes him with a leather fart. I sit opposite him. Hilary makes a triangle with his fingertips, elbows on the desk, and peers through the gap. He closes his eyes and I look at the picture on his desk, the picture of him, his wife and his spoiled daughter. I scan the books on the shelves, see the patina of dust that coats them, read the mug that says 'Trust me, I'm an ad man' and wait while he murmurs to himself.

'I don't want Collins on this,' he says after some time.

'What?' I splutter.

'I don't want Collins to manage this account.'

'I know I'm not his biggest fan, but he is at least partly responsible for winning this account. He worked hard on it.'

'Which is why I don't want him to have it. I want to keep him hungry. We've seen it happen time and time again. One big win and then stagnate on it for years. He's an ambitious little prick. I want to keep him that way.'

'Fuck me. He isn't going to like that one little bit.'

'That's the point.'

I consider it. Hilary's eyes are on me. Beady, intense, full of plans and schemes and intelligence. It occurs to me this could be more a test of me than Collins.

'I've got concerns,' I say.

'Okay, what worries you?' The triangle is now flat palms on a big desk, shoulders down, leaning forward.

'That it'll have the opposite effect. That it'll backfire on us. And anyway shouldn't it be his decision?' I tip my head sideways at the office next to Hilary's.

'I'll deal with him. You go and speak to Collins.'

'Oh come on. Me?'

'He respects you.'

'He's going to fucking hate me. What do you want me to say?'

'I'll leave that to you. You're a charming swine when you want to be.'

He stands and ushers me to the door, puts his hand on my shoulder, squeezes it, says, 'Well done. I mean it. Really well done.'

He knocks on Client Service Director's door. As I cross the office to find Collins I hear him say, 'Alan, can I have a word? We've got some good news.' He takes a confident, bow-legged stride into the room and then the door closes behind him.

As I walk through the office I'm aware of a commotion in the studio. Collins is leaning over one of the designer's shoulders gesticulating at the Mac screen with one hand, the other pressing his iPhone to his ear. I sidle over and stand behind him listening to his half of the telephone conversation. He is dictating changes to a press ad. I read the ad on the screen. He's changing the offer amounts and with it the lengthy caveat at the bottom of the ad. When he hangs up he realises I'm there. His face is flustered and evasive.

'What's going on?' I ask.

He shrugs. 'You know how it is, last minute changes.'

The designer snorts.

'Last minute?'

'Just past deadline.'

The designer snorts again. I realise I don't know his name.

'Quite a bit past the deadline,' Collins admits.

I lead him away from the designer and talk to him in a lowered voice.

'I'm not interested in how far past the deadline it is. I've got enough faith in you to assume you need to make this change, I just need to know what are you doing about it?'

He glances back over at the designer.

'He's making the changes. I've told the client they don't get another proof, then I'm sending it back to the paper on the same reference number. I've emailed them to tell them to expect it and to use the latest version.'

'Phone them for fuck's sake. You know as well as I do they never check the ads. You could send them a picture of your cock on the right reference number and they'd print it. Phone them and make sure they've picked up the new ad or you could end up looking pretty fucking stupid.'

He nods sagely and spins around, phone already to his ear.

'When you've finished sorting that, Collins, I need a word, come to my office as soon as you're done.'

12.

The silence is more disturbing than anything. This is not the contented silence of an early morning, not the calm of a snow-covered landscape, or the comfortable silence of an old couple deeply in love.

This is the silence in the eye of a storm.

The silence as the executioner raises his axe.

The silence as the explosion sucks all the air out of a room.

I pick The Pirate up again and hold him at eye level. There is the suspicion his silence is brooding, and picking him up somehow emasculates him.

That I will pay for this later. I always pay for it later. One thing I've learned about The Zoo is that it doesn't forget. It looks after its own. Hurt gets passed up the line. Dropping The Pirate doesn't mean I've just slighted The Pirate.

Because the order goes: The Cowboy, The Knight, then The Pirate.

The Pirate is the last of The Figurines and the first of The Plastics. His sheen and gloss is peerless amongst them. This is the reason he is first, because he is quite childlike in his rendering, certainly nowhere near as delicately drawn as The Knight. It is his sheen that saves him. As head of The Plastics he has his own subjects to lead, but he answers to The Metallics. The fact that there are only two of The Metallics must rankle with him. They are a pair. Confidantes. He has to control those below and report up to them. He is a Figurine, but he is more of a conduit between The Figurines and The Animals. In some ways he is more Animal than Figurine and the fact that he is a Plastic and not a Metallic can only exacerbate this.

He has black boots, a Tricorn, blue coat with yellow detailing. If he was a real pirate it would be gold, and a ruffled white shirt. I think of him as a brute enforcer; there is certainly not a hint of intelligence on his pink plastic face. His eyes are black dots, his lips as red as a harlot. He makes me uncomfortable with his brazen aggression and crimson lips, there is something almost sexually intimidating about him. I cannot deny his place because he comes third. I would like to remove him, but it is not up to me to do so. A parrot perches on his left shoulder, a smudge of badly formed yellow and blue and this represents his position in relation to The Animals.

He is a childhood of reading Treasure Island and all the mystery and romanticism that goes with it. He is hidden coves and smuggling. He is the Jolly Roger and scurvy. He is pieces of eight, plank walking and dancing the hempen jig.

He is William Kidd, Long John Silver and Blackbeard.

The camp of a Gilbert and Sullivan opera.

He is Captain Hook and Johnny Depp doing an impression of Keith Richards.

Peg leg. Hook hand. Eye Patch. Cutlass. Gold earring.

He is about taking what is not yours by force, the lure of gold and the evil men will commit for it.

He is third in line to the throne and I dropped him on the floor.

I focus on the pay phone, becoming aware that I am holding the receiver in my hand. A string of drool from my bottom lip joins to it like a smile. I poke my head out from

44

under the drug blanket for a second and I'm not where I was. Press the phone to my ear and the interrupted drone sounds like the accusatory twitch of a lie detector. I wonder who I called.

Look at the handset. Seven holes to hear from, shaped like a starburst, one lonely hole to speak into. I run my fingers over them, blocking them one at a time with the swirl of my fingerprint. More holes to listen through than to speak through.

We are told to talk here, to share, but by a simple ratio of numbers we spend more time listening than talking. This seems important to me, like the phone holes, so I need to save this for later.

Then.

Group. We sit and we talk and we listen. I mostly listen. I spoke with authority about things I knew very little about for so many years, I just can't any more. I feel I am always lying, even when I am telling the truth. I've told them this, but I don't think they believe me or think I'm saying it for effect. They want me to talk about what happened. They want me to talk about the drink and the drugs. They'd love it if I told them how every part of my body is screaming for a drink. But I know that even if I did it would sound like a lie and cheapen me further. In both their eyes and my own.

Beth is talking. I decide she is the saddest person I know.

'It's about dignity,' she is saying again, 'it's dignity that is taken from us, I'm an intelligent person.'

She is. I can tell she is, though she too is dulled by the medication, and she struggles to make coherent sentences. They are a jumble of big words, trying so hard to form themselves into phrases that mean something, but falling woefully short.

She used to be a teacher like Sally. She talks about the

45

children. About letting them down. About what they must think. She bursts into tears and I can't watch her. I can't watch her cry.

I think instead of the day my boy was born. Him lying in Sally's arms in the hospital, his face screwed up, his fingers clenching. How everything had to change there and how from there everything was to be different. How I looked at them both and said, 'Harry'.

She said, 'Harry?' All the tiredness in her voice, in her eyes, in the way her head rolled back on the pillow, made me want to protect her. Protect him. Them.

'After my Grandfather. I want to name him after my Grandfather.'

She looked at him, considering it, trying the name on him.

'Harry,' she said and that was his name.

13.

I pick him up from school. He sees me waiting at the gate and his face is crafted from happiness. I pop the door for him to clamber in. All the way home he chatters and chirrups, telling me of his day, of his friends and teachers and I reach over and tousle his hair and he shows me his teeth.

At home I spread paper over the dining room table, get out poster paint and we make prints with our hands. I smear paint on my lips and kiss the paper and he laughs, calls me 'stupid Daddy' and my heart somersaults.

When Sally comes in from work I point at a glass of wine on the sideboard and return to the painting.

'What's that?' I ask my son.

'Mummy, Daddy, me.' Pudgy fingers moving over the images.

Sally comes up behind me, hand on the back of my neck, rubbing the top of my head.

'This is what I want,' she says.

'I know,' I reply.

'We still okay for later?'

She takes a sip of her wine, rests her head on my shoulder, her eyelashes tickling my neck. I know she expects me to say no, find an excuse, try to wriggle out of it.

'Yep,' I say instead.

She kisses me on the neck, blows a raspberry on my skin and then sticks her tongue out at Harry. He giggles and covers his mouth with his hand, eyes wide in mock horror.

'Not long until his B-I-R-T-H-D-A-Y,' she says.

I count in my head.

'No, not long.'

'Any ideas?' she asks.

'I c-c-can spell you know,' he says, looking up from his painting, 'I'm not a b-b-baby.'

'Go on then, clever clogs, what did I just spell?' Sally cocks her head to the side, hand on hip, matronly and sexy at the same time.

He makes a show of screwing his face up, rolls his eyes back until I can only see the whites and then shrugs.

'That's what I thought,' she says, then to me, 'get your thinking cap on. I'm going to have a shower. Can you ring us a taxi for about 8?'

I hear the water running and her muted singing and for a little while I think everything is going to be alright.

In the background Bob Dylan sings about trying hard but not understanding. Sally passes me the joint and I take a big toke, jump as the hot rock falls onto my shirt, curse as it bounces onto my knee, onto the floor. Sally giggles and cuffs me with the back of her hand. She tucks her feet beneath herself and leans on me. Lights are low. Dan and Lou sit on the floor at our feet. They could be from 1965, all loose hair and hippy smiles, flowing clothes and gentle voices. Earnest.

'Have you seen them in real life, though?' Lou's talking to me.

'No,' I reply handing the spliff to Dan.

'Makes all the difference.'

I realise I'm stoned and have forgotten what we're talking about. Sally shakes an empty wine glass at Lou who gets up and takes it through to the kitchen, talking all the while.

'I was like you. I thought they were art prints for students. All pretty colours and no substance.'

I whisper to Sally, 'Who are we talking about again?' and she replies, 'Rothko.'

'I don't think that's quite what I said, Lou,' I shout through to the kitchen.

She returns and hands Sally a glass.

'Sorry, did anyone else want one? Maybe you didn't quite say that, Jay, but same lines. I know where you're coming from. What those prints don't show you though is the sheer size of the things. I mean, they are fucking vast. And the texture. They look all smooth and sanitised in the piccies, but in real life they've got texture. They're ugly and lumpy. They move too. No, fuck off, Dan, don't pull that face at me. Seriously, they move. They vibrate. Honestly, I'm not joking.'

'Actually, I'll go with her on that one,' says Dan. 'There is something a bit weird about them when you see them all together.'

'I can't imagine them in a restaurant. No way are they conducive to a nice relaxing meal. We didn't speak to each other for at least an hour after we left.'

'Jesus, Dan, I'm amazed you don't take her every day,' I say, then laugh to show I'm joking. Lou makes a point of melodramatically punching me on the knee.

'You used to know about Art, didn't you, James? Before you sold out to the Man,' she says.

'Everything's for sale, Lou. You know that. Even creativity.'

'It's not your creativity I'm worried about.'

'What then? My soul?' I ask.

'Your soul,' she confirms.

'Gone years ago. A tiny blackened peanut is all I've got left.'

'If that,' says Sally and kisses me on the cheek.

Later, in the taxi on the way home I'm warmly drunk. Sally has her head in my lap, big eyes gazing up at me. I stroke her hair.

'They're such dicks, your friends,' I say.

'They're your friends too.'

'Only by proxy,' I say, 'Friends by association.'

'Come on, they're alright. You like them really.'

'They're pretentious.'

'They're arty.'

'My taxes pay for them to do fuck all.'

'You're just sour because they took the piss out of you.'

We stop at some traffic lights. I look out at an angular city shrouded in mist. Hard frost on all surfaces.

'Tossers,' I slur.

'Are you trying to pick an argument with me, mister?'

'Yes, so we can have angry make-up sex when we get home.'

'Oh really? I can think of loads of things to be angry with you about if that's the case.'

'Yes please.' I lean forward and knock on the glass between us and the driver, 'can you hurry up please, mate, the missus has got the horn.'

'Oi,' shouts Sally and tries to sit up. I hold her still, her head in my groin.

'That's it,' I say, 'Make yourself angry.'

14.

Beard is praying. Or at least it looks like he is. Hands clasped together, eyes screwed up, his mouth working quickly, pink lips moving rapidly and silently.

I sit next to Beth at the table. She is reading a paperback, the pages folded back on the table so I can't see the cover. She smells of soap. When she speaks, her voice is too small, like a child's.

'I don't know how he can do that.'

It takes me a moment to realise who she is talking to because she doesn't raise her eyes from the book.

'Pray?' I ask.

'Uh-huh,' she says, her voice so quiet that I have to lean in to hear her.

'Whatever gets you through, surely?'

She studies me, then closes the book. It's a copy of 'One Day in the Life of Ivan Denisovich'. 'I would think that this place would be a recruiting ground for Atheism.' she says.

'I don't think you can recruit for Atheism, can you?'

'How so?' Her eyes are clearer. Now they are brown and intense.

'Isn't it a reaction to something rather than a philosophy?'

'Go on.'

'Well, it's a negative response to having belief and not a set of beliefs itself, so I don't think you can recruit for it, can you? It's a not having something rather than a having something.'

The way she looks at me I'm doubting myself.

'What do you think the default position of a human being is then?' she asks me.

I try to think of something, something clever, something pithy, but I can't. Shrug my shoulders instead.

'You've not really thought this through, have you?' Her voice has a laugh in it now, teasing.

'No. I've not. Just came out with it.'

I smile at her, a proper smile. Beth is reading me again. Her eyes narrow, as if she is trying to work something out about me.

'Do you find that about being in here? That you can't think things through properly. Like there's something that stops it.'

'The medication?' I ask.

'No. Well, yes. But more than that. Even now, when I've not been given anything, my thoughts aren't quite all there.'

I consider it. Beth's hand hovers over her book. I don't want her to start reading again.

'If I'm honest I would say that I haven't been thinking straight for quite a while.' I gesture for her to come closer, as if I'm going to tell her a secret. I look around with theatrically wide eyes. 'To tell you the truth I'm pretty sure everyone in here is guilty of not seeing things quite right.'

I throw myself back in my chair and wiggle my eyebrows up and down. She snorts with laughter. The whole room turns to us. It feels naughty. For a second it feels like us and them.

'Do you fancy a cup of tea?' I ask her.

'Yes please.'

We don't speak as the kettle boils. We're a facsimile of domesticity. I can hear the TV from the other room. I make sure my body is turned away from her all the time so she can't see my left hand. I don't want to draw attention to it. I pass her a mug and we take our drinks out into the courtyard.

'Wish this was something stronger,' I say and squeeze out a thin smile at her.

The air is cold and wet and a childhood break in my arm aches. I remember the feeling, how I couldn't understand how something inside me was breakable. That I wasn't solid. That there were parts inside me and these parts were fallible.

Out here the size of the world is threatening me. The closeness that I felt with her inside now is awkward and false. We are small. It should pull us tight but it doesn't. Need to speak. Need to say something. The tea is warm between my hands and I can feel my face getting warm too. Something close to panic. My gaze is on the space between my feet, the dimpled concrete of the slabs, the glistening track of a snail trail. I focus on a light green moss clinging to the gap between two of the slabs. When I dare I sneak a glance at Beth and she looks comfortable and is rotating her head to take in the sky. It calms me.

'I love this time of year,' she says. 'Or I did love this time of year. It's hard to tell. I'm not sure what I love any more. Or even if I can love. Do you know what I mean? Love is about dignity and respect and they don't allow you to have either of those things in here. You take away a person's choices and their dignity follows. I'm not even sure who I am.'

I want to touch her.

'Fuck. I sound like some horrible teenage cliché.'

I want to tell her she doesn't.

The door opens and Beaker sticks his head through.

'Newbie,' he says. His voice is all excitement and smugness and pride that he is the one telling us.

53

Beth looks at me for guidance, again I shrug.

'Come on,' says Beaker, 'We've got a Newbie.'

He turns to go, then stops and raises his hand like a traffic policeman.

'Wait there,' he says, points his invisible camera at us and says 'beautiful'.

He squints an eye at an invisible viewfinder, turns an invisible focus ring and mimes a clunk click. With a satisfied grunt he goes back inside. Beth follows him. I sip my tea for a moment. Waiting for the door to close behind her I remember when I was brought here: the commotion and the crowd, the way it felt.

Then I go inside.

The Newbie is a middle-aged man. He looks like Accountant or Solicitor or Doctor. His dark hair is greying at the temples. The rest looks dyed, like he's left these bits to appear sophisticated, thinking it looks like Clooney. His suit is slightly too big as if he's lost weight recently. Boat shoes. I hate boat shoes. His eyes are frightened, darting between us. He's carrying a battered leather briefcase, holding it tight to his body. His mouth is a snarl. He looks like he'll attack. There is murmuring amongst the group. Someone sniggers behind a hand. They stop short of pointing and laughing, but not by much.

'This is sick,' I whisper to Beth.

'It's all they've got,' she says and she's right.

15.

I take Baxter to the first meeting. When I tell him he's got the account he thinks I'm joking. I wish I was. It occurs to me that Hilary is laughing and it's at my expense. I suppress the thought and spout some nonsense to Baxter about deserving it and the board having noticed him and all the time imagine Collins' poisonous eyes on my back.

As we drive to the meeting the rain lashes the wind-screen so heavily the wipers can't keep up and I find myself hunched over the steering wheel, face against the glass, squinting and following the scrape of plastic against glass and the millisecond of clear vision that follows it. I feel shit and cheap and try to make friendly conversation in the car. I can't suppress the sensation I'm cheating Collins even though I don't like the prick and I struggle to find myself in the politics. On the radio there is an advert for a homebuilder, based around an old 50s hit, I sing along and admire the artistry, wishing I'd thought of it and feeling manipulated all at the same time.

Baxter looks at me and I realise I'd laughed. I shrug at him.

'What's the plan for today?' he asks.

'Immersion. We meet them. They talk and we listen. We take it all in. We introduce you. We let them know how we're going to run things. Agree some timescales. Come on, Baxter, you know how these things go.'

I am starting to worry that he's out of his depth. He

nods. Tries to look thoughtful and says, 'This is turning out to be quite a good month all in all.'

'How so?'

'Melissa's pregnant.'

His face is all smiles and schoolboy charm.

'Congratulations.' I reach across the car to shake his hand.

Sally's face, slick with sweat, exhausted, but so happy. My son in her arms.

'Congratulations, Baxter, I'm really pleased for you,' I say and mean it. I stop the car, turn the engine off, reach into the back and grab my Moleskine, my pen and the iPad. I undo the top button of my shirt and loosen my tie just the right amount.

'Ready?'

Baxter is checking his business cards are in his wallet. 'Yep,' he says.

I wrap a scarf about my neck and turn the collar of my jacket up. Outside, the wind howls about the car, hurling rain against the windscreen in loud slaps. As we run across the car park the sound of the car alarm arming is lost in the hurricane.

The receptionist shows no signs of recognising me. I tell her my name again and add Baxter's. She waves at the visitors' book, her attention already somewhere else. When she calls up to Berkshire she asks me my name again. While we wait I check my emails. One from Alan – *J, let me know how Baxter gets on, A.*

Berkshire arrives, clasps me on the shoulder and shakes Baxter's hand. At the reception desk he leans over and asks the girl what room we're in.

'Tanzania,' she says.

'All our meeting rooms are named after countries,' Berkshire says as the lift silently makes its way up and up and up. 'Reminds everyone that we're global. That they're part of something bigger.'

'Good idea,' says Baxter.

'No, not really. Just makes everyone want to go on holiday. Amazing how many people actually go on holiday to the same place as the meeting room they spend most of their time in. Would love to know what Freud would say about that. No, if it was up to me I'd just number the things. But some dozy marketing consultant came up with it sometime in the nineties and they've just stayed. No offence.'

'None taken,' I say.

Tanzania looks nothing like Tanzania, or what I imagine Tanzania to look like. It's a room with no windows, a table that takes up most of the space and leather-backed chairs too close to the walls to be comfortable.

'Coffee?'

I nod. 'White and one.'

'Same please,' says Baxter.

Berkshire turns on a laptop, plugs a cable into a socket in the table and an overhead projector throws the bank's logo onto the rear wall.

'Back in a moment with your drinks, gentlemen. The others should be with us shortly,' he says.

The picture behind me is a waterfall, taken with a long exposure so the water is a misty blur. Tropical. Warm. Aspirational. Horrible. I tap Baxter on the shoulder and point at it. He scowls.

Berkshire returns to the room with a tray of drinks, some Marks and Spencer's biscuits and a group of men who do nothing to reduce the banker stereotype. Faceless suits. Good haircuts. Tans. Dull. Dull. Dull. Within seconds of being introduced I've forgotten their names.

He sleepwalks us through a presentation about the bank, where they came from, their board of directors, a couple of whom are the faceless suits, their financial history, most of which we already know, blah, blah, blah. It's hot in the room and there's no sugar in my coffee. Baxter is scribbling notes, his hand a blur, so I don't bother. Mentally I pat him on the shoulder. It finishes, they file out apart from Berkshire and a young man.

'Mr Marlowe, Mr Baxter, this is Mr Ben Jones. He will be your day to day contact on the account, so I will leave you in his capable hands for a tour of the office. Gentleman, it's good to have you on board.'

He flows out of the room. Jones pours a glass of water, passes it to me.

'Just Ben, please.'

'Hi Ben, James and this is Michael.'

'I'll take you on the tour. Not a lot to see really. Not very exciting places, banks.'

We follow Just Ben through floor after floor of people squashed into identical cubicles, gunmetal, glass, marble tiles, chrome handles. Very slick, very designed, very dead. Before we leave he grasps my arm and says in an urgent, clipped voice:

'I'm so glad they've got someone new in. That singing piggy bank was just plain embarrassing.'

I pause for just long enough and then tell him it's a shame he feels that way because that's the only thing we're planning on keeping from the previous campaigns. I let him stare at me in horror for thirty long seconds.

'Only kidding, Ben. Consider that gone. First thing out the window. There'll be no gimmicks this time. Just honest communication.'

The relief is palpable on his face. It occurs to me that if he is given any sort of authority then we might be alright.

'Thank Christ for that. I thought you were serious for a moment.'

58

Outside the wind has died down and the rain has refined into the tiny needle drops that feel like nothing but go right through your clothes. Baxter trots after me. As we slump into the car I turn on the heater and spark a cigarette.

'That was okay, wasn't it?' asks Baxter.

'Yes,' I reply, 'not bad at all.'

16.

In the hospital every day is pretty much the same. It's a place of routine and rule. And for the most part this suits me just fine. Lack of routine is what caused most of my problems. Routine keeps away all prepossessing thoughts of drink and drugs. There are some rules you're told when you get in and despite myself I try to follow them. Some come from the orderlies, some from doctors, some from other patients, but they build up into a collective whole and they seem to make some sense.

Firstly, remember that everything you do in here is geared towards getting you back out *there*. It's not *ill* and *well*, it's *here* and *there*. No matter how much you want to, never beg them to let you go home, never plead and tell them you're ready to be sent back out *there*, because this means you're not. They decide and that's that.

Always tell the nurses the truth. I've learned this the hard way. It goes totally against my instincts. But I don't want to end up as a Randall P McMurphy, so being facetious and argumentative has been toned down. Of course the constant medication helps with that too. I'm aware of the irony about replacing self-medication with real medication, although it seems entirely lost on my keepers. Lying to them will get you nowhere, can get you stuck in *here* and certainly won't help you to get back out *there*.

Don't stay in bed all day. It would be so easy. The oblivious embrace of sleep is always there, beckoning. Don't do it. It only leads to isolation and isolation is not healthy.

This leads straight onto the next rule. Get dressed. Dressing gown and pyjamas are the costume of the unwell. We are not unwell, we are just in *here*, working towards getting back out *there*. Getting dressed, being involved, will get you noticed by them and can help reduce your stay. Moping around in your nightwear will only help convince them you're in *here* for the long haul.

Do what you are told. Again, this is the McMurphy rule. You can't win. They watch and mark everything down. Picking fights with the nurses and other patients will go against you and keep you in *here* longer. They like us placid. So placid we are. Not that they trust us to be placid of our own volition of course. They fill us full of pills and potions that turn us into the walking dead to ensure that we are placid. But there really is no use in fighting it.

Remember there is a blame culture here, point scoring, stool pigeons, snitching. If you do something wrong and someone sees you doing it they will tell on you and it will be detrimental to your stay. So either don't do anything wrong or don't get caught.

The aide is standing next to my bed. I open one eye. Think he is about to shake me. He sees my eye and takes a step back.

'You need to get up,' he says.

'I didn't sleep very well.'

'You still need to get up.'

'I dreamed I was being chased by a wolf, then I was the wolf and I was doing the chasing.' I'm still shaking. My heart is hammering inside my chest.

'You still need to get up. Hold onto the feeling you have now. It's no use sharing it with me. Keep it for group.'

'I wasn't trying to share. I was explaining why I couldn't get up,' I want to argue, my eyes are itchy with tiredness. I am all irritation and compressed aggression.

'You have to get up. Everyone has to get up.'

He grabs hold of the corner of the blanket, to pull it off me. I relent. Sit up. Rub sore eyes. The world changes from black to green to purple to blue to yellow under the heel of my pressing hand. From the window sill I feel the vibration of The Zoo. It quivers. Then rumbles. I take my hand away from my eyes to look at the aide. His image ripples. I shake my head, squeezing my eyes shut. Push the tips of my fingers into them. It rumbles again. I scream 'noooooooooooooooo' inside my head. Count to thirty and when I open my eyes again the aide has gone. I get out of bed and pull the blanket back over it, tuck the corners in, all the while avoiding the gaze of The Zoo.

In the ward the day staff are settling in. I go through to the day room. A nurse is writing on a whiteboard.

On the wall in the corridor there are little photos of the nurses, the team. I stand in front of them and study the greying pictures. 'I could get to you all,' I say to them, 'I probably have got to you all.'

Head Psychiatrist, I read. Janet Armitage. I reduce her down to a target. To a sector. Female, 45-50, paid between thirty and fifty grand, homeowner, about to become an empty nester, interested in gardening, reads *Elle Decoration* and the free aspirational magazine that plops through her letterbox monthly, drives to work in a luxury saloon bought on HP, passes a slog of 48-sheet poster sites upon which I would place a carefully designed selection of words and images designed to influence her whether she knew it or not.

'I know you, Janet,' I say to the picture. Kiss my fingertips and touch them lightly to its glossy surface.

The whiteboard reads, *Today is Monday. It is the 23rd February. It is raining.*

17.

Collins is brooding. He spends a lot of time on his mobile in one of the side offices. I suspect he is looking for another job. The rest of the time he has his head buried in his MacBook. He's barely spoken to me.

'I'm worried about Collins,' I say to Hilary as we drink espresso in his office.

'He'll be fine. He'll come out fighting,' he says.

Hilary looks tired. More tired. His skin is grey, his eyes bloodshot.

'Are you okay?' I ask.

'Hmm.' He studies his coffee, appears to be considering something, then says, 'Angie has moved in with her sister. A trial for a trial separation.'

'Shit. Sorry.'

He slurps when he drinks.

'Can't be helped. Certain irony to it all though. The one time I actually haven't done anything is the one time the silly old broad flips her lid and takes action.'

I watch two raindrops race down the window. He's muttering something.

'What was that?' I ask.

'Can't even iron my own bloody shirt. How pathetic is that? No idea how to use the washing machine. I've been buying a new shirt every day. I'm completely incapable of looking after myself. 59 years old and I'm like a bloody baby. Should be ashamed of myself. You can use the appliances in your own house I presume?'

I nod.

'Thought so. Different generation. Truth is if she goes through with the trial separation I'm going to have to buy someone in. Hired help. A nanny or something.'

'Buy a Thai bride,' I say and then regret it looking at his thin smile.

'Baxter's going to need some help with the bank. Start looking for an exec.'

I meet with Baxter and the creatives. The original presentation is spread out across the table on A3 boards. I push them around. Pick one up and put it on an easel in the corner.

'Start with this,' I say, 'This. But not this. They liked the pitch, but don't want to run with anything we presented. The idea is right, but the execution isn't.'

I turn over a sheet on a flip chart. Uncap a pen. Sniff it.

'Okay, who wants to start?'

Later I phone the newspaper and book an advert in the recruitment section. I speak to our web developers and get the job put on the website. *Account Executive required to work on blue chip client. Experience in the finance sector preferable. Good basic and potential for promotion.* Something like that. The web developer types it in without looking at me. I expect him to type 'something like that' at the end. He doesn't.

I put my head back around the door of the room where Baxter and the creatives are still working. They are huddled around the whiteboard surrounded by snow drifts of discarded paper. They don't look up.

I leave the office. It's 4.30. The roads are quiet. I stop at the Cock Inn on the way home. Drink a pint of lager and think about banks and money, what it means and how we rely on them, how they let us down and how we don't have any choice. I find myself getting angry and realise that this is going to be harder than I thought. I drop three pounds on the bar top and leave. Phil Collins serenades me out into the world.

When I get home Sally and Harry are curled up on the sofa. I kiss them both on the tops of their heads. They're watching Fawlty Towers. John Cleese is contorted with rage, his body screwed up.

'He's f-funny,' says Harry looking up at me.

'Yes he is,' I say, imitating Cleese's walk.

They both laugh at me then return to the TV. I go into the kitchen and get a beer from the fridge, then smoke a cigarette out the back door. Sally joins me, takes the cigarette from between my fingers and drags on it. I watch her lips on the filter. When she passes it back she's kissed it red.

'I know what we should do for his birthday.'

'Yeah?' she asks.

'Let's take him to Monkey Kingdom. I think he'd love it.'

'You'd love it.'

'Yes. But he would too.'

'I think he might.'

She kisses me on the cheek and goes back inside. I gaze up at the night sky and try to recognise some of the constellations, but I can't grasp them at all.

18.

Mark is talking, telling us about his family.

'I don't want them to see me like this,' he is saying. 'I don't want me daughter to think of her Da as a mad person. I want to get better so I can hold her again.'

He begins crying, his greasy hair falling forward and touching the table, and I can't help but think that someone has to eat their dinner off it. A nurse puts her arm around him. He's crying silently, shoulders shaking, rising and falling. The room waits for him to stop.

'Sorry, everyone.' There's a quiver in his voice.

I try not to think of my boy, aware of the parallels. Push him down. Push him down.

'When it started getting hard I tried to keep myself away from them. Was worried what would happen.'

He takes a passport photo from his pocket and hands it to the person next to him. It's passed around the group. When it gets to me I meet Mark's eyes and smile. He manages the tiniest quiver of his lips back at me. I'm surprised at how pleased I am about this. The picture is of Mark and his daughter. His hair is shorter, a ring in his eyebrow. His daughter is dimples and smiles and straw-coloured hair. I reach back across the table and put it in front of him.

'She's beautiful.'

'Thanks, mate.' He puts the picture back in his pocket.

'Are you okay to go on?' asks the nurse, voice warm and gentle and passive-aggressive insistent.

'Yes,' he says, takes two deep breaths and then continues.

'When I lost my job I began to resent them. I couldn't help it. They needed me and I failed them. I know now it was my failure that was hurting me, but at the time I thought they were blaming me. I didn't know what to do. I'd always worked at the same car factory. I thought I was going to lose my job before when they automated stuff. Thought I was going to lose my job to a robot. They retrained me then. But they just let me go this time.'

I know who he's talking about. They had some serious problems with the brakes, recalled thousands of cars. People died. Brakes failed. Smashed through the central reservation and into oncoming traffic. People got trapped in their cars. Whole families burned to death. Never good for sales, that. Nothing puts the consumer off more than the chance of a violent death and the smell of burning flesh. No amount of fancy seats and good stereos can make up for that. Recalls we can deal with. News pictures of burned corpses are an entirely different matter. Once the doubt is there in the public's mind it's very hard to get rid of. We got the chance to pitch for their account – turned it down, no chance, too risky.

'I went to work for six weeks. Or pretended to. I just sat in the car in a lay-by. I took the sandwiches my wife made me and sat in a lay-by.'

Someone sniggers. I scan the group and see Newbie smothering his mouth. I scowl at him. He's still got his briefcase on his lap, his arms wrapped around it.

'Something funny?' I ask,

He looks at the table. The person next to me puts their hand on my arm.

'It's okay,' I say to them, a little too much aggression in my voice, and they take their hand away.

In my room. I'm thinking about another room from the past: an oak table with chairs that cost more than a month's salary. A salesman from one of our suppliers. I remember the smell of his aftershave. Sharp. Lemony.

'I can guarantee you 20,000 visits. Guarantee,' he assures me. Freckled skin and eyes that can look only to the close of the sale. His top button is undone under his tie. His neck is fat and sweaty.

'Can you geo-target it to the North-East?' I ask him.

'No, I wouldn't do it if I had to narrow it that much. I can say North of England. But no more than that. If I have to reduce to North-East I would have to do too many sends and, to be frank with you, I feel I have to be honest at this stage, it just wouldn't be worth my while.'

'Whose lists are you planning to get the names from?'

I know I have to buy this data. I have promised I'll increase visitors to my client's site by fifty percent in eight weeks, but he's putting me off. My gaze is drawn to my cuff-links. Sterling silver, a ring of diamonds. A present from Sally for our first wedding anniversary. A stay at a country hotel. She's dancing on the bed, a towel around wet hair, laughing as it unravels and she whips her hair around and around, and I'm laughing too.

"These are all our names. All of them opted in and all of them are used to receiving offers from us. These are hardened Internet shoppers. They look forward to our mails."

I doubt this. Instead I look out of the window. An aeroplane has written my initials in the sky.

"These are people who love offers, they wait for them," he continues. "If you get the creative right, which I'm sure you will, you guys know what you're doing, then they'll fucking lap it up."

"Okay. I'll get accounts to raise you a purchase order. How soon can I have the data?"

"You get me a PO now, I can put a call into HQ, and you'll have it asap." He holds his hand out as if he is going to spit into it. I shake it, feel like I am arm wrestling, testing his strength and wonder how many poor people are going to have their in-boxes invaded with mindless crap to generate 20,000 visitors. It must run into hundreds of thousands. Information waste on an unprecedented scale.

When he has left I get a bottle of vodka out of my desk drawer, lock myself in one of the tele-conferencing rooms, pull the blinds and drink until my throat burns.

Now in the room, *here*. This room. Now.

There is a noise. It sounds like music.

I get up from the bed. Scrabble around looking for the source. Too quiet to hear, I can't work out the tune, but it's there. I know it's there. Louder now, nearly loud enough for me to find it. On my hands and knees under the bed, I follow the wall, until I can just make out the beginning refrains of *Helter Skelter*.

I am on my knees in front of The Zoo listening to it sing and I know that it is coming. It is coming for me and it won't be long.

19.

Jessica wafts through the office on a wave of Angel. Heads turn. Collins mouths 'fuck me' in my direction. It's the first real communication we've had since I told him. I arch my eyebrows back at him and lead her into the boardroom. Hilary joins me. Alan is already there, peering out over his laptop. We sit either side of him. Jessica demurely arranges herself opposite.

'Good morning, Miss Hardy,' says Hilary, eyes over glasses, 'You've met Mr Marlowe, and this is Mr Reach, our Client Services Director. Whoever gets this role will be reporting directly to him.'

'You're the one I need to be nice to, then?' she asks and Alan laughs like a little girl.

We talk her through the role and what is expected of her. She takes it all in. When she concentrates there are small furrows either side of the bridge of her nose. From the corner of my eye I can see Hilary trying to lean forward enough to look down her shirt.

'You know what we do here?' I ask.

'You're a full service agency.'

'Yes. But you know what we do?'

There are those furrows again. Nose all wrinkled up. 'You help people sell things?'

'Well, yes we do. But we essentially make people do things they don't want to do by being smart-arses. Can you live with that?'

Furrows. 'I think so,' she says.

'Look at it this way. The gap between person and product has been reduced to a microsecond. It's not just a case of making your product better than the next one on the shelf, it used to be but it isn't anymore. What we do has been narrowed down to a simple point of differentiation. You either have a product that someone loves or you have a product that isn't as annoying as its competitors. An annoying product is never going to be loved, but if it's less annoying than the other products on the market it will become a leader. A product that someone loves is the goldmine, because they'll always buy it and will tell others to buy it. As long as it doesn't become annoying. And aside from that it is just a matter of degrees, how much do you love it opposed to how annoying is it? It is our job to provide the information that lets people make the desired choice. Make sense?'

Hilary is looking at me as if I'm insane. Alan is closing his laptop lid. Jessica is searching the ceiling with her doelikes. Between them the furrows.

'Yes,' she says, 'I think it does.'

'Christ, you're better than me then. Are you sure you're going for the right job. You don't want mine?' Hilary is all professional smarm now. He asks her some questions and her answers are adequate if not inspired. When it becomes obvious they've dried up he rises from behind the table, reaches across, takes her hand, which looks clean and white in his liver-spotted paw.

'Thank you for your time, Miss Hardy,' says Alan, showing her to the door.

Hilary leans back in his chair and sighs. I can hear Alan talking to the Office Manager outside. When they return he says, 'What the fuck was that?'

I shrug.

'Are you trying to scare the shit out of her, James?'

71

Again shrug. Don't know what to say.

'Sometimes I swear you speak another fucking language.'

'When does she start then?' I ask.

They don't answer. Alan finishes packing his laptop. Hilary makes a show of checking his phone.

'Alan? I asked you a question.'

'You were being a prick. You know we've got 3 more candidates to interview.'

'Come on. Let's be serious. They're going to have to be unbelievably good to beat her. Or better looking, and I doubt that's going to happen. What do you think, Peeping Tom?'

Hilary flicks me the Vs. 'Due diligence. Employment law's a bugger nowadays.'

'Come on then. Let's get this over with then, I've got work to do.'

Two days later I'm talking to the receptionist as Jessica, Miss Hardy, walks in. She's wearing a light grey trouser suit, hair pulled back, black rimmed spectacles. She looks like the stereotypical horny librarian. My heart sinks as the rest of me rises.

'Morning,' she says and her glasses slide down her nose. She pushes them back up with her index finger. I lead her to Alan's office. When she opens the door I can see him arranged in his thoughtful pose and it's all I can do not to snigger.

The same evening I'm in a gallery for the launch of Lou's exhibition. The gallery is glass-fronted so we can all watch the wrath of God hurl entire oceans onto the street outside. Despite the biblical weather there is a healthy turnout. We get there late and the guests have already begun tucking into the free wine. I take a glass of red. It's too cold and it's cheap and I'm quickly onto my second.

'James.' Lou is wearing a dress.

'Fucking hell, Lou. Look at you.'

She clutches her hem and curtsies.

'Don't tell me you've shaved your legs too?'

She grabs my cheek and pinches it.

'Where's Dan?' I ask.

She points to a group of people in the main gallery space, takes Sally by the arm and leads her away. I walk over to the paintings. A man joins me. He's wearing a trilby. We both stand back from them, arms folded, cocking our heads. I imagine I'm looking artistic and appreciative.

'I don't get them,' I say eventually.

'They're about noise,' he says. He's got an Australian accent, faded from living here for a long time.

'Okay.'

'Yeah. They're about noise. These ones on this side are about human noises. Or the noises we make. Those ones over there are about the noises we can't hear. The ones that are out of our spectrum of hearing.'

'Like dog whistles?'

He walks over to one of the paintings behind us and examines the painting closely.

'Yes, look, a dog whistle.'

I join him. He's right. In the bottom of the painting, scratched into the thick oil painting is a tiny dog whistle. We return to the original painting.

'And this, I think, is supposed to suggest that we, the viewers, are responsible for the consequences shown in the painting. This here is a nod to the fourth wall.'

I think he's right again.

'You really get these?'

'Yeah, I guess so. Seems fairly obvious. You not?'

'No. And I know the artist.'

I go back to the bar. They're out of red so I grab a glass

73

of white. This time it's too warm and cheap. Work my way around the paintings. The Aussie could be right. They appear to be about noise. There is lots of reference to white noise. Some satellites. One looks like the inside of an ear. One has a childlike drawing of someone holding their hands over their ear to block out sound. A loudhailer. Two paintings are connected by a telephone cord. They are created using lots of media, some virtually collages. I find one with a picture of us all at university. 'Bitch,' I say under my breath. I look young and happy with my arm around Sally. I move closer and see that she has drawn little stitch marks across all of our mouths. I'm wearing a Levellers t-shirt.

Another glass of wine and I meet up with Sally at the dog whistle picture.

'What do you think?' she asks. I steal a Twiglet off her paper plate.

'Don't tell Lou this, but they're actually pretty good.'

'Fucking hell. Are you going all soft in your old age?'

'I think I'm a bit drunk.'

'They've invited us back to their house for a party. That okay?'

'Is there going to be more drink there?'

'I would expect so.'

'Drugs?'

'Fair possibility.'

'Can we make out in the kitchen?'

'Depends how drunk I get.'

I hand her my glass of wine.

The party turns out to be about 20 or so people that I don't know. We are in the lounge, the lights are low, the room is full of the sweet smell of incense. I keep looking at the bongos in the corner and wondering whether I should hide them. A group of people are talking about how the government is cutting funding and how artists are having to pay the price for capitalist greed and I know they're right, I know it's true, but I'm still having to bite my tongue.

My glass is empty. I push myself up from the floor, slightly light-headed, and stroll into the kitchen. Pour myself a generous measure of vodka. Add some lemonade. And then some more vodka. I'm scrabbling in my pocket for cigarettes when Lou and Sally join me. Sally is drunk, her cheeks flushed. When I pull the crushed pack of fags out I feel a lump in my lighter pocket.

'No way,' I wave the bag of coke in front of Sally's face, 'I forgot about this. Shall we?'

'Don't mind if I do.'

'Still on the yuppie drug of choice then, James?' says Lou.

'You won't be wanting any then?'

'Ah, I didn't say that.'

'Didn't think so.'

I curve three big lines on the work surface.

'Where's Dan?'

'He's about somewhere. He won't want any.'

'Anyway, Lou. I'm doing this to help the poor Colombian farmers. Think of it as an act of benevolence.'

'Helping the people who make baby laxative more like.'

I hand a rolled up twenty to Sally. It takes her two snorts to get the whole line up her nose. She grimaces and rubs at her nostril.

'Speaking of poor farmers, Sally tells me you've got a new client.'

'Yep.'

'You do know what they're doing in Nghosa, don't you?' says Lou, taking the note from Sally and doing her line. Up in one.

'Fuck off, Lou. They're from Holland. The Dutch don't do anything bad.'

'Look it up,' she replies.

Sometime later I've plugged my iPod into the stereo in the kitchen and it's John Lennon, 'How do you sleep'. I'm talking to a tall dreadlocked man, who has tattoos on his hands, about films that are better than the books they're based on. I can't think of any. He asks me if I want some Ket. I can already hear Sally saying 'don't do it. Don't take that. You know what it does to you.' And she's right. I do know what it does to me, it sends me mental. So I say yes.

Later still and I'm sitting on a log trying to explain to someone how everything is a square, literally a square and someone says, 'I just want to understand time,' and I want to write this down, the way everything happens, but the way everything happens makes it too hard to write things down and I'm right, everything is a square, along up, back, down, to the beginning, and I try to explain this to the person who was asking about time because this is the answer, but I'm talking to the wrong person then I realise I'm not talking to anyone. Then I'm standing in the back garden by the fire pit with Dan and he tells me that a log looks like a crocodile and I look and I see it. I see it, I say to him and point and he says, no, no, that's the wrong end and I say, Swopodile and splutter laughter into the flames and he says Flipodile, Switchodile, then I'm in the alley puking onto a bin, then I'm back in the garden, by the fire, cross-legged, one side of my face is red hot and I'm digging my feet into the gravel and I've lost my shoes and the man with the dreads says 'Apocalypse Now is better than the book' and I ask someone where Sally is and they say 'she's gone, man', and I am too.

I'm gone.

20.

When I wake the atmosphere in the house fills the gaps in my memory. Sally doesn't look at me when I stagger into the kitchen.

'I need to pick Harry up from my Mum's,' she says, addressing the sideboard.

I try to get a mug out of the cupboard and drop it onto the sideboard. It reverberates around inside my head and I squeeze my eyes shut.

As Sally leaves, she says, 'I think you need to apologise to Lou.' I can't think why and I can't think how I got home. Upstairs I search through my clothes for my phone, find it in my shirt pocket, go through it for photos or texts, any clues, but there either aren't any or I deleted them last night, so I climb back into bed.

I can't sleep. I try to phone Dan. He rejects my call. I try again. And again. Leave a whingy message. Eventually he takes my call.

'Mate, if Lou knew I was talking to you she'd fucking flip.'

He goes quiet. I don't know what to say. My head pounds.

'Sally says I should apologise to Lou.'

'Well, yeah. Maybe not just yet though.'

'Tell me.'

'You smashed one of her sculptures.' There is a sigh in his voice, like it pains him to say this. Like he experienced the aftermath.

'Accidentally?' I ask, although I know the answer.

'You said so.'

'But she doesn't think so?'

'No.'

I scrunch my face up. Feel blood hot in my cheeks.

'Is Sally okay with you?'

'Not really. Why?'

'You were a bit of a twat to her.'

'Oh Christ.'

'Tell me if this is none of my business. But you might think about calming it down a bit.'

When he hangs up I pull the duvet over my head. I am sweaty and sticky and my eyelids scratch my eyeballs. I give up. Grab my phone, open the browser and Google 'Nghosa'. It doesn't make me feel any better and I can't see the connection.

21.

I'm streetwise. Or as streetwise as someone who works in advertising can be, but I've learned some new terms for female genitalia in the last few days. Turns out Newbie can't refer to women as anything other than slang for their bits. I found it funny to start with. Particularly when he was shouting 'gash' at one of the nurses. Gash. Gash. Gash. Most words are funny if you say them long enough, words for genitals especially.

Cunt. Snatch. Twat. Pissflaps. Beef Curtains. Slit. Muff. Lady Garden. Vadge. Fanny. Poontang. Front Bottom. Punanyi. Bearded Clam. Minge. Beaver. Box. Camel Toe. Pussy. Cunny. Flange. Fuck Hole. Fur Burger. Quim. Box.

You can see him trying to stop it. Trying to hold them in. Trying to find a name or a term of endearment. He says 'minge' like someone else would say honey or darling or love.

I don't know what he's got, don't think it's Tourette's, it grips him though, squeezes him. You can see him inside it looking out. It's like a python of vagina slang.

Up close he smells of soap. A women's soap maybe, perfumed and flowery. The taint of female vanity. He clasps his briefcase still, tight to his chest. I want to know what is in there. I need to know.

I remember my Gran's house. There was a box on a shelf up high, too high for me to reach. My Gran leaning down, her face big in mine, saying, 'Don't touch that box. That box isn't for you.' I spent years wondering what was in that box. As I grew taller the box got closer, until I was at eye level and I could study it. Leather with metal corners, a gold lock and her initials engraved into the leather of its front. All I wanted to do was to crack the lid and see what was inside. One day I waited until she was in the kitchen and opened it. Inside was a dried rose. When I heard her coming I struggled to push it back inside and it crumbled in my hand. I later found out it was from her father's coffin.

I involuntarily reach for the briefcase. He pulls it tighter and utters 'snatch' at the Asian Radio Lady as she passes.

I realise I have subconsciously categorised him. He is 'Corporate Leader'. Returning late at night to his big house in extensive grounds. Type A. Aspirational. Premium. Will pay more for the correct product. Extensive investments. Private education. Corporate career. I know him. I know you, Newbie. You play golf. Drive a marque. Your wife has weekly therapy to hide from the cold distance your work has put between you. I could run through a roster of clients whose products I have targeted you for.

Quite a fall.

Beth sits next to me. She smells of rain and grass and open air.

'Hi,' she says.

I smile at her. Sincere.

Newbie glares at her. His fingers knead the leather of his briefcase like a kitten kneading at something it thinks is its mother. Hungry. Nervous. His mouth is moving.

I hear a noise I recognise coming from my room. A click and a whirr like the pilot light on a boiler starting up. A whumpf of air and flame. The Zoo is awake. Its gaze has turned to me again. The hairs on the back of my neck stand up.

Newbie glares at Beth. Silently I will him not to.

80

Don't do it. Not now.

'Cunt,' he says.

Beth looks at me, then at him. Confused.

'You. Cunt,' he says again.

Beth raises her finger to her chest, as if to say 'me?'.

'Axe wound.'

I register the hurt and confusion on Beth's face, see her eyes glaze with tears.

He says it again. Slams the briefcase on the table.

'Axe wound.'

She jumps up, hand over her mouth. Her chair topples backwards, clattering across the floor. She bursts into tears, spins and runs into the corridor.

Click. Whir. My fists clench. I'm on my feet, jabbing him in the chest with my finger, all the while knowing it's not his fault, not really, that he can't help it. I'm calling him a prick and he's taking it, taking each prod of my finger. 'Keep your fucking names to yourself,' I'm telling him. Prodding. Then I'm in the corridor, arms around Beth and she's crying on my shoulder, I'm asking her if she's okay and behind her I can see my room and the gap under the door is red and it's rattling my teeth. I can feel it in my legs. In my head. So I hold her tight. It's awake now and she's hugging me and I'm hugging her and after a while it's hard to tell who is consoling who.

22.

By the time Sally returns with Harry I am somewhere near decent. Sober at least. She leads him into the lounge and he plonks himself in front of the TV. I sit down next to him. Put my arm around him and he wriggles away, moaning 'D-d-d-d-daaaaaaaad'. Sally's eyes are red and puffy.

'Do you want a drink, Harry?' she asks.

'P-please,' he replies, eyes always on the TV.

As she passes me she whispers, 'We need to talk.' I turn my head and raise a questioning eyebrow and she mouths 'Later'.

'What are we watching?' I ask Harry.

'Ceebeebies.'

'Okay,' I say and allow myself to be zoned out by the colours and the noise and try to forget the mess that is all around me.

In our room, voices hushed, we argue with the volume turned down.

'It has to stop,' she says.

'I know.'

'You're just saying it, James. I know you're just saying it. Agreeing with me so I stop talking and it'll be fine for a couple of weeks. For a couple of weeks you'll be great. You'll be my husband again. And then it'll slowly go back to this.'

She is propped up on pillows. Her hair is a wall that

divides us. I see the anger knotted in clenched fists and the tendons in her arms and neck. She means it.

'I can't take it anymore. I really can't. I'm sick of being both adults in this relationship.'

'That phrase has come straight from your mother,' I say and regret it as she turns to me with real hatred in her eyes.

'Fuck you. *Fuck* you. This is not about my mother. Don't try and score points. I'm not playing. I am at my wits' end. I can't bring Harry up and look after you. It's like having two children. And I'm just so tired.'

She's crying now. I reach for her arm and she shrugs me off, aggression in her movements. I let her talk. Let it all come out. All the hurtful words. Allow them to ricochet off me.

'You're all as bad as each other. You, Hilary, Alan. You act like you're rock stars, when you're really just a bunch of boys playing, acting like you're heroes to the younger ones, and the worst thing is they flatter you and play up to it. It's pathetic watching them fawn over you and the lot of you lapping it up. It makes me sick. I mean who the fuck really wants to be Hilary? It's not real. None of it. It's make believe. There's a boy next door who does worship you and you can't even see it anymore.'

'Now wait a minute . . .'

'No. You listen. Listen to me for once. You can pull the wool over everyone else's eyes, God knows that's what you're good at. What you do all day. All of you, you think you're being so smart. What good have any of you ever done?'

I stammer, stumbling over words. Try and get something out.

'We work with charities,' I manage, knowing it sounds pathetic.

'Lip service and you know it. So you can appeal to the

Corporate Social Responsibility of those wankers you work for. You know what you are? All of you? Corporate cocksuckers.'

'Fuck's sake.' I sit bolt upright, spin my head around so that I am facing her, but she turns away again, still won't look at me.

'I think that's why you all get so drunk all the time. You know what you're doing is vacuous and selfish. You promote greed and it hurts you.'

I am hurt. She's hurting me.

'Thank you Sigmund fucking Freud. Is it all my mother's fault?'

I know I sound childish and yet I can't stop myself.

'Don't be facetious. I'm being honest with you. If I don't tell you this now I don't know how much longer . . .'

'Sally, please . . .'

'You know, that might be why you smashed Lou's sculpture. Because it had some emotional truth and you don't any more. You're not the man I married. If I showed him the way you are now he'd be horrified. You were an artist. Now you're a cliché.'

'You're not exactly following your artistic dream are you?'

'I'm a teacher, James. I teach children to take joy in art. To learn how to express themselves. I make a difference. Maybe not to all of them, but some of them and that's enough.' Her voice is cracked and clipped with anger.

'Have you finished the character assassination?'

'I've barely brushed the surface.'

'Look. I'm sorry. I'm sorry about last night. I'm sorry about Lou's sculpture.'

I've got my hand on her arm. Her skin is cold. I can feel the shake of her muscles through my palm.

'Forget Lou's sculpture. That's just you being a prick. You

know what it reminded me of? One of Harry's tantrums. When he thinks we're not giving him enough attention.'

'Maybe it's a cry for help,' I say and am filled with such a wave of self-pity that I think I'm about to burst into tears.

'You do need help. But the only person who can help is you. You need to look at what you've got and make some very hard choices. You can carry on playing with the boys or you can be a father and husband. But you haven't got long to decide.'

She turns her light off and rolls over, her back to me.

I sit there blinking into the dark, wondering how I got here.

23.

The floor of the corridor ripples like a carpet being shaken, as if someone has grabbed the other end and shaken it. When it passes us I struggle to keep my feet and pull Beth even tighter so she doesn't lose her balance. I can feel the beat of her heart against me, small and fast as a bird's. The light from under my door is growing, flickering, the light of flames. I can hear it too, a whirring and clunking of chains and gears and things moving. Something warming up. Static. The sound of voices. Fragments from an oratory. A place name I recognise and that fills me with dread. How can that place have followed me here? I look at Beth in my arms and shout, 'No'. I grab her by the hand and lead her through the day room. Behind me I hear the door burst open and the noise is louder. Louder. Louder. The powerful rhythmic chunt of a stream train. The groan of metal on metal. The door to outside is getting smaller, the walls have changed so they meet in the centre, the ceiling gone, vaulted now. My feet are moving as if in treacle. Beth is looking at me, terrified. I hold her head so she doesn't look back, look forwards, always forwards and keep her moving towards the door. The diminishing door. The noise behind is growing. A tsunami. Metal. Steam. Water. Waves. Building. Building. Building. I push Beth out through the door. See the fear on her face, tell her to wait there and turn to face it.

Turn to face nothing. Just the day room. No-one is

looking at me. Asian Radio Lady is turning the volume of the TV up and down, so the words are cut in half and the speech is stuttered. Beard and Beaker are in the armchairs. Mark is singing quietly to himself in the kitchen.

I blink into the room.

I expected maelstrom and instead I see domestication.

I edge my way back to the corridor. Pluck up the courage and poke my head around the corner of the door, look left and right. An orderly is sweeping up, iPod headphones in, mouth pursed in a silent whistle. At the desk at the front a nurse is speaking on the phone. I look at the door to my room and in my peripheral catch a glimpse of movement. I freeze. Looking back into the day room I see Beth's scared face through the glass. Then there's the sound of something smashing in my room. The orderly doesn't look up from his sweeping and his musical earplugs. Swallowing heavily I take a step towards my room. Another. Look at the shake in my hands. Clench my fists tight. Then I'm at the door. My mouth is dry, fear is whispering in my ears, don't do it, don't do it, go and sit with Mark, watch TV, have a cigarette outside, don't go in. Don't go in.

I step into the doorway. Everything is still. There's no one in here. I take another step into the room. Nothing happens. Nothing at all. I laugh to myself , laugh at the situation. What did I think was going to happen? My shoulders relax, hands unclench. I'm in the middle of the room now. I look at The Zoo. Something is wrong with it, something not right, something is out of place. I can't quite figure it out. My head is muddled, confused, heavy. I step closer. The door slams behind me. I jump, spin round and, as I do, something moves. So quickly it's just a blur, a dark shape. I can't get out of the way and it hits me hard in the face. I can't feel any point of contact, not a fist, not even solid, but something with weight and matter and pain.

My vision blurs and I taste blood in my mouth. My legs go from beneath me and I hit the floor. Everything spins, my vision turns orange, then white. The blur of movement goes past me. I pass out.

As soon as I wake I know something is wrong. Very wrong. I am propped up against the bed. My neck is stiff. I stare at my hands for a long time. The skin is white, veins tracing patterns beneath it. Dirt is packed under the fingernails. The nail of my index finger has been bent back, a blue-black mark across the middle of it, crusted with blood. My throat is dry and sore. I try to speak my name, but it barely comes out. I touch my head and flinch. Probe my sore eye socket.

I can feel the eyes of The Zoo on me. I try to stand but my legs won't hold me, so I move sideways across the room like a crab, the floor clinging to me. I'm lower than ground level, my legs have gone. It takes me decades to reach The Zoo. With one eye closed I count The Figurines and The Animals with an outstretched finger. They're all there.

But there is a gap.

On the second level there is a gap. One of them is missing. Yet they are all there. A gap where there wasn't one. A space where there shouldn't be. What is it? What is missing? I reach back and find nothing.

I collapse back onto the cold floor. Creeping, creeping cold against my skin. Then I pass out again.

I wake in my bed. It's night. For a while I listen to the sound of the sleeping world. The tick and tock of the sleeping ward. I run fingers over my face and find nothing, no pain, no bruise. Nothing. A slight tenderness to my skin, but aside from that – nothing.

Lights from a passing car sidle across the ceiling, drawing

my eyes with them. I can hear the rumble of the heating. Music from somewhere, it sounds like 'je ne regrette rien', warbling and indistinct. I am cocooned by my blanket, wrapped tight in it, a chrysalis. I free my feet and clench my toes against the cold. I try to go back to sleep, but it is elusive and I lie shivering, alternating between staring at the inside of my eyelids and the ceiling. I grow restless and irritable.

Getting out of bed I wrap the blanket around my shoulders and go out into the corridor. The world is bathed in a blue light. It shimmers like water. The reflections of a swimming pool against the walls. My feet stick to the floor and the sound of my skin peeling off the floor tiles as I walk is loud in the ward. Afraid someone will hear, I slow myself to a creep. I don't know where I am going, only that I can't stay in bed.

The day room is still. There are Snakes and Ladders spread out over the table, left there against the rules. The door to outside is locked. I press my cheek against it, watch my breath fog the glass, and trace a smiley face in it. For a while I sit in the armchair. I'm unsure of how long I stay there, but when I stand I have a memory of shapes and colours, of movement, but nothing distinct, everything shaded with the pallor of a dream, narcotic and distant. I find myself in the corridor again, making my way along it. I realise the destination as a sudden burst of panic and fear, but can't stop my progress.

I stop at the door to his room. Wonder where the night porters are. Why I am on my own here. Someone should stop this surely? Someone should be here to see this. To stop this happening.

I push the door open.

Despite not being able to see anymore, he recognises movement in the room, shifts his weight up and turns his blind head towards me. I pad across to him and sit on the edge of the bed. I push him back into the bed with a palm on his chest, whispering 'ssssssssssssssshh'. There is a sound from under the briefcase. I press my ear against the leather, try to hear what he is saying. The leather holds his muffled words captive. He tries to kick out, but his limbs are bound to the bed. I study the knots, sheets wrapped into cord and knotted tight. Around them his skin is red raw and blood crusts the sheets. The briefcase is over his face. Over his head. The ripped handles are securing it around his neck. His naked body is an ugly mass of blue/purple bruises. The weapon is a sock full of soap, pulled over his penis like a balaclava.

I put my hand over my mouth to hold the noise in, not sure if it is a laugh or a gag or a noise of revulsion. Somehow I keep it in, shoulders shaking with the effort. When it subsides I kneel down on the floor. The contents of his briefcase are arranged as a cityscape, tower blocks of personal items, the landscape of the life he was trying to keep private.

Books, classics, piled so the bands of colours match perfectly: The Picture of Dorian Grey; Wuthering Heights; The Scarlet Letter. I allow my finger to trace their spines. They feel waxy and unreal.

Three photo albums. I hesitate, then open the first onto family holidays – kites and picnics and laughing on a beach. I drop it like it burns.

A birthday card. When I open it, it plays Happy Birthday. I allow the first bar of warbling, wavering notes to play before snapping it shut.

A comb, blond hairs woven around its teeth.

A stuffed rabbit. One eye missing, an ear falling over the other.

These things, these totems, they were his life. I understand why he held them tight. They are personal, deeply personal and I am trespassing. I feel dirty and invasive and ashamed.

I leave him there. Briefcase over his face. Limbs stretching against their bindings.

I leave him them and return to my room, where I vomit into the toilet. I don't flush the chain, afraid of the noise.

Sleep still hides from me. So I think of The Zoo.

24.

The next of The Plastics is The Soldier. The order goes: The Cowboy, The Knight, The Pirate, then The Soldier.

Logic would dictate that The Soldier should be nearer to the top than this, and he may well have been above The Pirate were it not for his defect.

He is a cripple. The veteran on the street. A cardboard sign between his legs. He is the guilt in all of us over the horrors of war in a foreign land. The reality of death and maiming we all want to hide from. He brings it all home and we avoid his eye. Study our phone and hurry on. He is the chink of coin in a paper coffee cup. He is the TV news reeling out casualty figures like football scores. He is divided opinion.

He is moulded out of green plastic, an American Marine from the Second World War, and the mould has left a ridge of plastic that runs along the centre of his fried-egg-shaped base. The ridge is too small to gnaw away with my teeth, though I have tried, scraping at it, the sharp plastic scratching at my gums. I worried away at it, trying my eyeteeth, forcing it into the side of my mouth to test it against my molars. In the end, which could have been ten minutes or four hours or three years later, I gave up and picked at it with my fingernails, discovering at the same time that he felt very satisfying in my hand, the end of his rifle pricking the inside of my thumb – an inoculation against the hopelessness of the chewing.

He doesn't stand, he can't stand, he leans and rocks on his ridge like a weeble and for this reason, despite the sensory pleasure I derive from him, he is lower in the ranking than you would immediately think he should be.

He is the following of orders. The debasement of having no choice combined with the masculine ideal of killing for a cause. He is brute force and ignorance. He is the grunt.

He is the taker of lands and the defender of lands.

The Soldier makes up the last of The Figurines; beneath him are only the Animals, which make up the main part of The Zoo. He is the last that understands; beneath him are those that can only listen and obey.

In the morning Newbie is gone. When I ask Mark where he is, he looks at me blankly. I check Newbie's room. The bed is made, the blinds up. The window is slightly open, shifting the plastic of the blind against its frame with a rhythmic slap.

At dinner I sit next to Beth. Her hands shake as she eats. She takes tiny mouthfuls, barely a spoonful each time, then leaves half her meal.

I push my plate away. I can't face it. She asks me if I want a cigarette. I say yes and numbly follow her outside. The cold hurts the bones in my hands as I draw the smoke into my lungs.

I ask her how she came to be here. I immediately want to withdraw the question. She examines me. Momentarily I think she is going to slap me: her hand is raised, her palm flat, then she rubs it against her face.

'How does anyone end up here?' she says, 'how did you?'

She waits for me to answer, but I don't, so she starts talking.

'I was an infant teacher. It's a great age. They're just starting to be people, but too young to have been affected by the world. They're beginning to understand things, there's no cynicism there yet though, just an intrigue. I tried teaching older kids and found it heartbreaking to see that gone. They change so dramatically, so quickly nowadays.'

'Hasn't it always been that way?' I ask.

'I know I'm sounding nostalgic. Think back to when we were kids though. Think about what we did and hat we had access to, then think about today.'

'I've got a son.'

'You must know what I'm talking about then? How do you keep it all away from him?'

'I can't keep him away from anything from in here.'

'Of course. I'm sorry. I didn't mean to suggest anything. Where is he now?'

'His mother.'

'Are you still together?'

I consider answering her properly and telling her everything.

'Sorry, that's really personal,' she says, 'Don't answer if it makes you feel uncomfortable'

'No. It's okay. We're not. Weren't, even before this,' I gesture to the building with my head. 'She'd taken him away from me before I came here.'

She rests her hand on the top of mine where it lies on the bench. Her fingers are minute against mine. Minute and pale. Doll's hands. I can feel the pulse in her thumb. She makes no attempt to move it away. I stroke her little finger with my remaining thumb. Neither of us looks at each other.

'I became very depressed,' she says. 'I watched them leave me and go into the main school. Watched these beautiful, innocent little children turn into something else entirely and it hurt me much more than it should have, to be honest. I struggled to deal with it.'

94

'Do you mind talking about this?'

'No. It helps.'

She closes her eyes.

'Each year I felt they needed me more and more. And each year without fail I could help them less. I don't want to sound like a cliché, but I spent less and less time teaching.'

'My wife. My ex-wife is a teacher.'

'You know then. You know what it's like. There's this machine behind us all. A big, clumsy juggernaut of a machine. Don't get me wrong; education has always been something of a production line. But the end product is less important now. It's as if it's the actual production that matters now. It doesn't matter now what comes out the other end as long as we tick all the right boxes on the way through.'

Her eyes are still pressed shut, but tears are rolling down her cheeks, dragging mascara with them. I let her cry, dabbing at her swollen cheeks with the sleeve of my jumper. Still she doesn't make a sound. When she eventually begins to talk again her voice is staccato with concealed sobs. As she talks I become aware that she's never spoken about this at length before. I get the impression this is a long rehearsed internal monologue, which has never been shared. I can see it in her body, the way it unfurls, her shoulders becoming looser. I realise I am doing something good by listening, by letting her simply speak. I don't interrupt her or interject at all. I put my arm around her shoulder and she buries her face in my neck so I have to strain to catch the words. Her tears are hot against my skin.

'The irony is,' she says, 'as the council take more and demand more, there is less opportunity to give to the people you actually want to be giving to. I always knew who I was and what I was doing, or at least what I wanted to do, but this was steadily being eroded and I became little more than a bureaucrat. I was worried the kids could sense it in me. They're like animals in that respect, children. They sense weakness. You must have experienced it as a child, a supply teacher coming in and being totally destroyed by the class. As soon as I acknowledged the change I think it became inevitable that I would fail. I thought of nothing else. I lost all my faith in myself, and what I was doing. Of course when it happened it was in front of a class. It's my own fault. I tried to fight it. You can never beat the system. I should have realised my hands were tied and tried to make the best of it, but I couldn't because I cared too much.'

She pauses. Pulls herself from my grip, fingers fumbling for another cigarette. I light it for her.

'If you try and fight anything of that size, with that much momentum, you are bound to lose. And I became more and more depressed. Found it harder and harder to get up, to go to work. It's pretty standard from there on in. Everything just collapsed and here I am.'

We stay outside for another half an hour or so. The air gets noticeably colder. Beth is shivering. As we get up to go in she whispers 'thanks', and I tell her she is welcome and mean it.

25.

The first day of filming. Ben Jones is there from the bank. Baxter, myself, Hilary and Jessica are seated on uncomfortable plastic folding chairs behind the camera crew, talking in hushed voices. I wonder why Hilary is there, showing off, clinging on, trying to be involved. It irritates me. Jessica is wearing a grey skirt suit, dark tights on impossibly shapely legs. I keep looking at them as her skirt rides up. I'm sure she sees and makes no attempt to pull it down.

In front of the camera is a mock-up of a family kitchen. From where I'm sitting I can see the plywood backing to everything. The orange make-up of the actors under the lights, the plastic whiteness of their teeth and perfect hair.

Ben puts his hands on the back of my chair, leans over my shoulder and says, 'I almost believe it myself'.

'Let's hope so eh?' I reply.

He claps me on the shoulder and goes and stands next to the director, who shouts 'action' and the proxy of daily life begins in front of us again.

They repeat their movements, aim at crosses on the floor, say their lines, the director calls 'cut', they do it all again, like mechanical toys, actions by rote, perfect and the same every time. I look at the darkness behind the dome made by the studio lights and I can't see the ceiling, can't see the back wall, just black extending back and back and back, my eyes un-focus, a softness around the edge of things, it all falling away from me, and the girl in the set is Sally and the boy is Harry and the man is me and as they get smaller and further away I reach out for them and . . .

'I need to get a drink and some fresh air,' I hiss at Hilary.

'I'll join you,' he says and the others stand and come with us.

We're in the canteen drinking cheap coffee. The place is nearly empty. My phone vibrates an email into my pocket. As I reach in to read it Ben interrupts me.

'So,' he says, reaching across me for the sugar, 'talk me through the concept again. I've got to report back on this tomorrow. Mr Berkshire wants a full debrief.'

'Didn't they tell you? This has all been signed off, hasn't it?'

'Yes of course, but I haven't seen anything other than the original documents you showed us.'

'Okay,' I say. My coffee is cold. I wave at Baxter and point at my cup. He nods and leaves the table, 'it's about putting the public's mind at ease. We're writing you a whole new ethos. It's about not just knowing where your money is, but what it is doing, so you can get on with your life without worrying. We're playing on the guilt that people have that makes them have a load of direct debits for charities every month and the whole transparency thing. We're filming the life without worrying bit today.'

'Gotcha,' he says and I realise how young he is.

Once the shoot is over we go for dinner at a nearby chain restaurant to eat badly cooked steaks and drink house wine. Halfway through the meal I remember the email. It reads 'I hope you're proud of yourself'. It appears to have come from my own email address. Confused, I stare at it, phone in one hand, glass of wine in the other. I must stay frozen for a long time because Hilary asks me if I'm okay. I tell him I am and go to the bar to order another bottle of wine, but I am shaken and can't lose the feeling there is someone behind me. Back at the table I keep checking the phone. It stays blank, flashes the time back at me, which creeps inexorably to the early hours as the wine bottles multiply around us. Hilary is demanding karaoke, the waiter is trying to tell him they don't have it, have never had it and Hilary is accusing him of lying. Then I'm at the bar with the bill and Hilary is nowhere to be seen so I pay it and shovel mints into my mouth, filling my cheeks like a hamster and then we're moving to a bar nearby and Hilary is back, swaying as he walks, leaning on me, muttering about having no-one to go home to and I check my phone again, think about calling Sally, telling her where I am, opt instead for an easy text message: '*Shoot just finished having dinner won't be late,*' and I know it's a cheap, cheap lie, I know she knows it and my face burns red.

The pub is old-fashioned, traditionally English: a fire in the corner, Johnny Cash on the juke box. Baxter is telling the old joke about the man jumping from the Empire State building, as he's falling repeating 'so far so good, so far so good' and Jessica is laughing a laugh like wind chimes. Ben is opposite me with a big drunken smile on his face.

'I've got to go to work first thing,' he says, 'probably didn't ought to have any more.'

We scoff and tease him, order another round, organic lager, strong, yeasty. Surrounded by the wood and the red leather, the thud of darts into a board, the crackle of the fire, the rasp of Johnny Cash's voice and the lager sitting on top of it all, I'm starting to feel very drunk. Before I can stop myself I have turned to Hilary and asked, 'Do you ever question it, you know, what we do?' and he looks at me as if I've spat into his face.

'Bloody hell, no. Why would I?'

'I don't know. I was just thinking. Do you never ask whether we're doing a good thing?'

99

'What's good got to do with anything? People are going to buy things whatever we say. They're going to spend money they don't have on cars and clothes and get fat from food and booze. They're going to go on holidays and fill their credit cards until they can fill them no more. We can't affect that. We don't affect that. What on earth has got into you?'

'God knows, must be the drink talking.'

'Well for heaven's sake tell it to keep its bloody mouth shut. You're putting me off the evening.'

He studies me over his pint, glasses falling down his nose, glazed eyes struggling to focus.

'For pity's sake, man up. You're not going all commie on me now are you?'

I'm laughing, trying to make out I'm joking and he seems to be buying it.

Sometime later and I'm at the jukebox with Jessica and she's scrolling through the tracks, flipping the CD covers. Baxter joins us, putting his arms around our necks.

'I'm going to get going. Got to start being responsible now,' he says.

He hugs Jessica, looks like he is going to hug me, thinks better of it and shakes my hand instead.

'Good work today,' I tell him and he grins at me.

We turn our attention back to the jukebox and I look at Jessica's profile, at her neck, her nose with the hint of a bump in the middle, at the small silver hoops in her ears, the way she holds her tongue between her teeth as she reads the labels, at those furrows either side of her nose, at the hair fallen out of her pony tail. She catches me looking and smiles, so I turn away, suddenly bashful. Then she shouts 'Got it', thumps the glass and whirls away from the jukebox as 'You've lost that lovin' feeling' begins and she's singing, moving her hips, looking at me and singing and

I'm saying 'Tom Fucking Cruise' and watching her hips, watching her hips, watching her hips.

At a different bar somewhere deep in the centre of the city, polished, crisp and modern. Three of us looking down the jaws of a line of shots. Multicoloured jewels of shots in a wooden plank. There's a reflection of us in the mirror behind the bar, too far away to see anything other than misty pink shapes. Drink the shots down, peppermint, chilli, apple, toffee, pure vodka, something else.

In a booth and Jessica is in the toilet and I'm making a lechy comment I know I shouldn't. Ben shows no sign of hearing it, then he says something about the campaign, something about whether we should be saying what we're saying and I mean to ask him what he means, mean to pin him down to it, but Jessica is back and we're in the street, hailing cabs, saying goodnight to Ben, then we're in a cab, just the two of us, and the glass is cold against my face, the world spinning, looking at her legs, her beautiful legs, close to mine, feel the heat from them and we're outside her house, she's looking at me and we hold eye contact too long, then I kiss her on the cheek and she gets out and we pull off and I'm drifting off to sleep in the lullaby of the motion and the last thing in my head is 'so far so good, so far so good, so far so good, so far . . .'.

26.

The office is soggy with hangover. Hilary hasn't turned up yet, Baxter is his desk, head down. I've avoided Jessica. Alan takes pleasure in slapping me on the back of my skull. I pour glasses of water down my throat one after another and eat too many Nurofen. I phone our IT department and ask them to check if anyone could have broken into my email account, they tell me no, no-one has been in it, so I check my sent items and see only the stream of business mails I sent yesterday. The email is no longer in my inbox either.

Mid-morning Sally texts me and reminds me that we're going out for Harry's birthday at the weekend and asks if we can have a nice family day. I reply 'yes, of course', then after a second add a kiss to the end of it. She doesn't reply.

The director of the ad phones and tells me the rushes of the shoot are on our FTP. I spend the next couple of hours in a darkened room watching hours of silent footage with Baxter. It's good, if not inspired, and I hope it can be enriched by a well-chosen soundtrack and the rest of the footage.

Hilary arrives after lunch, a pair of sunglasses on and a trilby pulled over his face. He goes straight into his office and closes the door. I don't see him for the rest of the afternoon.

One of the designers asks me to look at some work he

has been doing for another of my clients. It's based around semaphore. A series of flags arranged to make up the name of the company. I tell him it's too complicated and that the consumer just won't get it. He argues we shouldn't be pandering to the lowest common denominator and I inform him that that is exactly what we should be doing. I can tell he is annoyed, that I've offended his artistic pride. He argues with me for a while longer and I can feel myself getting angry with him. I bite my tongue and in the end I walk away from him mid-sentence.

I hide in the kitchen for a while, write offensive messages with the fridge magnet letters, sit on the sofa and make a cup of coffee. Jessica comes in. Tight black trousers. White vest top. Grey cardigan. She looks like she had a full eight hours and a session at a beauty spa.

'Heavy night last night eh?' she says, leaning against the work surface.

'Not compared to the old days,' I reply and press my coffee cup on my cheek.

'Don't think I would have been able to handle them then.'

She looks like she could handle just about anything.

I struggle through a conference call by making grunts in all the right places, in the process filling an A4 sheet with doodles I can't decipher and don't remember making. I leave the office early, signing out in a hand that no-one will be able to read, and turn my phone off.

At home I play a game of Hungry Hippo with Harry, spend half the time chasing plastic balls around on the wooden floor as he laughs like a harpy and throws them at me.

Sally goes to bed early so I read Harry a story and kiss him goodnight. I sit by the bed as he falls asleep then listen to his soft breathing for a while, watching his chest rise and fall, and my heart is breaking.

I climb into bed with my wife, next to the forbidding wall of her back and pull a duvet over me that feels like a shroud.

27.

In a room.

Being asked questions.

Lots of questions.

Questions I don't know the answers to.

While I'm thinking about the missing piece of The Zoo.

Thinking back trying to remember what it was or whether it was, thinking back and trying to answer questions I don't know the answer to and not to answer questions I do know the answer to.

Questions about Newbie and the briefcase and the stacks of his life.

Head Psychiatrist. Janet Armitage. Female, 45-50, paid between thirty and fifty grand, homeowner, about to become an empty nester, interested in gardening, reads *Elle Decoration* and the free aspirational magazine, luxury saloon bought on HP.

Interested in Newbie and what I know and what I don't know.

'We're not accusing you of anything,' she says, 'we're asking everybody the same thing.'

I say nothing about the briefcase and the sock and the bruises and the little piles of his life.

'It's important we all trust each other here. We're all committed to well-being, but we can only achieve that through total honesty.'

I say nothing about The Zoo and what it showed me.

Janet is earnest and smiling and not accusing me of anything. She just wants to find out what happened.

I'm saying I don't know what happened, asking where he is now and she's saying it doesn't matter.

I don't know, I really don't know, but she seems to think I do, seems to think I know exactly what happened.

She looks at me patronisingly, as if she's waiting for me to tell her something she already knows. That she knows but wants to hear it from my mouth.

So I search my memory and only find the ward and the light and the man on the bed with the briefcase on his head and the piles of his stuff arranged on the floor like a ritual.

I'm asking her what she wants me to say and she's saying, 'The truth, just the truth. Somebody got hurt and somebody needs help and we can't help if we don't know the truth. We just want to know the truth.'

Janet is all smiles that hide her age and her pay, the fact she's a homeowner, that she's about to become an empty nester, is interested in gardening, reads Elle Decoration and the free aspirational magazine, and her luxury saloon was bought on HP.

All hidden behind the smile and the questions and the lack of accusation that feels like it is one anyway.

Outside the room I hear a clatter, metal against tiles, something heavy dropped. I look at Janet Armitage. She doesn't flinch, shows no sign of hearing it, or if she does she doesn't want me to see that she has.

Something mechanical starting up, metal grinding against ceramic. A circular saw or a grinder. Workmen shouting. It drowns out her words. I have to really focus on what she is saying, something about how we are a community and we rely on each other and I cup my hand to my ear, her words lost in the din until I can just watch her mouth move. It's hurting my ears. I flinch, shy away from it, press

106

my palms against my ears and see the disappointment on her face, so I say, 'no, not you, I'm trying to listen, I can't hear you because of all the noise, all the noise out there. What are they doing?'

She is getting cross, I can see her trying to suppress it, not hiding it well and I want to explain, I don't want her to think I was ignoring her or being rude, I wanted to listen to what she is saying, but she is getting up to leave, saying, 'I'm glad we talked,' and I'm saying, 'Yes, me too' but it sounds sarcastic and she's gone and the sound goes with her until I'm left in the room on my own with an echo.

Back on the ward the noise is there again. Down the corridor by Newbie's room. Getting louder and louder as I pad towards it. The end of the corridor is blocked with opaque plastic hung from the ceiling. From behind it I can see movement, the shadow of bodies passing from left to right. The grinding is there too, but quieter now. I go closer. The plastic is attached to the walls on either side with yellow and black tape. The plastic breathes rhythmically. In and out.

I watch it for a while. I can't make out what is going on back there. There is some pattern in the movement. Definitely bodies. But too abstract, muffled by the plastic and dampened. On the floor in front of it a layer of dust coats the tiles. In it is a trail of footprints, small footprints, child's, leading up to the plastic. The last cut in half by the drop. I kneel down and study the swirl and patterns in them. Bare feet . . . I put my ear to the plastic, feel it slap against my skin, now there is just the hint of work and enterprise behind it.

I go back into the day room. Beaker approaches me.

'Do you know what they're doing down there?' I ask him.

He doesn't acknowledge my question, instead raises his imaginary camera to his eye and pulls focus on me. I put my hand over the lens. He seems annoyed, shoves it away.

'Stop taking my photo,' I say, 'what are you? Some sort of paparazzi?'

'Evidence,' he says.

'Evidence of what?'

He raises a finger to his lips, whispers 'shush'. Says, 'I can't tell you, they can't know, otherwise all my work is wasted.'

On his way out of the day room he pauses in the doorway, takes my photo and grins as if he has got one over on me.

I'm suddenly aware of how tired I am, so I return to my room and lie on my bed, hands behind my head. I reach for sleep even as it mocks me. Sometime later the door opens and an orderly puts his head round it. He says my name. I raise my head and grunt at him. He nods and leaves.

I try again to sleep.

Half an hour later the orderly is back. I realise that something has changed in the way I can lead my life here.

28.

In the car on the way to Harry's appointment we listen to a CD of animal songs and in the back Harry happily sings along. I join in with the noises. A goat. A monkey. A cow. Struggle with a goat, causing Harry to guffaw with laughter and call me stupid Daddy. The roads are busy and I realise we're going to be late. Before we left I had a muted argument with Sally. All in hushed voices and gritted teeth where she accused me of trying to play the fucking hero and only wanting to take Harry to his appointment to score points. I resisted the urge to say something about paying for it all and left the house in a temper, dragging the boy along behind me, his little arm stretched up and his hand warm, gripped too tight in my palm.

When I see the time I swear and then flinch as he repeats the word. Telling him not to say it only makes him repeat it and laugh. So I try to distract with some monkey noises.

When we get there I'm flustered, sweating and barely holding it together. The receptionist tuts at me and tells me we'll have to check whether we can still be seen, then leaves us on uncomfortable plastic chairs to wait.

We're surrounded by stacks of out of date magazines, piles of games with the pieces missing, oh-so-fucking-happy posters on the walls.

It's hot in here.

Harry is bored and fidgety. He knocks an avalanche of magazines onto the floor and, as I'm sweeping them back

109

up, the receptionist returns to tell us the doctor will squeeze us in. I look around the empty waiting room, at the empty, uncomfortable plastic chairs, at the lonely oh-so-fucking-happy posters and say 'I should think so too.'

The doctor is a young girl, who looks too young to know anything about anything, a plain young girl in a white coat that hides a drab grey jumper and scruffy jeans. As she takes Harry through his exercises, la la la la, fa fa fa fa and helps him roll through tongue twisters, I sit on another uncomfortable chair and check my phone. There are two text messages, one from Sally which I scroll over without opening and another from a withheld number saying 'It'll catch up with you'. I stare at it for a while and roll possibilities through my mind before coming up blank. I consider deleting it, instead open Sally's. 'I'm going to be late back, going to Toys R Us'.

I reply with a simple 'okay' and think back to a pub, ten years ago, twelve, maybe twenty. A Sunday afternoon in Nottingham, rain crashing against the windows, a table covered in graffiti. I was scratching at it with my nail and trying not to look at her, knowing we were there for her to put an end to it. Turning my pint glass around in my hand as the words stumble from her mouth. 'We shouldn't be doing this. We live together. I'm finishing my degree soon and I'm going back to Leicester.'

I want to say, 'no', to tell her that we should try, we should carry on, that things will be all right, but I go to the bar instead and order us another couple of pints and when I look up she's smiling and I know she doesn't mean it, that she's saying it because she thinks she should.

'I don't want to stop,' I say and sound so childish and petulant that we both laugh. Then I reach across the table and take her hand, her chewed nails, the softness of her hands, the weight of a ring on her thumb. We're both

110

smiling now and I lean across the table to kiss her, she turns her head, then turns it back and her mouth is warm and my other hand is on the back of her head, pulling her close, our teeth clash and we laugh while we're kissing, butterflies in my stomach, a thrill in my groin and I say, 'shall we go back to the flat.'

We fuck on an unmade bed with the curtains open and she bites my neck, sucking the skin into her mouth until it burnishes blue and later, when we lie there smoking, I run my fingers over it and she says, 'I want people to know you're mine'.

I sit on the uncomfortable chair listening to my son repeat 'the ragged rascal ran round the ragged rock', listen to my son trying to find a way to bring together his mouth and his mind, and think about how everything else is unravelling, how I miss my wife, and know that it is not in me to stop it from happening.

29.

Beth's reading a book, her mouth moving, tongue stuck out between her teeth. Listening hard I can just hear the words, breathy and so quiet as to nearly be non-existent. All vowels whispered between bitten lips.

The day is tight about me. Everything is compressed and there is a pressure in my skull that makes my eyes hurt and my vision explodes in pins and needles when I turn my head. So I sit stock still, any movement exacerbating the pain, sit stock still and reach out for whispered words. She doesn't seem to notice me, or shows no sign of doing so if she does. I watch her eyes slide down the page. Watch her mouth form words I can barely hear and wonder what she is reading.

A layer of dust coats everything and I can taste it in my mouth. The building work has moved further down the corridor and the noise is constant: hammering and metal against metal. The crash of bricks on the floor. It has been incessant for the last couple of days, starting early in the morning, 6 or 7, then continuing throughout the day, before stopping at around 3 am. They don't even seem to break for lunch.

Earlier, as I stood chasing shadows through the plastic, someone's hand crept between the plastic sheets and split them slightly like theatre curtains. In the gap I could make out movement, the flash of a fluorescent jacket, a stack of bricks next to an upturned wheelbarrow and then the curtain closed, leaving just the calloused fingertips and then they were gone too.

I don't know how Beth is reading her book.

The expression on her face is of rapt concentration. She looks at peace for the first time since I met her. A flash of jealousy explodes through me like ark light. I squash it down.

'What are you reading?' I ask.

She holds the book up so I can read the cover, her eyes continue to trace the words. *The complete short stories of Franz Kafka,* I read.

'Is it any good?'

'You've not read any Kafka?' she asks, incredulity in her voice.

'No,' I say, feeling acutely embarrassed.

'You know about him though?'

'He's the one with the beetle, yes?'

She peers over the top of the book and laughs. 'Yes, he's the one with the beetle. That's not the one that I'm reading though. I'm reading the one with the talking monkey.'

'It's about a talking monkey?'

She checks the number on the page and lays the book down on the table, careful not to break the spine.

'It's about a monkey that has taught itself to be like a human,' she says.

'Go on.'

'You're really interested?'

'Yes.'

'Okay, it's a about a monkey. Well, a chimp really. So not a monkey at all. It's been caught by hunters and taken home by them on a ship. They keep it locked in a cage, so small it can hardly move. It realises it can buy its way out by becoming one of them. The first thing it learns is to spit on the floor, then smoke a pipe and then drink booze.'

113

'Typical bloke.'

She smiles. There's a tiny gap between her two front teeth.

'The whole thing is a monologue that the chimp is giving to a group of scientists.'

'Do you know how it ends?'

'Oh yes, I read it for A levels. He tells them he can't remember what it was like being a chimp anymore and he's quite pleased about it.'

She picks her book up again. I let her read, watching her eyes devour the words, listen to the rasp of the paper as she turns the page and think about changing myself to fit in with what is expected.

I feel a hand on my shoulder, look around into the eyes of an orderly and he asks me if I'm doing okay, if everything is alright and I tell him yes, even though I'm sure it's not. He seems satisfied and leaves, something furtive in his manner, so I follow him, down the corridor to the plastic sheeting, which he splices open with his palms held vertically, pushed through the gap and pulled apart, then, with a glance over his shoulder, he is through them. The sheets fall back, slapping the floor and causing a cloud of dust to hang in the air. I go to follow him, treading as lightly as I can so as not to leave a trace. Pressing my ear against the plastic I can hear an engine start up inside then man's laughter. I put my hand against the gap and tease my fingers through, feel heat on them from the other side.

Then I hear a voice down and to my left, thick with vowels and unintelligible. I jump. Asian Radio Lady is holding her radio up to me. It spits and crackles with white noise, focusing momentarily into music, haunting Gregorian chants, then descending again into the hiss. She says something else I can't understand. I ask her to repeat it. She does, but I still can't make it out. Then the third time I get it.

'It's for you.'

'What is?' I ask and she forces the radio into my hands. Taps her ear.

'I don't understand what you want,' I say.

Taps her ear again. Then my chest, repeating, 'it's for you.'

So I put the radio to my ear and sink into the white noise. Somewhere deep in there I hear a voice I recognise, a deep baritone speaking words I recognise. An accent from a dark land. A speech from a long time ago about freeing the country from the yoke of capitalist imperialism, something about the resources. Nested in amongst the fizz and pop of distortion. Barely there.

I'm forced to go back and remember and for the first time since I've been in here I am truly terrified.

30.

Harry has been awake for hours.

He scrabbled at our bedroom door at 6 am and curled up on the end of our bed like a cat. I tried to get him to go back to sleep, but in the end gave up and went downstairs with him to make breakfast. When Sally joined us we were sat at the breakfast bar eating Coco Pops, Harry's head cocked over the bowl, telling me the noise it made.

'I heard a p-p-pop Daddy. And a c-c-crackle.'

Sally kissed him on the side of his head. I thought she was going to kiss me as well, but instead she brushed her hand against my cheek and perched on the bar next to our son.

He opened presents that were as much a surprise to me as they were to him.

In the car on the way to Monkey Kingdom he chunters and titters in the back and sings along with the jungle CD. I make monkey noises with him and Sally reaches between the seats and tickles his bouncing feet. I study the greying sky, my mind vibrating with trepidation. Turn the air-con up until the heat makes my eyes hurt.

We park in the overflow car park. I help Harry pull on his wellies, zip his parka up to his neck and pull the hood up.

'You look like a monkey now,' I tell him.

He giggles and jumps about, tickling his own armpits.

We trudge through the mud on the long walk to the

entrance. The air is damp and cold, the wind picking up, sweeping the car park of leaves. I yank my coat around my neck.

'How cold?' I ask no-one.

'Stop being such an old woman,' says Sally.

There are only three pay kiosks; the queues meet us as we pass under the welcome sign. I go to say something, but Sally catches my indrawn breath and shoots me a warning glance.

As we wait I check my phone, erase a heap of spam emails. Sally plays pat-a-cake with Harry, their gloved hands making whumps. Kids bounce and jiggle around us, one behind bumping into the back of my legs repeatedly. I want a cigarette, want to ignore the fact that we agreed not to smoke in front of Harry. The kid behind slams into my legs again. Sally gives me Harry's hand and goes to the front of the queue. Harry looks up at me, his big eyes a question framed by a sloppy fringe, I shrug. 'I never know what your Mum's thinking. Best you learn now never to second guess what women are thinking.'

He looks confused.

'How c-c-can you second guess something?'

I begin to explain but am interrupted by Sally's return.

'Here,' she says to Harry, 'They've got maps. You can choose what you want to see.'

They huddle around it. I find a pen in my inside pocket, put it in my mouth and chug on the lid like it's a fag.

'He's your son all right,' says Sally.

'Uh?'

'Not even slightly interested in the rides and kiddy stuff. Wants to go straight to the monkeys.'

'Well, at least he's got one of my good traits.'

She looks at me as if she is going to say something but stops herself.

At the kiosk I hand over my card, amazed at the figures on the till display. As the attendant hands it back wrapped in a coil of receipt, Sally and Harry are already off into the park. I jog to catch them up. They're hunched over a sign attached to the wall of an enclosure. Harry turns to me, bangs both fists against his chest.

'It means gorilla,' he says, points at the sign, 'it's a language for people who can't hear anything. T-t-they speak with their hands instead.'

Then he's away again pulling Sally by the hand.

We watch Spider Monkeys run rings around the edge of their enclosure. Get close enough to watch their nostrils flare as they breathe, look into their eyes, at their black fur. Then notice a pair of tiny hands amongst the hair, see the tiny face of a baby monkey pressed tight against its mother.

At the glass wall of another enclosure, hands pressed on divisive glass. Inside there are tottering towers of rain-drenched wood, a tyre spinning in the growling wind. A member of staff lobs food over the top, it cascades and rattles off the dead trees and Harry follows it with wide eyes, shouting, 'he's eating it, he's eating it', as simian hands scrabble in the dirt for grain.

We stand with soggy families at the Orang-utang enclosure. Sally and Harry are talking, their words stolen from me and swept away into the air. The Orang-utang pulls a blue blanket over its head and shuffles its body around so it faces the wall, back to the watching crowd, like a child playing hide and seek, hand over its eyes, can't see you so you can't see me. The wind snatches at the blanket, billowing it up, trying to take it into the sky as a kite.

In every cage the monkeys huddle together, the wind whipping furrows in their fur. It screams between the enclosures and slaps the loose plastic covering of a sign against the wall with a crack.

118

We take cover in one of the inside viewing areas, gagging at the smell of shit and food. A young chav couple, all neck tattoos and gold jewellery, fight against the door, smashing their pushchair against its frame. As the door slams closed, chimps swivel and stare at us. One climbs to the top of a tower of trellis, puts both palms against the ceiling and pushes, trying to force open an imaginary trap door. The muscles in its massive arms ripple, but the ceiling doesn't give.

The chav baby screams, struggling to get out of its push-chair, the mother swearing and grabbing at kicking legs.

Harry tugs at the material of my jeans, so I pat his shoulder, saying, 'It's okay. It's okay.'

I attempt to distract him with a picture attached to the wall at child eye height in a metal frame with screw heads filed off. A smiling chimp with paint all over its face, brush held skew whiff between wonky teeth. Harry points at the sheets of paper in front of it, splashed with random colours and lines and shapes.

'N-n-not as good as mine,' he says and I tell him the story of the chimps from the TV commercial that used to live here. The longest running TV advertising campaign ever. The chimps dressed as a family, lips quivering in mimicry of speech along with the voiceover.

'H-h-how long was it on telly for?' he asks.

'40 years.'

He thinks for a while, then says,

'That's older than me?'

'Older than me,' I reply, ignoring Sally saying, only just.

He studies the picture again for a while.

'Was it always the same m-m-monkeys?'

'I don't think so,' I say, 'I think they just used ones that looked the same.'

Sadness clouds his face.

119

'Do monkeys d-d-d-die?' he asks.

'Everything dies eventually darling,' says Sally, picking him up and kissing his face until he giggles, dead monkeys forgotten.

My reflection in the glass as I look into dark chimp eyes, at a foot hanging over the edge of a hammock, the swirl of fingerprints, calloused and grey, a lip curled over human teeth. It picks at its nose and the gesture is familiar. The blink of an eye and in it I can see recognition, understanding, empathy.

Harry shows me the sign language for chimp.

He calls at the chimp, calls its name at the glass until the chimp turns to look at my son and Harry is screaming, 'It heard me, Daddy it heard me, it knows its name,' his stutter lost in hysteria. The chimp jumps from the hammock, crosses the floor and cuddles up to another chimp, stroking its face.

Later we sit on a bench with a plaque dedicating it to a dead girl and wait for a leopard that never shows.

I suggest a drink, but Harry won't leave until he sees the leopard, so I make my way across the park on my own, leaning into the wind, spots of rain flecking my face.

The trees bend down to touch the ground. On a bench under their swaying canopy a small boy sobs into his hands. I walk past. Then go back. He is only wearing a t-shirt and shorts, sandals on his feet.

'Are you okay?' I ask, squatting down on my haunches in front of him.

Black hands are pressed against his face. He has short, tightly curled hair, soaking wet.

'Where are your parents?'

Behind his hands the sobbing becomes wailing. I reach out for him, try to peel his fingers away. He screams, jumps away from me, cowers against the arm of the bench and shouts something at me in a language I don't understand. I reach out for him again. He pushes himself into the wooden back of the bench, climbs it, feet scrabbling.

'It's okay, it's okay. Can you tell me where your parents are?'

Yellow eyes filled with terror.

Then he is up on his feet and running away into the bushes lining the path. It takes me a second to react and then I am chasing after him, shouting at him to slow down, that I want to help. The branches push back against me, the top of one springing back and cutting my face. I reach a tall metal fence and he is nowhere, all I can hear is the wind bullying the trees, the branches ricocheting off each other and the rain lashing down.

I scramble back onto the path. Search about for an employee, but can't find one and when I return to my family I am shaking.

'What happened to you?' asks Sally.

I tell her about the boy. 'Did you tell anyone?'

'I tried,' I say, 'I tried, but couldn't find anyone.'

She grasps Harry's hand and leads us through the deluge to the information desk where I splutter out a description of the boy. The attendant copies my words onto the back of a paper bag and repeats them into a crackling radio.

In the cafeteria I cradle a cup of over-sweet tea and listen to Harry chatter about painting chimps.

The rain increases, turning the paths into streams and we run splashing to the Gorilla house, Harry leaping from puddle to puddle, the wind pushing us about like chess pieces, where I press my hand against a bronze cast of a Gorilla's hand and a Silverback prowls around in front of us.

The car park is nearly empty, most people having left as the weather worsened.

Harry sleeps in the car on the way home and Sally stares out of the window. I drive home in a daze, gusts of wind smashing into the car so hard I have to grip the steering wheel tight to stop us meandering across lanes. I think of the boy running through the bushes, his yellow eyes and bare feet and haunting screams.

In the night I reach for Sally and this time she responds, never opening her eyes and we have familiar, mechanical sex and I force myself into her harder and harder and her nails scratch at my shoulders until I collapse off her and she rolls away from me. It's so dark I can't tell if my eyes are open or closed.

31.

The order goes: The Cowboy, The Knight, The Pirate, then The Soldier. That's all of The Figurines and then it's The Animals.

The Animals break down like this: The Lion is the first of them. This needs no explanation. He is the king of the beasts, the master of the savannah, the top predator. But even he is below The Figurines; because on the seventh day God blessed us with the recognition that we were superior to the animals. But there is a disconnect, a gap between The Figurines and The Animals. It occurs to me that here is the gap. The missing piece. I can remember nothing being there in its place though. As far as I can remember it has always been The Soldier then The Lion. I try and imagine something else, but I draw only blanks and my memory always arranges them like this: The Cowboy, The Knight, The Pirate, The Soldier, The Lion, then The Animals. The logic seems right. The order seems right. The nagging feeling is just that. Like leaving your home convinced you left the iron on, or having to go back to check the front door is locked. It has to be an illusion. So I push it down.

So, the order goes: The Cowboy, The Knight, The Pirate, The Soldier, then The Lion, his mane a proud quiff, brushed up and to the side like that of a sixties rocker.

He sits like the Sphinx and there seems to be a trace of a smile on his face.

He is the endangered species that is also the top of the

food chain. He is losing his fight with Man the species and paradoxically is individually more powerful, more instinctual and more deadly.

Daniel was snatched from his den and Hercules stole his pelt.

He is bravery. He is stoicism. He is the messianic figure in an imaginary world through a wardrobe. He is the roaring introduction to a film and he is Born Free.

He is a star sign that represents leadership, confidence and creativity.

But he is also hunted, killed, traded and penned back.

Beneath The Lion it is more difficult, they are much of a muchness, the categorisation is looser and less sure. So here I push them aside and think of other things.

The fifteen minute checks are grinding me down. I try to hide from them. Avoid the concerned gazes and the earnest head nods when I tell them I am fine.

Since they began the building work I am struggling to sleep. I am irritable and tired. I think about my son constantly. I wonder what he is doing and whether he is thinking of me too.

The speech from the radio is with me at all times. I stretch for the words, but the harder I try the further away they retreat. Asian Radio Lady won't let me touch her radio again. The last time I tried she hollered so loud the orderlies came running and I backed away with raised palms, struggling to convince them I wasn't doing anything. I imagine a note on a form somewhere, about me attacking fellow inmates and *there* never seemed so far away.

Numbness. A plastic tray on a plastic table in a bright canteen. My teeth clenched under a spasming jaw.

Beaker sits opposite me. Slides his tray onto the table and huffs his way into the seat. His knees touch mine under

124

the table and I angrily shift mine away, stare at him, but his attention is focused on cleaning the lens of his camera. He blows onto it and then polishes the glass with his shirt sleeve. When he's satisfied he raises it to his eyes and examines me through the viewfinder. I put my hand up over my face like a cheap celebrity stumbling out of a bar in the early hours.

'Stop it, will you?'

He ignores me. Clicks the shutter. Again.

I lash out, hitting only his hands.

'I said, stop it.'

He whispers something.

'What did you say?' I demand.

He whispers it again.

I lurch over the table and repeat myself.

'I said, I need to,' he replies.

'Need to? Why would you need to?'

I sit back down, the anger gone and now looking at the hurt on his face I feel selfish and stupid and aware of myself. The canteen is too quiet, just the clash of cutlery on plastic plates and the low chatter of the dining staff.

His tone is conspiratorial as he gestures for me to lean in close and says, 'I'm not crazy, you see.'

'Well, none of us are, are we? We're just having difficulties with living in our high pressure modern society.'

'It's all an act.'

Someone drops a tray, an explosion of metal against tiles, the smash of crockery breaking. A cheer builds around the canteen, like in school. Beaker looks as if he is going to stop talking. I put my hand on his forearm. Nod encouragement at him.

'I work for a paper. A major paper. I'm doing an article on the mental health system.'

I can't stop my look from being incredulous.

'Really,' he says, patting his invisible camera, 'And these are going to go with the article. With your permission, of course. We wouldn't publish your photo without your permission. Unethical.'

'Of course,' I say. 'How did you get in here then?'

'Faked it. An undercover reporter has to be an excellent actor.'

'Aren't you afraid that you're going to end up stuck in here?'

He taps his nose. His eyes magnified by his glasses.

'I wrote down my intentions before I came. I just have to say the words and,' he mimes taking off with his hands, forces a whizzing noise between his teeth and says, 'don't tell anyone though. I'm trusting you. You're the only person I've told in here.'

As he leaves the table he winks at me and grins.

I lay my head on the table, cheek against the surface and look at the world down its expanse. I can see my breath steam momentarily on the plastic and when I try to raise my head I find I can't.

Then there are hands on my face pushing it into the table, pushing my nose against the table until I feel it crack under the pressure of hands on the back of my head. I can feel ragged breath on the back of my neck, heat, screams. The smell of sulphur harsh in my nose.

I gag.

Something is pushing me harder into the table as I struggle, trying to wriggle from the grasp. It's holding me tight, a weight on my back, rancid breath moving the hairs on the back of my neck.

My own panicked breath lifts the dust off the table in snorts of white. The touch of lips on my ear and a voice in my ear, in my head.

'I am coming for you.'

126

I'm screaming, but my mouth is held shut against the table and I feel as if I'm going to explode.

Then the weight is gone. The voice is gone. The breath is gone.

I'm on my own, spinning my head round and round looking for the perpetrator. The canteen is as it was – groups of people huddled over trays, scooping colourless food into mouths, the chatter of the dining staff, no-one near me.

I look down at the imprint of my face in the dust of the table and see my cheekbones, the flat of my forehead. The pout of my lips and the wet ellipses of my eye sockets.

Eventually the shaking stops and when I stand to leave I realise I have pissed myself.

32.

A slapping fight between Beard and Asian Radio Lady causes the staff to run into the day room and, seeing my chance, I slip away to the plastic sheet. Some instinctual respect for authority nearly stops me, then I force my hands through and pull it apart.

On the other side the corridor is unrecognisable.

The plaster has been stripped from the walls, revealing pockmarked breeze blocks. Most of the floor tiles have been ripped up and the concrete underneath is water-stained and chipped. The fluorescent tube lights are smashed and hanging down from the ceiling. The doors to all the rooms have been removed, in their place gaping black maws into darkened rooms. Scaffolding runs alongside the left hand wall, a bucket of bricks still swinging from the lower planks. The air is thick with plaster dust. There is a sense of recent desertion.

I take one step through. Leave a trailing foot on the ward.

Above the scaffolding I am sure I can see daylight. The feet of a ladder sitting on the top planks, even when the top of it must be above where the ceiling level is. A stack of corrugated metal leans against the other wall and over the top of it a piece of material. Gold, red and black stripes in an order I recognise. I strain my eyes into the gloom and think I can see the outline of a gold crown in a white circle.

I shudder.

Noise behind me in the corridor.

Beard shouting.

I pull myself back onto the ward, brush the dust from my shoulders and, scuffing at my footprints on the floor, turn straight into the face of Janet Armitage. She looks concerned. 'Are you okay?' she asks. Her voice is soft as lambswool.

I stutter, nod and try to push past her.

'I just wanted to know what they're doing in there.'

She peers over my shoulder.

'Same as they always are I would say.'

She has a grip of my arm, steering me back towards the day room.

I want to ask her what she means, what she means by same as always, but she is talking to a doctor, at the same time easing me through the doorway into the day room so I stand there, nullified, impotent and I am sure I hear her say my name.

I sit at the table in the day room. Dust is covering everything like snow. Someone has written my name in it with their fingertip. It isn't my writing.

I can't stay here. I go to the sofa area and lump into a seat. The dust puffs up around me with the force of my body. Mark is in one of the other seats, the dust heavy in his hair like dandruff. I smile at him. He returns a weak smile then turns away. The hair at the back of his neck is spiky and aggressive in the place of his pony tail.

Later.

I am sat at the computer. The internet is ponderous. I watch the blue bar creep across the screen. Most pages I try to look at are blocked. Instead I open Wikipedia and type in *Nghosa*. On the right of the screen I see those colours again. Stripes of gold, red and black in an order I recognise. The outline of a gold crown in a white circle. Nghosa – officially the Republic of Nghos, a country in East Africa, the Indian ocean to its south east and bordered by The Islamic Republic of Nerjeru to the north.

I feel someone sit next to me. Without looking I know it's Beth.

'What you looking at?' she asks.

'My past,' I say.

She squints at the screen and then looks at me quizzically.

'You lived there?'

'No. It's hard to explain.'

'Okay, I don't want to pry.'

'You're not prying. It really is hard to explain.'

I scan the screen again. I know everything that's on there. It's telling me nothing new. The keys are cold on my fingertips. I trace my name out on the keyboard, touching the keys lightly. Lose myself for a moment and when I come back I see that Beth is staring at the scars on my left hand. At the gap where my thumb used to be. At the criss-crossed scar tissue, white and tight. I instinctively pull my hand away, then acknowledge the concern on her face and put it back. She rests her hand on top of mine. Then turns it over so I can see the recently healed scar running vertically up her wrist.

I want to tell her, to explain everything, instead I say,

'We did it to ourselves.'

She nods.

33.

I'm walking back from a meeting at a new recording studio in a digital cinema to see if we can use it to record the voice-over for the new Dutch bank commercial. We've got a well-known Shakespearian actor in to do it. A voice people can trust.

I'm regretting not driving. There's drizzle in the air. The scarf around my neck is already wet. Jessica is walking next to me, her heels clacking on the pavement. She's wearing a long coat, so there's only denier-clad legs showing underneath and shoes with tiny leather straps around the ankle. A rut in the pavement causes her heel to turn over and she falls into me, grabbing my arm. When she rights herself she doesn't let go, just loops her hand through my arm. I can smell her perfume.

The studio wasn't good enough. They spent more money on the plush green leather sofas in reception than they did on the equipment. I only went to look at it because Alan asked me to. Friend of a friend or something. I'm looking forward to telling him it was shite.

We stop at the ring road. Jessica unlinks my arm and presses the zebra crossing button.

I look up at the building which houses the regional newspaper. Grey plastic and stark black glass against an apathetic sky. On the tower a digital clock displays the time, then flips to the temperature.

We wait for the lights.

I glance back up to the clock. It says 'wait' instead of the time. W. A. 1. T.

Jessica tugs my arm and we cross the road. At the other side I glance back at the clock. 7 degrees.

As soon as I get back into work Collins knocks on the open door of my office. I ignore him and turn on my computer. As the Apple logo appears in the middle of the screen I gesture him in. He closes the door behind him.

'I wanted to ask you something,' he says.

'Okay.'

'I don't know if you know this, but my father is head of security at a technology company?'

'I didn't.'

He starts to talk again. I raise my hand. Pick up the phone and dial my PA. Ask her to bring me a coffee. I'm cold. My knuckles hurt.

'Do you want anything?' I ask Collins. He shakes his head.

'I spoke to my father last night and he told me there had been a big shake up in the office. The marketing director walked out,' he says conspiratorially.

'Okay. And you're telling me this why?'

'They're bringing in the marketing director from Diamond Homes.'

We worked with Diamond Homes for years. For a long time they were our biggest account, we looked after all their advertising for the Midlands region. We lost the account when they pretended to take all the marketing in-house and then pimped the creative to a big London agency.

'I texted her and congratulated her on getting the job.'

My coffee arrives. It's scolding hot. I blow onto it. Watch the ripples on its surface.

'She asked me to put together a creds pitch,' says Collins.

'And you want my help?'

'I want you to help and I want it to be my account.'

I take a sip of the coffee. Feel it burning down my throat right down into my stomach.

'Okay,' I say, 'Good work. Get a date and we'll put something together. Keep this between us for now, yes?'

Selfish, wanting to claim the win, not wanting it in my pipeline.

'That's what I wanted,' he says and I understand how he can swallow his pride and come to me for help. Hilary may have been right.

When he leaves I follow my mouse around my screen and feel empty. The coffee doesn't warm me up. I turn the air conditioning up in my office. It has no effect and I shiver, clasping my arms around myself and stare at the back of my door until I notice that all the lights have been turned off outside. I get up and open my door. Everyone else has left. The office is black and quiet and lifeless. As I'm locking my door I think I hear somebody moving about in the corridor. Turning the lights back on I search all the conference rooms, then the board room. Nothing. As I lock the outer door of the office and make my way down the stairs I am sure I see movement on the stairs below. I shout out. No-one replies. I pick my pace up and half run, half tumble down the stairs. As I hit the bottom the main door is swinging shut and there's a blur of a small leg bursting through it.

The car park is empty. I can hear the groan of the city. Nothing else.

As I'm driving home I pass a poster for Lou's exhibition and experience a crushing pang of guilt. I pull the car over and dial her number. She doesn't answer. I light a cigarette and the car fills with smoke. After a while I notice the phone flashing. When I answer it Lou just says, 'well', and

133

waits for me to speak. Now that I'm faced with the reality of talking to her I don't know what to say.

'Look Lou, I just wanted to say I'm really sorry about what happened,' I spit out eventually. It sounds false, hollow and not even close to near enough.

'That's it?'

A lorry rushes by, close enough to buffet my car. It continues to rock for a minute, like a pedalo in the wake of a tanker.

'Nothing I can say will make it better. I was an asshole. I know I was.'

'You were more than an asshole. You were a childish, stupid, violent asshole.'

'I know. I'm ashamed of myself.'

She falls quiet. I listen to the echo of my breathing through the phone.

'I don't know how to say what I want to say. It's not my place to have to say this but you made it my place when you ruined my party and wrecked my sculpture. My fucking sculpture, James. You of all people should know what that means.'

'I'm really fucking sorry. I was off my tits. I know it's not an excuse . . .'

'You're right. It's not an excuse. But it is always your excuse,' her breathing is quick and angular, 'You've changed. That sounds clichéd and horrible and is nowhere near strong enough for what I mean. But you have. I barely recognise you anymore.'

'Lou . . .'

The anger is rising in her voice. I can imagine the face she is pulling, blotches of red rising on her cheeks.

'We've known you for a long time. Even Dan says he doesn't recognise you anymore.'

This hurts more than it should, hurts more than her

thinking I've changed. Ridiculous, but I don't want Dan to think ill of me. I can handle Lou being pissed off with me. Dan is somehow different. I stammer another apology.

'You need to take a long look at yourself. Look at what you're doing and who you're doing it for. I know you don't believe in karma, but what goes around comes around and you're racking up a huge debt.'

'You're talking about the bank aren't you?'

'Yes, I'm talking about the bank.'

'What do you think they've done.'

'Watch the fucking TV James. I'm not your teacher.'

The tone of her voice has changed. Softer. Still angry, but there seems a way forward.

'Are we going to be okay?' I ask.

'We're going to have to be okay because you're married to my best friend. This doesn't mean I've forgiven you. I'll be polite to you for Sally's sake, but I want you to stay away from me as much as is possible. And know this, I'm watching you.'

'Thank you,' I say, 'I am sorry Lou.'

She hangs up. I open the window and the smoke spills out into the night.

34.

The thing that gets you in here, the thing that makes it unbearable, is the boredom. Human beings aren't supposed to be kept locked in the same place day after day. We're not supposed to repeat the same actions over and over.

Get up. Eat breakfast. Go outside for a cigarette. Sit at the table in the day room. Art therapy. Once a week go down into the gym to swim twenty lengths in a pool full of piss. Weekly doctor's rounds. Eat dinner. Watch TV for a couple of hours. Go to bed. Get up. Repeat.

Then there's group therapy. Sit in a group and share your most private thoughts. Spill out the reasons why you're so fucked up, so a group of strangers in the same position can nod and sympathise and applaud your misery. Led by another stranger in a white coat and dirty trainers who will cajole and prod and push you and try and make you give everything up in the name of your recovery. So you can get from in *here* to out *there*.

'Mr Marlowe.' The surname, always the surname. Formal and respectful.

I move my gaze from the tiles to the voice coming from a coat and a jumper, a face that is too young to talk to me with authority, a face kissed with a hint of stubble and eyes that are free of lines. Eyes that hold mine and will me to talk.

I return to the tiles. Count the number between my foot and Beaker's sock to my right. One. Two. Three. Study

136

the dirt in the grout, the dust over everything, the curl and twitch of Beaker's toe in his threadbare sock.

'Mr Marlowe.'

Again.

'Mr Marlowe?'

I raise my head.

'Have you anything you'd like to share?'

I have. I'd like to tell them about a lost wife, a lost son, a lost boy in a zoo, a lost life. But I don't. I bite my lip and shake my head. I want to tell them about how the time in here is filled with a longing for the drink and the cocaine that will take away the boredom and the doubt and the fear. But I don't.

'It helps, you know. It helps to share with the group. No-one is judging. There's nothing to be afraid about.'

But he's wrong. There is something to be afraid about and I can hear it. It's always there now, beneath everything, as a constant. It wants me to know it can do what it wants when it wants and I am powerless to stop it.

He's moved on. The doctor or the intern or the orderly or whatever he is, with his near moustache and scruffy shoes, with his clipboard and pens and questions. He's moved on to someone else and they're talking. They're telling us things they wouldn't share with their closest friends or with their families. We're lapping it up, nodding and clapping and making sympathetic ohs and ahs. This circle of loonies perched on plastic chairs, each one of us with a halo of baggage above our head.

I push the dust about on the floor with my feet, drawing figures of eight. It's everywhere, settled on everybody's shoulders like the first snow.

It's hot in the ward, the heat on too high. It makes me apathetic and drowsy.

The day stretches out before me, a highway of wasted

minutes. I trudge along it. Given my medication by the pudgy hand of a nurse, put them in my mouth, swill them round, consider hiding them under my tongue, then swallow them down. They stick in my throat. Two waxy lumps and I swallow, swallow, swallow, until I can dislodge them, splay my mouth wide open so she can see my fillings. Then the highway weaves and winds and becomes softer round the edge as the day is spent in confusion and the embrace of the armchair, of cigarettes and the wooden plank of the bench outside. Then it is time to go to bed and I lie, eyes on The Zoo, afraid to turn my back on it, it being made of whispers and accusation.

The heat is rising, until the air is full of it. Hot and dry like the air in a sauna. Hot in my lungs as I breathe it in. The heat on my chest is like a black dog.

The Zoo.

All the while, pointed fingers and implicit threat. I dare not turn my back because I know it is there. I don't have the courage to move it or face it, so instead I watch it through itchy eyes, fighting off sleep until I can't any longer and I fall into a well of dreams of crowds and motion, that push me this way and that, people all around me, so close I can smell the food on their breath, their sweat, my feet are off the ground, washed along on them, trying to look over my shoulder. When I manage to turn my head I can see my son, way back, way back behind all these people, all these faceless people, his arms raised, his mouth moving, calling 'Daddy', as all the while I'm dragged further away from him, then pulled under, into the world of chests and arms, screaming out for my boy, then I'm lifted up, spun around, looking down on the hands that are bearing me along, the hands that belong to The Zoo, I see them all, and I'm screaming his name again, but he's long gone and all that is left is this. I'm filled with a sense of loss and hopelessness

138

that I could never have imagined, so complete, nothing of me left.

When I wake it takes me time to realise that it was a dream.

The sheets are kicked off. I'm slick with sweat and panic.

When I am calm enough I sit up in the bed. On the floor is a piece of paper torn from a spiral-bound notepad.

I pick it up. When I read the words, bile fills my mouth and I remember the dream, am there again and I thrash about on the bed, try to find purchase, something to kick against. I kick myself weak like a toddler, and when I am spent the paper is still there.

Written on it in a childlike hand, is one word.

Beth.

35.

I scrumple the paper up into a ball and throw it at the wall where it bounces and rolls to the feet of The Zoo. I hug my knees and avoid looking towards the window, towards The Zoo, towards the paper.

Beth.

The intention is clear.

I think of her – delicate, damaged with big, teary eyes. The scars on her wrist.

I unfold myself and go to the door. I put both hands on the frame and lean out into the corridor. The ward is quiet; even the workmen have stopped. The heat is oppressive, the air hardly moving. I close the door as quietly as I can and, cushioning the handle, push it until it clicks. Leaning against the wood I face The Zoo. Swallowing fear I kneel on the floor in front of it, clasp my hands together and push the ball of paper away with my knee.

I look up at The Cowboy, The Knight, The Pirate. The Figurines. The Animals.

'Why her?' I plead. I squeeze my hands together until they shake, close my eyes and whisper, 'Not her. You don't have to have her. Take me instead. You don't need to have her.'

Even as I say it I know why it has to be her, know that I have played my hand and become acutely aware of the danger I've placed her in.

'Please,' I say, 'anyone but her. Take Beaker. Not Beth.'

Silent amid drifts of dust on the shelf, The Zoo won't bend or deviate. It will always do what it intends to do, so the only reason it has shown me is to hurt me, to taunt me about how little I can do.

Not this time. I won't let it happen.

'No,' I shout at The Zoo. 'You won't hurt her.'

I make a decision. I haven't got long – they will check on me soon.

I take the chair and wedge it under the door handle, testing the movement. It holds, it is a start, but it won't go on holding. Around me the atmosphere is beginning to crackle and hum, static all about me, the hairs on my arms upright. Through the window the sky is darkening, a bank of cloud rolling over the horizon, angry and full of rain. Still the temperature is rising. I am drenched in sweat as I drag my desk across the room, move the chair and wedge the desk up against the door. I put the chair in front of it and sit challenging The Zoo.

The whole room is full of electricity now, sparking about me. There's pressure in my head, thumping behind my eyes. The door handle flaps up and down. Someone is calling my name but I blot it out. Stare at The Zoo through the heat haze. A roll of thunder tears the bank of cloud open and rain begins pelting the window. My head is full of the sound of The Zoo starting up. Clanking and whirring and grinding and I know it wants to get out, out through me, out into the ward, at Beth.

I grip the seat of the chair, squeezing hard, as if the pressure of my fingers alone will keep her safe from it.

Then the smell again – sulphur and burning. In my mouth. In my throat. In my chest.

And the voice.

'You cannot help her.'

I'm shouting that I can. That I *can* help her. The world

141

is shaking around me, the door handle wrenching up and down, my chair rattling on the floor. Rain is slamming into the window in waves and all about me the sound of The Zoo, so loud my ears ring with it. Someone thuds into the door from the outside, the voices telling me to open it calm at first, then more urgent, distracting me and I turn away from The Zoo for a second. Something smashes into me from the side, launching me from the chair. I hit the wall, my head striking it first. They ram into the door again. The room is lit by lightning. Ram the door again. The chair flies across the room. I pull myself up, drag myself across the room and sweep my arm through The Zoo, sending it skittering across the floor. The sharpest of pain in my chest, neck, a vice tightened on me.

A shoulder rattles the door again. There's a hand on my chest holding me down, sharp nails against my skin, another hand around my throat squeezing. There are people are all about me grabbing my arms. I kick out, connect with someone's shin and they fall next to me. Then they've got hold of my legs. I'm screaming her name, telling them to keep her safe. My sleeve is rolled up. A spike of a needle and a coldness spreads through my body. I fight against it, determined to stay focused, but it is like ice in my veins, down my arm to my fingertips, up my arm to my shoulder, across my chest. My eyelids are heavy and I am loose in their arms. Underwater. They lift me and carry me from the room, down the corridor with my head lolling upside down. Faces watching me. Into the isolation room, onto the bed, straps over my arms. The door closes then a hatch in it opens and a pair of eyes look through.

The Zoo is quiet. It can't say anything.

From in here it can't say anything.

I allow myself a smile.

36.

A day or a week later. They've upped my medication; I am weighted down.

Initially I was checked on constantly. Sporadically a nurse came in and injected me with a substance that made me feel like I was sinking. Then after a while the door was left open and the visits became less frequent. I didn't have the energy to stand, let alone walk, so I lay in a stupor on my bed.

The dust gathered on me, filling my eye sockets and coating my tongue. It built up around me like snow drifts. Then the injections stopped and I steadily regained my focus.

No-one has mentioned me moving back to my room, so I stay here. At least from here I can't hear the building work.

An orderly enters and helps me to my feet.

I'm led to Janet Armitage's office and plonked into a tall-backed leather chair opposite her. It's the most comfortable thing I have sat in in a long time.

Janet is reading a sheath of papers in a brown A4 folder. She doesn't acknowledge me.

I study my nails. They're longer than I normally wear them and encrusted with dirt.

She grunts, a satisfied noise, and closes the folder. Puts it down on the desk, leans back in her chair and folds her arms.

'How are you feeling?' she asks.

Manners win and I say, 'I'm okay thank you.'

It sounds ridiculous as soon as I say it.

'I've been reading your file.'

I nod. I am childishly small in the chair as I swallow a snivel in my throat.

'You were, are, a very successful man.'

I shrug.

'Intelligent too.'

I shrug again.

'There's no need to be modest,' she says, tapping the folder, 'it's all in here.'

One more shrug.

'I'm sure you don't want to be in here.'

I shake my head.

'You haven't spoken to anyone since you got in here. If you don't speak to us we can't help you. And if we can't help you, you won't be able to go home. A man of your intelligence is wasted in here.'

I study the grime under my nails.

'You've got a family, haven't you?'

A tear rolls down my cheeks. I'm nodding, yes, I have a family. Janet is waiting but she is no more than a shimmer through the mirage of my tears. Through the tears I'm trying to say, 'it's always someone else gets hurt, always my fault, but it's always someone else who gets hurt', but the words are lost in the spasm of my throat.

'Are you ready to talk to me now?' Her voice is velvet.

I nod. 'It all started falling apart because of a television programme.'

37.

The day it begins I pick Harry up from school. He's excited, showing me a picture he's made: shells and pasta and glitter stuck to a sheet of pink crepe paper. He's scrawled his name in huge letters with a blue crayon along one edge.

'It's a m-m-monkey,' he says, pointing at a shape, which looks nothing like a monkey. I coo at him with parental pride.

When Sally returns from work she is carrying a grey tray piled high with exercise books and spends the evening working through them with a red pen. I make us a stir-fry and Harry, fish fingers. I've been trying to quell my drinking, to come straight home from work, behave like a husband, so when she asks me to open a bottle of wine it feels like we're heading in the right direction.

I choose a bottle of white Burgundy. I place the glass in front of her and take away her plate. She waves a thanks at me, eyes still on the exercise books.

Harry is nagging at her, trying to get her attention, so I sit him on the sideboard and get him to help with the drying of the dinner dishes. He chatters away all the while.

'The monkey looked at me D-d-dad. Did you see it? When I called its name it looked at me. I-I-I-I'd like a monkey. Do you think we could be friends? I don't talk monkey, but I think it could understand me. M-m-m-maybe I could teach it sign language like at the z-z-z-zoo. Do you think?'

'I don't know Harry, maybe. It's nearly time for bed.

Go and say goodnight to Mum and then I'll read you a story.'

He reaches out with his hands, I help him down and he trots into the lounge. I follow him through. He kisses and hugs Sally.

'I'll put him down,' I say to her. She mouths thank you.

Upstairs I help him brush his teeth, pull on his pyjamas, tuck him into his bed. He insists on me reading him The Gruffalo for the 30th time. He is all smiles and reciting the words, halfway through though I can see his eyelids going and he's asleep before I finish. I kiss him on the forehead and turn off his light.

Sally's pile of books is going down.

'Do you mind if I turn the TV on?' I ask her.

'No, just keep the volume down,' she says without looking up.

I flip through the channels until an introduction stops me dead. The BBC logo on screen and a voice over: an investigation into mineral mining in Nghosa.

Bookmark this moment, Janet, because this is the beginning.

I sit cross-legged on the floor in front of the TV so I don't have to turn it up. It begins in a hospital, an interview with a doctor who treats women who have been the victim of rape and sexual violence. It's the only hospital in the country with the facilities to treat forgotten women. Can that really be possible? One suitable hospital in a nation of millions. There's a 14-year-old girl with a baby on her back, a baby that is the result of gang rape by a group of soldiers. The interviewer talks to a woman whose father's eyes were plucked out before he was hacked to death with a machete because he refused to rape her. Her own eyes are empty, her words unwavering. She is the walking dead. A prickly heat covers my back. The camera cuts to the interviewer. He is a mask of unbelieving horror. He chokes out questions, his shoulders shaking with anger as he talks to a young girl who had a plastic bottle stuck into her, heated with a lighter until the plastic was red hot and molten. Another woman, 19 years old, had her clitoris removed. Bile is rising in my throat. 'Why does this happen?'asks the interviewer, 'what sort of man could do this to a young girl?' The answer is matter of fact. 'Soldiers. Boy soldiers.'

I want to turn the TV off, I want to stop watching, but I can't, I have to see this through.

Behind me Sally slams shut a book and sighs.

'What are you watching?' she asks.

I think for a minute, consider explaining it, then say, 'the end of civilisation.'

She yawns.

'What do you want to do? Watch a film, listen to some music?' I ask.

'I wouldn't mind going to bed. I'm really tired. Do you mind?'

'No, of course not.'

Upstairs we brush our teeth and get ready for bed in silence, then lie under crisp duvet and sheets. After a while I can hear her taking deep breaths as if she is about to say something then stopping herself.

'Are you okay?' I ask.

'Saturday night. Shall we leave Harry with my Mum. Go out, just the two of us?'

'Like a date?'

She laughs, and the tension in the room dissipates. 'Yes, like a date. Maybe go for dinner, then the cinema?'

'Yes,' I say. 'I'd love that.'

And I would. Right now, I'd love it. In the dark I roll over and try to find her mouth, miss and plant a scruffy kiss on her forehead. She grabs my hand and squeezes it. We hold hands, her palm small and warm in mine, and then she lets go, rolls over. In seconds she is asleep.

Saturday night. I watch her dress, pulling on a flowing black dress then sitting at her dressing table applying make-up. She catches me watching her in the mirror and says, 'What?' But she's smiling when she says it and I smile back. I wrap my arms around her neck and kiss the top of her head. She squeezes my arm.

Sally's mother arrives, a flurry of mac and scraped back hair, all ageing glamour and pragmatism. Harry explodes in excitement at her arrival, shouting 'G-G-Gran's here,' running back and forth down the corridor.

'I wish you wouldn't call me Gran, it makes me feel old,' she says, trying to catch him as he brushes past her.

'Evening Sandra,' I say, kissing her on the cheek.

Sally comes down the stairs.

'Oh darling, you look wonderful.'

I have to agree with Sandra, she does. She looks wonderful. Elegant. Beautiful. A whole list of superlatives.

We take a taxi to the restaurant. Butterflies dance around my stomach. The day is closing down. Across the city street lights blink on, shops close, bars open. The Yin Yang of the city.

As the taxi slides through the inky evening, I'm thinking 'so far so good, so far so good . . .'

The Opera House restaurant is in the Lane area. It's pedestrianised, with boutique shops overwhelmed by the massive new glass shopping centre that I catch glimpses of through side streets as we make our way there. We tentatively hold hands.

A French maitre-d' greets us and leads us to our table. The restaurant is a warren of booths and alcoves, private

148

tables, shadowy, all lit by candles. I hold the chair out for Sally. She folds her dress under her thighs as she sits. In the light of the flames her eyes are moist. I make a show of ordering the most expensive red wine and then feel like a prick.

Around us there is the low hum of conversation. I realise I'm listening to other people and not talking to Sally. She checks her mobile.

'How's the new account?' she asks, putting the phone in her bag.

So I tell her about the bank and the creative, about how the advert will run and feel like I'm giving a presentation. Halfway through my phone beeps. I check my messages while still talking, no idea what I'm saying, words spilling onto the table. The message, from a withheld number, says, *you're a fucking fraud.* I delete it.

Our dinner arrives.

We eat. My steak is too rare but I don't complain, don't want to make a scene tonight. I drink my wine too quickly, it goes to my head and the darkness, the candles and being here with Sally makes me woozy, like I'm underwater and Sally's face shimmers in the heat from the flame. Over the table, she's in the distance.

We talk about Harry, how he's doing at school, how his stutter is getting on. She moans about her job, about the headmaster, about government cuts and as she's talking I think back to another date. More like a pub crawl. The two of us in a sports bar. Dressed in tattered jeans, her hair lank and eyes rimmed with kohl. Standing talking about Nirvana and Kurt Cobain and arguing whether Bleach is a better album than Nevermind, Sally passionately standing up for Nevermind and me pulling out clichés about Bleach being more real. Her calling me a snob, that it being real has nothing to do with whether it's a better album. Then it's closing time and the bouncer asks us to leave. I've still got most of a pint left and he's telling me to hurry it, so I neck it in one and as her laughter chimes about us both his anger grows and suddenly I'm vomiting the beer onto the table, onto the screen embedded into the table and onto the bouncer's shoe. He's grabbed me by the throat and dragged me down the stairs and thrown me out the door and Sally is punching his back with little balled up fists. I'm face down on the tarmac, tasting the blood from my nose and she's hunched over me, brushing my hair from my face, kissing my eyelids and we're both laughing. We stagger down the hill from the centre. Stop at the park and drunkenly clamber over the fence. The moon's reflected on the boating lake. We fuck on a basketball court, grazing my knees. Then go back to our new home. Our first home – with damp walls and borrowed furniture, a TV on a box, books in a shelf from the wood they pack glass in and mismatched crockery.

We leave the restaurant and walk across town, Sally's arm through mine. There's no weight to it, it might as well be made of air. Outside Lloyds Bank a beggar and a dog lie on a patchwork quilt.

'Have you got any change?' Sally asks.

I root around in my pocket and pull out a handful of shrapnel, her painted nails pluck two gold pound coins and drop them into his polystyrene cup.

At the cinema we watch a Mexican film about a drug dealer who discovers he's only got a few months to live because of cancer. It's full of haunting imagery of reflections that don't follow the person making them, shadows that move on their own, dead immigrants washed up on a beach like driftwood. It hollows me out and when we leave I can't vocalise my feelings about it.

We take a taxi through the muted city to an empty house.

38.

I've been allowed back in my room. It's been tidied since I left, it smells of disinfectant now. My bed sheets are new and taut and there's a new desk and chair. They must have cleaned fairly recently as only a thin layer of dust has settled on the surfaces. I run my fingers through it on the desk top, drawing veins and road maps and spaghetti and . . . something is wrong. The room is dead quiet.

Flat. No noise at all. Not the road. Not the ward. Not the heating. Nothing. I sit on the bed, looking about. The Zoo back in its place on the windowsill. Someone has tidied it up from the floor and replaced it. Put it back in the wrong order. I get up and stand before it. Nothing. Nothing there. The Zoo is silent. I can't help but smile.

I lie back on the bed and look at the ceiling, try and make patterns from the shadow of the chip paper. My eyes get heavy, then I drift off.

A dream of Harry holding hands with the boy from Monkey Kingdom, they're both talking in a language I half understand.

I wake with a banging headache, a pain in my stomach and a crippling feeling that I've forgotten something. Something important. I try to remember the dream as it fades quicker than I can grasp it and within minutes I'm left with a vague sense of unease and nothing more.

Lying there I remember Beth and want to make sure she is okay, to check that nothing happened to her while I

151

was away. I feel anger at myself for not finding out before. I push myself up against a bass drum in my head, using the wall as support I leave the room. I trace it along the corridor like a blind man and when I reach the day room the gap across the corridor is as wide as the Atlantic, my head as turbulent. It takes me three attempts to get across. Stumbling forward, washed back, forward again. The TV threatens to break my head in two. I rest in a chair at the table, lashed with sweat. At the back of my mind the disarray of The Zoo is a constant. I do a circuit of the room, swaying, keeling, mumbling. She's not there. Panic grips me. Mark is outside in the courtyard. I grab him by the arm, demand if he's seen Beth. He pulls away from me, fear on his face, shaking his head violently. The sun bores into my skull so I narrow my eyes against it. Leaning against the wall I try to motivate my body to move again, battling against the inertia that wants to hold me there. Somehow I'm up and moving again, back through the day room, the world rolling, kaleidoscope colours, my vision like oil on water. Down the corridor again where the cramps hit me, snap me in two like a mousetrap and I'm crawling now, back towards my room, when I see her, near the door, reading the notice board. I make it to my feet, using the wall as scaffold and in jerking, strobing steps approach her. She sees me, tries to hide the look on her face, grasps my elbow and in an urgent whisper says, 'James, are you okay?' and I get out a grunt, nod, but that causes the world to explode and I feel my legs going again.

'You need a doctor,' she says.

'No, no doctor,' I force out, voice cracked and desperate, 'fresh air.'

She helps me back out, feeling the eyes on me, shying away from them, burying my head into her shoulder, her hair, until we're outside. She helps me onto the bench, then

152

stands facing me, her hands either side of my head, palms so hot they scald my skin.

'What happened? What's the matter?'

I can't speak. Squeeze my eyes shut. I know what it wants. The inside of my skull is a frozen scream of no.

She cups my chin with her hand. I open my eyes and the world is her face, behind it shadows and depth and in this depth shapes move.

'Your beard has grown,' she says and I run my hand across my face, find thick hair.

She sits next to me. I rest my head against her, shiver and shake.

'You need to see someone,' she says, gentle and insistent.

'No,' I say, 'I just need to be here.'

I feel for her hand and find it, she allows me to take hold of it. Our hands fit together. Perfect and airtight. I become aware that I'm squeezing her hand tight, too tight, that she hasn't let go, hasn't complained, has just stayed there. With the back of her other hand she tests my forehead. Strokes it.

Despite the pain that grips me I feel myself begin to drift away. The pain seems to sense it. It's as if a dial has been turned and it jumps up a level. I grit my teeth. Listen to the shout of no in my head. Focus on it.

No. No. No. No. No.

The more I strain against it the more it ramps up the volume of pain. My head is ready to split in two, my stomach full of twisting knives. Tears fill my eyes. My teeth feel as if I'm grinding them into powder from the pressure of my jaw.

All the while she is there. Holding one hand. Stroking my head with the other.

All the while I'm thinking. No. No. No.

I know how to make this stop, how to make it all go away.

I taste death in my mouth and can't stay there any longer. I wriggle my hand from her grip. The cramp pushes into my stomach and I barely make it to the toilet before I'm pole-axed with violent diarrhoea. I hold my knees and pray for it to stop. It does momentarily and then cripples me again. I hear Beth outside the door calling my name, asking if I'm okay. I'm too weak to answer. I hear her running down the corridor calling for help. When it's over I am so weak I hardly make it back to the bed.

When my door is opened to check on me I can't lift my head, instead remain curled like a foetus, a doctor over me, shining a light in my eyes. I feel the pressure of fingertips against the inside of my wrist, then someone is holding my head up, pouring water down my throat, tablets washed down on it. Through it all I hear Beth's voice, and a male voice, though I can't make out their words. The light is turned off and I'm left alone. The room spins slowly.

This carries on at intervals for what seems like days. Each time I barely make it to the bathroom on time and then return to my bed on shaking legs, with watering eyes and a headache stamping black spots in my vision.

I try to sleep my way through it, a disco inside my head, flashing lights and explosions of noise.

At one point I wake standing over Beth's bed, watching her sleep. She looks so peaceful, all the angst that is present when she is awake has gone. She snores slightly, her mouth open, displaying the tips of her teeth. The bed cover is pulled back and the skin on her neck is pure white in the moonlight, porcelain, fragile. I reach out, touch it with the tip of my index finger, trace her collarbone.

'Do it', says The Zoo. 'Do it'.

I run my fingertip across her throat. She turns onto her side, mumbles something unintelligible. I am numb. The Zoo moves my other hand so it circles her neck, only

154

millimetres away from touching her skin, from closing round it. I can see the shake in my fingers.

Hurt her.

I snap out of it, the panic coursing through me. I clasp my hand to my mouth and the headache washes back over me. The cramps return to my stomach. I spin away, hurl myself from her room, race back to mine.

I know what I need to do.

It wants order and I have to supply it.

'Okay,' I say, 'okay. Just leave me alone long enough to do it.'

I lay still and the headache recedes like the tide. The pains in my stomach become more sporadic until there is just a dull throb remaining.

I pull the chair over from the desk, place it at the window, facing The Zoo. I hate myself for being this weak. Tell myself that this way I can watch it, that I can stop it, so I pick it up and place it all on the floor, then one at a time put The Figurines back in place. The Cowboy. The Knight. The Pirate. The Soldier. Then begin on The Animals. The Lion. Then The Rhino.

The order goes: The Cowboy, The Knight, The Pirate, The Soldier, The Lion, then The Rhino. The Rhino is stocky and grey as an English winter. He is frozen in time as though charging, head down and red eyes blazing. You can see knots of muscle under his thick hide. His stumpy tail is stuck straight in the air like a car aerial. The comical effect of this negates all his ferocity, and ensures that despite his size and strength he is below the Lion.

Of course there is also intelligence to take into account. He is an automaton. A tank. He is bullish and instinctual. He is prehistoric. The past in the present.

He is thick skin.

155

He is point and go. A machine. Trampling. Squashing. Barging.

The irony is that despite his looks he is a vegetarian. He is a one ton hippy.

The horn that is his weapon is also his Achilles heel. The thing that protects him, the thing that makes him hunted. His defence is what makes him prey. The sword on his head becomes ornaments and pretend medicine. It is made of keratin, as lacking a solid core as our fingernails.

He is all front.

39.

When Janet asks if I am ready to share I tell her I am, but only with her. She is to be my confessor. Her and her alone. I will say nothing to anyone else. I will not talk to doctors. I will not talk to orderlies. I will talk to Janet and she will share the burden with me.

'What happened next?' she asks.

I sit in the chair, feet dangling, and I begin to talk again.

I'm late for work. A traffic jam. An accident. An old lady crossing the road has been mowed down by a delivery van, causing an avalanche of fruit and bread rolls to block the road. When the traffic starts moving again I can see the wet patch on the road where they hosed her away.

Jessica is sat on the front desk talking to Ruth, the Office Manager. I hunch over the desk and sign in.

'I can't believe anyone would do that to a woman,' says Jessica.

'A girl. She was a girl really.'

Jessica nods. Neither of them acknowledges me. Jessica holds her phone up, taps the screen.

'All because of these,' she says, 'all those murders so we can have mobile phones.'

'Morning both,' I say.

They notice me. Jessica's smile flashes like a toothpaste advert. Ruth waves at me.

'Ben something from the bank has been calling for you.'

157

I sit at my desk and turn on my computer. The Apple appears on the screen. In the kitchen I make myself a cup of black coffee. When I return to my office I see that the desktop has been changed to a picture of Charles Manson.

I open the door to my office and shout out, 'whichever of you fucking clowns thought it was funny to change my desktop, think again. If I catch anyone messing with my computer I'll cut their fucking hands off.'

I slam the door hard enough to make the pictures rattle on the wall. I revert the desktop to a picture of my family.

After checking my emails I go to the Sky website and look at the details about the programme about Nghosa. An investigation into the mining of Cassiterite and Coltan in the African nation. The civil war fought over the control of the mining. I open Wikipedia and type in Cassiterite. A tin oxide mineral, it is black and crystalline and looks like something from outer space. Used for solder on circuit boards. I type in Coltan. Again black, but shards this time, like iron filings, it's used to make electrical capacitors in mobile phones, DVD players and computers. Next to the text is an image of children digging in an open mine. I see the word Nghosa. I see the words European markets. I close the window down.

The morning drags. I do my billing. Check the hours spent on each job against the price quoted, hand-write invoices that I know Ruth will struggle to translate.

One of the creatives brings in the first draft of the press ads for the bank. I can't concentrate on them.

At 11.30am I take a bottle of vodka from my desk drawer and take a slug from it. The burn wakes me up. I make myself another cup of coffee and pour some more vodka into it.

I remember that Ben called, dial his number and get his answerphone. A minute later he calls back.

'James.'

'Ben. How we doing?'

'Good. Good. You?'

'Yeah, fine. Sorry I missed your calls. Anything I can help with?'

'I've been speaking to Michael', he says and it takes me a while to realise he's talking about Baxter, 'he says we're looking good, that you'll hit all the deadlines?'

'Yes, of course. We've got a planning meeting later this week. After we've finalised that side of things we'll be ready for final sign off.'

'The board is keen to see the whole campaign.'

'As we all are. Nearly there, Ben. Nearly there.'

I take another gulp of my coffee, the forgotten vodka making me wince.

'I need to go back to Mr Berkshire with a timescale.'

'End of next week,' I say, worried he'll hear the drink induced cough in my voice.

'Excellent,' he says, 'that'll get them off my back.'

'Don't worry, Ben. We'll give you something brilliant and they'll love you for it.'

I can feel his relief down the phone. I hang up, turn on iTunes and scroll through it, settling on Thom Yorke, Eraser. The melancholy cradles me. I lie back in my chair.

Everything fades into the background apart from his voice and when I put my hand to my face it is wet with tears. I rest my forehead on the desk. As I pull myself up I see my tears have smeared the ink on my invoices.

At lunch I cross the road to the local. Sit by an unlit fire with a flat pint and flick matches into the hearth. The rasp of the match against the side of the packet. The flare of the flame. I drink the pint and order another. As I cross back to work my legs are unsteady.

I close my office door against the world.

159

Mid-afternoon there is a knock on it. When I ignore it there is another.

'Come in then,' I shout at the wood, barely even trying to cover my irritation.

Baxter looking uncomfortable in the door way. He shuffles and fidgets.

'Are you coming in?' I ask.

He looks back into the office as if deciding and then comes in, closes the door behind him.

'I've just had Ben on the phone asking about the campaign. I told him we were on track. Nothing I should know about?' I ask.

'No. Not at all. I think we'll come in on time and on budget.'

'Good,' I say turning the music off on my computer, 'how's Jessica doing?'

'Well, she's doing well.'

I nod sagely, then say, 'you tried it on with her yet?'

I regret it immediately, aware that I sound like a dirty old man. Baxter shifts uncomfortably in his seat. I shrug to show I was joking.

'Do you mind if I ask you a favour?' When he asks me, he doesn't meet my eye, instead focusing on the floor in front of him.

'I guess that depends on what it is.'

It looks like an effort for him to be asking me this. I wonder when I became the monster.

'Go ahead, ask away,' I say to make it easier for him.

'I haven't told the others yet, but I'm getting married. I asked Melissa to marry me and she said yes.' He is all coy schoolboy pleased with himself. I want to tell him of the pain of marriage, about the work, about the death of love, about uncomfortable silences and empty beds. About how it used to be and how far I've let it all fall.

160

'Mate. Congratulations,' I say instead, work my way around the table, pump his hand, clap him on the shoulder.

'Thanks. Thank you. I'm proper chuffed.'

'I bet. It's not just because she's up the duff?'

'No, no, hell no. That's just an added bonus.'

I go to the bookcase behind my desk, grab a couple of glasses and pour two healthy measures of scotch, chuck in some ice cubes and hand one to him. The liquid is sharp. I struggle to hold it down. Baxter grimaces when he drinks it.

'The favour?'

'Oh, oh yes. We're having an engagement party. Everyone at work will be invited of course and I was wondering whether you'd do the invites for me?'

I think for a second about how I feel about this, then realise I'm really pleased he's asked me.

'Of course. It would be an honour. Email me all the details and I'll sort it out for you.'

He thanks me, I promise I won't tell anyone until he makes the official announcement and when he leaves I drink another Scotch, then another until my throat is numb.

40.

The dust is getting worse. It's on everything. In everything. It amazes me how quickly it amasses. It's piled up against the walls. There are trails through it where people have moved about the ward. I've been trying not to think about what it is and about where it's come from. The bits of us that the rest of us don't want any more. We're not as literal as snakes or moths. We don't shed ourselves in such an obvious way, but we're always losing parts of ourselves and rebuilding. A lifelong metamorphosis. We're a process. Along the way we leave these reminders of ourselves. Hoover or sweep them up and move on. So here I am tramping through the leftovers of all the people who share my confinement or who have been here before me. I breathe in their memories, I traipse through their past as it finds its way into my tea, into my food, under my nails, crunching in my teeth and making my eyes itch. It doesn't seem to bother anyone else. When I mention it to Mark, ask him if it bothers him, he simply shrugs and continues to read the paper. And all the while it grows, this snowy landscape of memory.

I try to avoid Beth. I can tell it's hurting her, but I can feel The Zoo in me. I know what it wants to do and have to stay in a state of constant alertness against it. Several times I have felt it building, seen the first shimmer of light, or felt the pressure building in my calves and have locked myself in my room and shook, shivered, screamed my way through it until a group of nurses have rushed in, held me down and pumped me full of oblivion.

Janet continues to try and goad the past from me and sometimes I give it to her in bite-size chunks. She thinks I'm making progress, but I see only a trail of dust that leads to here and behind it all The Zoo is mocking both of us.

On the way to the canteen I follow Beaker down the stairwell. He is chuntering and muttering. I attempt to fit my feet in the footprints his slippers have made in the dust. It's a game. Like not treading on the cracks. Or balancing on the kerb. He stops and turns to me,

'You've not told anyone, have you?'

His eyes are wild with aggression behind his milk bottle glasses. For a second I'm actually scared of what he might do.

'No,' I say, hands up in surrender, 'of course not. I said I wouldn't, so I'm not going to.'

'Good. Because I'm close.'

He pats the camera which hangs on his chest.

'I've got some great stuff on here. Pretty soon it'll be time to make the call and go out there to tell the truth. They're going to be really pleased. All this will be worth it and I don't want it messed up. I shouldn't have told you. But it's hard, you know?'

I nod agreement, I do know, it is hard.

He seems satisfied by this, pats my arm and then trundles off down the stairs again. I let him go down one landing and then start after him.

Three floors down I pause under a flickering light. The cover is off. I study the W shape of the bulb as it struggles to ignite, the glow working its way around the bulb, nearly far enough to ignite and then fading back to nothing. Starting again. Failing again. All the while it buzzes like an egg timer. It's a familiar sound. I am mesmerised by it. Can't move. The weak bulb illuminates only a few feet around me, the rest of the landing is in shadow.

Somewhere beneath me Beaker's footsteps drift away.

A moth smashes into the light, making me jump. A massive moth, all big hairy body and flapping wings. It throws itself at it over and over. The light fights to ignite. The moth hurls itself at the glass, chasing the fading and resurrecting light. Another moth joins the first and they take it in turns to hit the bulb.

I watch with car crash fascination as another moth joins them. Then another. There are five of them. Six. Seven. I can't work out where they're coming from. There's more now. Maybe ten. Maybe more. Throwing themselves at the light with suicidal intensity.

One of them clips my face. I feel the brush of its wingtip on my cheek. Flap at it with my hand. They're all over the light now, hoards of them. The corridor is full of the buzz of the light and tiny thuds as they crash into it. They're all about me. The weak glow of the light swallowed by the flap of their wings. They're like a dust devil or a tornado and I'm at the centre. A swirl of movement and wings against my face, against my arms, in my hair. I flail about, feel the connections with every swing, but they're everything. The noise of them fills my head. I squeeze my eyes shut and take a jump forward, hit the first step, stumble down it, reach out and find the banister, but fall heavily down the next door, spin around and collapse into the wall, my head hitting it with a thud which shakes my teeth. I stay there, gulping down air, look back at the landing above me, full of moths now, so densely packed they're almost a solid mass. When I can breathe again I take the stairs two at a time, panic a wolf on my back and when I burst out into the canteen I am wet with sweat. Unable to explain myself to anyone I sit away from them all and wait for my heart to calm.

41.

The next day. Enclosed in the leather embrace of Janet's chair. I want a cigarette. I want alcohol. I want a line. She gives me coffee instead. Her office is the epitome of organisation. The books on her bookshelf are in alphabetical order. An array of framed certificates behind her enforces her credibility. The desk is sparse, just a jotter pad without doodles and by the side of it a fountain pen in a velvet lined box, exactly in parallel with the edge of the jotter. I think she's probably got mild OCD. I snigger. She looks up from her computer.

'Something funny?' she asks me.

'No. Thinking about something.'

She turns her professional attention to me.

'Anything you want to share?'

I'm the naughty boy at school. She is the severe teacher. I can only shake my head. She returns to the computer and I turn my attention to the window, to the flat grey sky, to the rain hanging in the air.

'What are they building at the end of the ward?'

'Building?' she asks.

'Yes, behind the sheets.'

'What sheets, James?'

She looks at me like I'm mad. Which of course I probably am. Why would I be here otherwise? I go to continue, but she interrupts me before I get a chance.

'They tell me you've distanced yourself from the group,' she says, fingers dancing on her keyboard.

'I was never really part of the group.'

'It's not healthy. We want you to interact. It's important that you integrate in order to get better. We're a microcosm here. If you can't exist as part of our smaller society you're inevitably going to struggle with the larger one out there.'

'I know,' I say, 'it's best I stay away from people right now.'

'Really? Why would you say that?'

I don't want to go into it.

She stops typing, says 'will you tell me why?'

I don't reply, instead turn around a picture on her desk. Janet and a small jolly looking man, two children.

'Your family?'

She reaches over, turns the picture back.

'Yes. Do you want to talk about your family?'

I want to say something smart-arse, something like, no I want to talk about your family. Instead say, 'which part?'

'Your parents?'

I haven't thought about them for a long time. A flash of pain. Think of a kitchen full of pain and recrimination. An angry car drive away. Ignored phone calls.

'Okay. How about your wife?'

And there is our bedroom. Not long ago. Sally sitting on a chair, her naked back to me. A pad on my knee as I trace the shape of her body with a charcoal. The delicate turn of her shoulders. I draw the curve of her side, smudge the charcoal with my little finger, give a hint of her vertebrae through the slats of the chair. The pinch of her shoulder blades as she turns her head to look at me, the shadow of her eyelashes on her cheeks, her hair swept over one shoulder, fanned out across her skin. The room is lit with just the bedside lamps, her body defined with shade. I put the pad down and go over to her. Kneel on the floor behind her, bury my head in the hollow of her neck.

166

She smells of vanilla and shampoo. I kiss her. She moans and rolls her head to the side. I kiss her again. Trace her collarbone with my lips. I reach around and cup her right breast with a shaking hand, leaving a trace of charcoal on her pale skin. I gently turn her head, find her lips, part them with my tongue, flick it across her front teeth. She reaches behind with her hand and strokes my head. I kiss her more urgently. Sense she isn't responding and kiss her harder. She pulls her head away from me. I hold her tight. Force my mouth against hers. She shoves me away. I grab for her again. Her arms locked, pushing me away, she stands and pulls her dressing gown around herself, saying, 'I can't. It isn't right. I just can't. I know why you're doing this. You're a man. You want to enforce your ownership.'

I reach out for her again and she spins and storms to the bathroom. Locks the door. I scream 'fuck's sake' and throw the charcoal at the door, snatch the picture from the bed and leave the bedroom.

I pull my jeans on, grab the car keys and drive into the night. I don't know where I'm going until I find myself on the street outside Hilary's house. I check my watch – 11.45 pm. As I crunch my way up his drive the security lights come on and the shadows from the stone dogs either side of his door stretch out to greet me with mute snarls.

He answers after three urgent rings on the doorbell. I can tell he's drunk. His hair is dishevelled. There are dark stains on the front of his white undershirt.

'Do you know what time it is?' he asks. Then his face changes, 'you'd better come in.'

The house is a mess. We go through to the lounge. It looks like a student hall. Wine bottles. Beer cans. Pizza boxes.

'You look like you need a drink,' he says.

I nod and follow him into the kitchen. He plucks a glass

from the sink, runs it under the tap then hands it to me, drops a couple of ice cubes into it and half fills it with vodka.

'You don't need a mixer do you?'

'I'll cope.'

We slump onto dirty sofas in his ruined lounge. Drink our drinks in silence. After an age he says,

'They're all bitches.'

I had been drifting off. His voice is a warm slur. He looks tiny on the sofa.

'Women – they're all bitches. Silly old cow won't return my calls. Don't even know what I've done. 30 years of marriage and the fucking mare won't talk to me. I've been round to Angie's parents' house and her old man threatened to call the police on me. I used to play golf with the cunt now he's acting like I'm the stable boy who's poked his rich daughter.'

I nearly tell him about the condoms. Think better of it.

He shakes an empty glass, and says, 'another?'

I nod and he stumbles from the room.

A couple of hours later I get back into my car. Too drunk to drive. Way too drunk to drive. As I reverse out I clip the back bumper on his gate.

I drive home bang on the speed limit. Hunched over the steering wheel, window open, hoping the freezing drizzle-filled air will keep me awake. When my head starts nodding I turn the radio on. The car is filled with the shout of static. Shocked, I lean over to switch over to CD and look up to see something in the middle of the road. Instantly I'm bristling with sweat. Slam the brakes on and swerve hard. Mount the central reservation, fighting with the wheel, all the while pumping the brake until the car skids to a halt. I rest my head on the steering wheel, my body in spasms. Don't want to look back. Eventually I pluck up the courage

168

and snatch a glance in the rear view mirror. In the centre of the road the boy from Monkey Kingdom is standing, hands clasped to his head. I push the door open and climb out.

'What the fuck are you doing?' I shout.

He doesn't move.

'What are you doing in the middle of the road?'

He drops his hands to his side.

I take a step towards him.

'Are you okay? I could have killed you. Why are you standing in the road?'

He starts to back away. As I take another step forward he turns and bolts into the night. I run after him, the sound of my feet slapping on the tarmac echoing behind me. He's quicker than me and soon I'm left chasing nothing on an empty street. My legs and lungs scream and I double over, hands on my knees and vomit onto the road.

It begins to rain as I make my way back to the car. Huge swerving rubber marks on the road. The grass on the central reservation ripped up by my tyres. When I try and start it the engine refuses to fire. I smash the steering wheel with the heels of my palms. I rest my forehead against the window and feel myself drifting off into a drunken sleep. I violently shake my head clear. My breath has steamed the glass. With my forefinger I slowly trace the word HELP into the mist. I begin to worry about police cars. When I try again the engine starts and I carefully reverse back onto the carriage way and limp my way home.

42.

We're all in the boardroom. Baxter is making his announcement. There's champagne and orange juice. Baxter looks bashful when he tells us. There's a round of applause. Jessica is standing next to me, her skin electric against me. Baxter hands out the invitations to his engagement party. On the front is the drawing I made of Sally, her face a blur. Crisp Helvetica text over a smudgy charcoal drawing. Alan passes out the drinks. Glasses clink and there's another round of applause. Claps on the back. As we file out Baxter waves the invitation at me.

'Thank you. They're great.'

'You're welcome.'

I collect up the bottles and take them through into the kitchen. Pour all the dregs into a coffee cup and sip it as I cross back through the open plan creative area. I stop at Collins' desk and pull a chair up next to him. Notice him quickly closing down his personal email.

'Any news?' I ask.

'Yes, we've got a meeting. On the 5th. 3 pm.'

I check the calendar on my iPhone, mark the time out as busy, but don't specify why so no-one else can see it in the shared calendar.

'Nice one,' I say, 'When are you free to go over the creds pitch?'

He brings his calendar up on his screen. We compare dates, settle on an hour tomorrow.

'Mum's the word,' I say as I get up. I think we've turned a corner.

So far so good. So far so good. So far so good.

Someone has written '*everyone is happy apart from you*' on the notepad on my desk.

Sat in the reception of the bank. Baxter. Me. Jessica. They're late. We've been here half an hour already. I take out the iPad, check the presentation one last time. Get up. Lean over the desk. The receptionist is on the phone. She waves a dismissive hand at me. I sit back down. Look at Jessica. She's polished and bright in a black trouser suit, white blouse, just a hint of a cleavage. Baxter looks pale. I straighten his tie for him.

Berkshire stalks across the reception. Ben two steps behind.

'Gentlemen. And Lady.' Berkshire shakes all our hands. I wouldn't be surprised if he kissed Jessica's.

We follow him to the lift and rise through the floors in oiled silence.

The meeting room is already dimmed.

Today we're in Italy. A picture of St Peter's on the wall. Terracotta paint scheme.

I plug the projector in. A square of blue appears on the back wall.

So far so good.

I plug in the iPad, pray that it's going to work. The projector thinks about it, then the square turns white with the agency logo in the middle.

'Are we ready?' I ask.

Seven sets of eyes turn to me. They glint in the light of the projector like wolves around a campfire.

'Proceed,' says Berkshire.

I swipe my finger over the screen of the iPad and begin.

I don't remember the rest. Opening slide, then closing. Sleepwalked my way through it. I come around to silence and a slide that says 'thank you for your time.'

The lights flicker on.

Everyone blinks the darkness away.

I find myself looking at Baxter for reassurance. He gives me a thumbs-up under the table.

'Excellent,' says Berkshire, 'let's get the coffees in and then we'll do questions.'

I take my seat again. Jessica puts her hand on my knee and squeezes it. She is all proud smiles. The coffee comes. I take it black and hot. It rips my throat.

Berkshire takes control of the room. Not sure how he does, a clear of the throat maybe that I didn't hear, but everyone's attention is on him when he says,

'Any questions? I'm sure we've all got loads.'

A man at the back left, wrinkly and tiny as a crisp packet cooked in the oven, raises his hand, leans forward.

'It's all very pretty. But how is it going to work?'

There's nervous laughter about the table, as if this question was inevitable.

I go to reply, but Baxter has already started.

'We're using the usual channels, but to a much lower degree than you have previously. We're going to give you a much higher return on investment because our media planning is much more targeted than your incumbent agency.'

Crisp Packet smiles.

'I like the sound of higher return on investment, young man. But what on earth do you mean by usual channels and targeted media planning? Excuse my ignorance, I'm just a bean counter.'

Again the nervous laughter.

'Assume you're talking to someone who is completely stupid,' says Crisp Packet.

'Okay,' says Baxter, 'previously you've used high rotation television campaigns, a lot of national press, some cinema advertising. Now, there's nothing wrong with this, and we've retained elements of all of these in our campaign, but there is a lot of wastage and they're expensive. Imagine a TV programme, that we advertise on either side of, is watched by 16 million people, then think about all the people who turn over for the adverts, all the people who go and make a cup of tea, all the people who've Sky-plussed it and fast forward through them, all the people who just aren't interested and you begin to get the idea of the waste implicit in this sort of advertising.

'Now, there is merit to it, particularly in a brand recognition capacity and to a degree that is what we are trying to do, but we primarily want to be talking to the people who are already looking at financial services and considering their financial futures carefully. These are the people we want to communicate with in order to increase your market share. And there are much cleverer ways of doing it nowadays than blanket media coverage.'

Baxter stops. Takes a drink of his coffee. A sheen of sweat on his forehead. They're hanging on his words. I can barely believe it.

'You've got an amazing database. We intend to use that properly, with timely and relevant communications to the existing customer base, as well as looking for new customers. Retention is at least as important in this campaign as finding new revenue sources.

'There are so many digital tools out there we can use to get to people without it costing you a fortune. We can run profiles based on your core products and send adverts directly to prospects through the websites they most often view. We set goals for each of these adverts; for example a potential customer to visit your website and fill in an enquiry form, then we put cookies on their computer and follow them across a network of websites displaying tailored display adverts until they complete that goal.'

'Cookies?' says Berkshire.

'Think of them as electronic breadcrumbs,' I say.

'Is that legal?' Crisp packet looks concerned. His face is even smaller and wrinklier.

'Oh yes,' says Baxter, 'there's an argument that it's actually better for the consumer in that they're receiving advertising for products that are related to them rather than the scattershot effect.'

Someone snorts. Baxter looks at me. I nod at him and he continues.

'We're buying up advertising space on social media sites. People put so much information into them we can be really, really targeted with our content and change it depending on their demographic. We know where they live, what level of education they've got, age, sex, job, relationship status. You name it, we know it. So the message we display to them can differ depending on their circumstances.

'We intend to buy a lot of data from Experian. This is more your territory so I don't need to go into it too much, but again the level of profiling is very sophisticated. We'll be supporting the traditional media and digital work with a hugely targeted direct mail campaign. We'll streamline the application process using Behavioural Economics. The long and the short of it is that with this creative and a meticulously planned delivery strategy we'll be able to give you much higher results with a smaller budget.'

Baxter sits back in his chair. Crisp Packet smiles.

The room is quiet.

Again Berkshire takes control.

'Well gentlemen, thank you for your time today. Can

174

we have a few moments to discuss your presentation? Mr Jones, if you could take our guests to Australia?'

Ben stands. I unplug the iPad and projector and follow him down the corridor. We sit quietly in a sand yellow room and wait. A few minutes later Ben's mobile rings. He leaves the room to take the call. When he returns he's beaming.

'They loved it.'

'I think I need to take you guys out for a spot of lunch to celebrate,' I say.

43.

In the car I call Hilary to tell him the news. He sounds like he's had a couple already. He's going to meet us at the restaurant. As we pull into the city, work is over and everyone else is driving out. I park by the station and we cross the ring road to our favourite Indian. The waiter puts us on a table in the back, through a set of beaded curtains. I order 4 pints of Cobra and a couple of bottles of wine. As I slide into the booth Jessica eases in next to me, her hand ghosting mine. Ben and Baxter sit opposite. We chat about the restaurant. It's a southern Indian restaurant, mostly seafood curries and actually really good as a restaurant not just a curry house. Baxter is telling us about his gap year, which he spent travelling in India, when Hilary bowls in.

'One of these for me?' he asks picking up the nearest bottle of wine.

'It can be,' I reply.

Hilary grabs a chair from a neighbouring table and scuffs it onto the end of ours.

'I hear congratulations are in order,' he says. His mouth is already stained red with wine.

'Indeed they are. And mostly due to Baxter I have to say. You were fucking excellent. Where did that come from?' I ask.

Baxter smiles and says, 'I've been preparing it. I knew that bank people, no offence Ben, were more likely to be swayed by the technical side of things, so I made sure I swotted up on the planning strategy. All the hard work was done, I just regurgitated it.'

'Didn't know you had it in you.'

I raise my pint into the centre of the table. The others clink theirs against it.

'Told you it would be brilliant and they'd love you, Ben.'

'Yes you did and yes they do. Now we just have to do it.'

Hilary clicks his fingers at the waiter, then says to Ben, 'that's the easy bit, son. We've been doing this for years. The hard part is convincing the bloody clients that we're doing the right thing. Once that's in the bag it's a turkey shoot. You just sit back and let the experts cover you in glory.'

The waiter is next to Hilary, who hasn't noticed, instead is fiddling with a wine menu. I nudge him.

'Oh, sorry. We're after a couple of bottles of champagne. And not the shit stuff either. Give us the bottles you save for your family. Best have three and make sure they're cold. Right. Anyone know what they're eating?'

'I can't really stay for much longer, Sally is waiting for me,' I say and soak up Hilary's best withering stare.

'Fuck off. We need to celebrate. All work and no play makes James a dull boy.'

I want to argue. I really do. I want to. Instead I text Sally: *The bank approved the creative. Just going for dinner to celebrate. Won't be too long x*

The curries arrive. Hilary takes drunken control, dishing them out, but spilling as much on the tablecloth as on the plates.

The waiter lights candles on our table, the house lights dim. The music is acoustic, Indian, the wail of a sitar.

We order more wine. It's as inevitable as it is pathetic.

I want to go home and I want to stay here. The wine wins. Just as it always has and right now I loathe myself.

Over the table Hilary's face is pits of shadow, his eyes

vanished in the caves of their sockets. His skin is bone white in the candlelight. There is a manic edge to his voice.

At one point in the evening Jessica asks, 'how did you all get into the industry?' and he laughs, loud, long and cruel.

'James is a failed artist, aren't you?' he says.

'I never wanted to be an artist. I went to Art College. Hilary thinks this makes me effeminate.'

'Smocks and paint smeared berets. I bet all the girls made art based on their periods.'

I want to argue, but he's right, they did. I tell them about a piece one girl made – a medicine cabinet, filled with jars filled with her own menstruation. Jessica mimes vomiting into her hand. Baxter sniggers into a pint.

'I hate my job,' says Ben.

'I don't blame you.' I'm relieved for a moment that Hilary's scorn is away from me. He's a nasty drunk when he wants to be and I can do without it. Then I remember that Ben's a client and not one of our friends, go to step in, but Ben is warming to it.

'Imagine knowing that everyone hates you because of what you do. They don't actually care about whether I'm a nice guy, don't wait to find out most of the time. As soon as I say I'm a banker I can see their faces turn. The inevitable wanker jokes come rolling out.'

Hilary is leaning back in his chair, his head almost gone in the shadows, his fingers drum on the arm of his chair.

'It makes a nice change some other industry taking the flack for a change,' I say before he gets a chance to interject, 'It's normally all our fault. I was relieved when you guys fucked everything up. The accusatory gaze turned away from us for the first time since the sixties.'

Ben smiles a sad smile and pushes his curry around on the plate. I notice he's separated his rice from the meat, two completely disparate piles of food.

I'm filling everyone's champagne glasses when my phone vibrates on the table. A text message from Sally: *what a fucking surprise.* My hand hovers over the phone, mind searching for the words to reply. Then I see my wife, waiting at the other end for my carefully chosen words, words designed to do no more than placate her and I can't do it.

'Why did you get into advertising then, James?' asks Jessica.

Before I get a chance to answer Hilary has lurched forward, elbows on the table.

'James has got a gift for seeing things from other people's perspective.'

'I don't think my wife would agree with you, Hilary.'

'Ah, I didn't say you can empathise with them, just that you can see why they think in a particular way.'

'Is there a difference?' asks Baxter.

'Oh yes, my boy. James here looks at things in a pragmatic, cold and calculating way. It's why I made him director. He's a ruthless bastard.'

Jessica looks at me. Reaching out for reassurance. I can see questions in her gaze.

'Fuck you very much, Hilary,' I say, getting up from the table, my knees hitting the underside causing everything on it to jump.

He guffaws again.

'Only joking, old boy. You're soft as shit on the inside. Honestly, folks. Like a teddy bear in a suit of armour.'

I cross the restaurant, stepping in and out of the pools of light around the tables, I can hear him ordering more wine.

In the cubicle I hoover up two generous lines of cocaine. It hits my head and everything is instantly flattened and simplified.

As I piss I lean my head against the tiles above the urinal. Realise I'm drunker than I thought. My piss is dark yellow, nearly brown and lasts and lasts and lasts. I struggle to do my belt up, now I'm away from the group and the table and the candles I am really drunk. I have to hold onto the sink to accept the towel from the attendant.

The lights flicker, fade quickly, come back up and then flicker off again. My head is heavy. The attendant gestures to the bottles of aftershave on the side, says something I can't make out, his words liquid, flowing away from me.

'What did you say?' I ask, aware of the violence in my voice.

'Freshen up?'

'What?'

'No splash, no gash,' he says and I half laugh, half baulk at the vulgarity, stumble backwards as the lights go down again and I catch sight of myself in the mirror, tie undone, shirt hanging loose, face ashen and the attendant is gone and the wall behind me is shimmering. In the mirror the boy from Monkey Kingdom stares back with black eyes and opens a bloody mouth, gaps for teeth and says in a voice made of broken bottles, 'we're dying so you can talk.' I stumble back, push out at him, but he's gone and the attendant falls into the bottles, sending them rolling and I realise what I've done, scoop them up, full of apologies, take a fiver from my wallet and put it on his tray, because money makes everything better, push the door open to the restaurant and am greeted by Hilary's drunken singing.

At the table I pull my seat in close, sit on my twitchy hands.

'Are you okay?' asks Jessica and I nod mutely, aware that she must think I've puked.

They're still wittering about work.

Jessica's hand is still on my leg.

'Where do you see yourself in 5 years, Baxter?' Hilary's speech is a message in a bottle floating on a boozy sea.

'Financially stable, with a healthy family,' replies Baxter, puffed with pride.

'Very admirable. Bloody boring, but admirable. How about you, young lady? What do you want?'

Jessica pretends to be thinking, a manicured nail to pouting lips and then says, 'I want your job, Mr Perkins,' and the whole table is laughing.

More wine. More wine. More wine. A predictable cycle. A weary predictable cycle which I give in to, all the while trying to suppress thoughts of my wife and son with wine after wine after wine.

Then outside. Leaning on a wall.

So far so good. So far so good.

Walking home with one eye shut – the only way to judge distance.

Wrapped up in a half-formed memory of kissing Jessica goodbye, and I'm saying to myself, it was on the cheek, it was on the cheek and that was it, nothing more, nothing more, though I can't be sure and the night is cold and the pavement wet and the reflections of the street lights are like rips in the earth. As I weave and stagger I'm aware I might topple into one at any misplaced step.

44.

Beth stops me in the corridor. I try to steer away from her into my room. She steps between me and the door.

'Have I done something to upset you?' she asks.

I should tell her, 'I need to stay away from you because it's marked you'. I should tell her, 'I'm doing this for your own safety'. I should tell her, 'the last thing I want to do is avoid you'.

How can I though? Whatever I say it's going to sound like the rantings of a madman. Because whatever The Zoo is, whether it's in me or from without, it does have the power to hurt people. I've seen it. There have been physical consequences, so I can't dismiss it. I have to take its threats seriously. She's waiting for me to reply. Her eyes are wet. I'm hurting her. I really don't want to hurt her. I should tell her.

'No, you've not done anything,' is what I say instead. I pull short of 'it's not you, it's me' but it's implicit.

'Well why then? Why are you avoiding me?'

'I'm not.'

She wipes tears from her face with the back of her cardigan sleeve.

'I promise you,' I say, 'I'm not avoiding you. It's just a place I'm in.'

A cliché again. A crap relationship cliché and I hate myself all over and she looks like she hates me too. There is incredulous disgust on her face. She turns away. I grab her arm. She stares into my face, then looks at my hand. I remove it.

'Sorry,' I say.

'I'm getting better. The doctors say I'm getting better. I feel better.'

'That's great. I mean it, that's really good.'

I reach for her hand. She lets me hold it for a second.

'And that's another reason why I should stay away from you. I'm damaged, Beth.'

Anger in her. Red hot and deserved.

'Aren't we all, James? Aren't we all?'

She walks away. I throw futile words after her, about how it's for her own good, about how I hurt people, about how damaged people need to hurt others to feel better about themselves. Until I am just a man on his own in the corridor shouting at a wall.

In the dust at my feet someone has drawn an approximation of a monkey. It's pointing down the corridor.

I stand in front of the plastic sheeting, push my hand through the gap, then my arm, then my shoulder, then step through.

The dust is deeper here, two or three inches maybe. I wade through it, down the dark corridor. Past work-scarred walls, shapes where pictures used to be. The light from the ward, filtered through the plastic, only reaches a few paces in and I'm soon stumbling along taking baby steps into the blackness. I reach about me and find nothing. I am the centre of a black void. Behind me I can only just make out the faint glow of the ward. I inch further forward. The heat is stifling and the beginnings of claustrophobia begin to grip me. I suppress an urge to turn and run back down the corridor, to emerge into the clinical light of the ward. Swallowing it, I press on.

The temperature is rising. A thick, dry heat, it tastes

warm in my throat and lungs. Sweat prickles my forehead. My legs become heavier. I want to sit and rest. I want my back against a cool wall. I have no idea how far above me the ceiling is, how far away the walls are from my outstretched arms.

A smell too – sulphur. I gag, retch, hold my hand over my mouth and nose, but it finds its way around my fingers and fills me.

This seems to drag on for hours, small steps forward as the pressure of the heat pushes down on me.

Then there is a change of quality in the light ahead. A slight blue tinge. Then that grows. Develops into a patch of light, a patch of light that grows into a defined shape, into a jagged hole of brightness.

I stumble into it, through a gap in a wall. Torn teeth edges where bricks have been punched through the wall. On the other side the light is too bright to define any shapes, a pure white light that hurts my eyes. I hold my hand up. The heat is intense. My palm bristles.

I climb through.

45.

I know it's wrong, but it pains me to watch Harry butcher GTA. It pains me the way he can't control the bike. The way he makes the character walk into the wall and round in circles. I want to take the control back from him and continue with my game, but he's perched on my knee and trying to snatch the controller off me.

'I w-w-w-want a go, Daddy. Let me drive the car.'

'There's more to it than driving the car, Harry. It's not for little boys, this is an adults' game.'

'It's a computer g-g-game. Computers are for children.'

I can't fault his logic. Every wife and girlfriend in England will agree with him.

The cat joins us, paws at my leg and then, resting its front paws on me, settles down.

I'm tired from the night before. My body is a maze of aches. The inside of my head feels like it's full of wire wool. I want to be left alone.

I realise Sally has come in from work when I hear her tut behind me. She goes through into the kitchen and clatters around, then comes back into the lounge.

'Can I have a word with you please?'

'Uh huh,' I reply without looking around.

'Out here.'

I look around now. Hands on hips, pulling off the angry school teacher look perfectly. I pick Harry up and dump him down on the carpet, shooing the cat away. I follow her through into the kitchen. She leans her elbows on the surface and talks in a hushed insistent tone that she is battling to keep down, because she wants to scream at me.

'What the fuck do you think you're doing?'

'What do you mean?'

'Letting him play that filth?'

I roll my eyes and lean back against the work surface.

'Fucking hell Sally it's a computer game.'

Her fists clench and unclench.

'It's a disgusting computer game. We agreed. We've got rules. There are things he can and can't do. We agreed. We're supposed to be a team.'

'Get a grip. It's a game. It's just a game. He's not hurting anyone.'

'It's a game where you can drive around indiscriminately killing people, running children over and raping prostitutes. It's not something I want our son to see. We've discussed this,' she is rigid with anger.

'He doesn't know what it means.'

'Of course he fucking does.' The *fucking* is a hiss between her teeth.

'Okay. Okay. I've had a hard day. I don't need this right now. I'll go and turn it off.'

'You've had a hard day? You've had a hard day? You've struggled to get through work because of fucking hangover. That's not a hard day. Working in A & E is a hard day. You don't even know the meaning of a hard day,' she leans back, runs her hands through her hair. Breathing out heavily through her nose, almost a snort, she appears to be counting under her breath, her expression a flickering montage. Hatred. Anger. Disappointment. Love. I understand them all. Because I feel them for myself too.

'Look,' I say, 'I'm sorry. I didn't think. I'll go and turn it off and I won't let him near it again. It's not like he can't see all this on TV anyway.'

'Good God. I can't believe that just came out of your mouth. You of all people. There's a difference between watching a news report and glamourising it in a fucking game. You know this. Why am I having to tell you?'

I just want this over. I just want to have peace. I haven't got the energy to argue with her and inside I know she's right. But there's stubbornness too. A sense of injustice that she's talking to me like a child. I am petulant and stupid and hungover and I want this to stop.

'I'm going in there now and I'm going to turn it off and sit him in front of Teletubbies or something fluffy and nice. I'll never play the game in front of him again. Happy?'

She swallows heavily.

'No,' she says, 'no, James, I'm not happy.'

I know she means more than this. I leave the kitchen before she has a chance to vocalise it.

After work the next day. Everyone already shuffled out at 5.30. Just Collins and I huddled around the MacBook Pro. We run through the credentials pitch. He is nodding as I show each slide, saying okay to prompt me to move forward. I let him control it, can see that he likes it, see the earnestness in each nod of his coiffed head. I scroll though examples of past work and, while a video of some PR we got for an energy company is running, I slip away to the toilets. I lock the main door behind me, then go into the cubicle and take out a plastic sealy bag of chop and trace a lumpy line on the cistern. I'd called for it earlier. Feeling tired and weak and not knowing how I was going to make it through the rest of the day, I'd nipped out and met my man in a local car park. He pulled up in a brand new Audi RS3 and I started to take the piss out of him for being conspicuous, then saw the growl behind his smirking lips, paid him the money and fucked off. A couple of lines off my car owner's manual and the day didn't seem too bad. Now, huddled in a cubicle at work, I hold the bag up and shake it. More than half gone. Still, no problem, just got to get me home. I check my face in the mirror, hold open a bloodshot eye with my index finger and the world blurs.

Through a world of mist I see the cubicle door begin to move. So slowly at first that I don't think anything of it. Then it slams, my body jolts with shock and I poke my finger into my eyeball. Inside the cubicle I hear the window being opened. I inch over to the door and with a shaking hand try to open it. Can't budge it. Locked from inside.

'Collins?' I ask, 'Who's in there?'

No-one replies. I try the door again.

I'm ice cold. The airs on my arms are stood straight up. Crackling electricity in the air.

I'm frozen. I know that I need to do something.

My breath fogs in the air in front of me as thick as cigarette smoke.

I half-heartedly ram my shoulder into the door. Then the window inside slams shut and the door swings open. There's no-one inside. I clamber onto the seat of the toilet and push the window open. It's only about 40 cm deep, certainly too small for anyone to fit through, but as I peer out the boy breaks from the shadows and runs across the car park. In the dusk he looks back up at me, his face is all smile in the murk, and he raises his left hand, index finger extended, then is gone. I shout after him. Words spat into the growing night.

This can't be real. This can't be real. Working too hard. Not sleeping enough. But, this cannot be real.

I slump back and sit on the toilet seat. Hold my hands up. They're shaking. Partly from the gak, partly from fear.

I squeeze them together, compose myself and return to Collins.

'This is looking good,' he says.

'Should do. It's tried and tested. Is there anything you want to add to it?'

My words are lies, trying to hide what I've just seen.

'No, I don't think so. She knows us. It's more of an introduction to the others there.'

'Okay. Set then?'

'Set.'

'I might nip over the road for a swift half. Do you fancy one?' I can't believe I'm choosing to spend my leisure time with him, but I'm pretty shaken up and can't face going home, even though that's exactly where I should be and I know it.

'Nah. Thanks though. Going round to a friend's for dinner.'

'Okay. I'm going to stick around for a little while and answer some emails.'

He says goodnight and leaves. Now I'm in the office alone, it suddenly seems dark and cold and I find myself shivering.

In my private office I take the bottle of JD and a tumbler from the shelf and pour myself a heavy glass. Already the effect of the line is dissipating. Cocaine. Such a teasing bitch of a drug. She grips you so quickly, promises so much then leaves you just as quickly. A one-night stand of a drug. I tap another line out onto to my desk. Roll a business card and hoover it up, run my finger over the residue and rub it on my teeth. Chemical taste – the numbness of novocaine a petty insult at the end of it.

'Time to go home,' I say under my breath. Steel myself. Gulp the JD down. Squeeze my eyes against the aftertaste.

The main office is lit by the glow of the MacBook Pro

screen. I turn on the corridor light and then make my way over to the laptop.

The laptop is still showing the presentation. But in the centre of the last slide the words read '*Your real life is at home and you're here jumping at shadows. Fucking joke.*' I angrily delete them. Collins wouldn't, would he? Probably would. But I'd have heard him coming back in. I hold down the power button and the screen turns blue. The fan whirrs. Without the glow of the screen the office is sharper, the shadows deeper, the windows gaping possibilities. I shudder. Run to the corridor, pull the door behind me, struggling to get the key in the lock. I have a sense of something behind me and can't help but look over my shoulder. Nothing there but the canyon of the stairwell. I take the stairs two at a time. I'm out of the fire door, not even waiting for it to shut and when it does the clunk makes me start, stumble, then I'm opening the car door, falling into the seat, clicking the central locking shut. I laugh. Ridiculous. You're ridiculous. I start the engine and make my way home on roads which are slick with rain and speckled with the spit of reflections.

46.

I catch my foot as I haul myself through the hole. Part fall, part roll through it and land on my back, wind knocked from me and eyes closed. When I open them I can only see white light and feel a burning heat on my face. My eyes adjust themselves and I can make out the shape of a chain mail fence stretching off in both directions. Slowly my vision returns and I am looking at an uninterrupted blue sky. I sit up.

Dusty ground, a rectangular space bigger than a football field, surrounded with 20 foot high metal chain mail fencing. Baking hot. My skin is burning, literally burning. I scan the area for shade. There is none. A bleached rectangle with the sun burning down on it. I am a bug under a magnifying glass.

Pull myself to my feet. Already my throat is dry. I am coated with a sheen of sweat. I make my way over to the fence, test my weight against it. It bends then pushes back against me so I jump up and grasp it with my fingers. The metal is red hot. It takes all my willpower to hold onto it as I heave myself up. About six feet from the ground, I can't bear it anymore and let go, drop down to the ground again. The palms of my hands are branded with the hexagons of the fence.

On the other side of the metal enclosure is thick brush, a plant I don't recognise, too high to see over.

I begin to work my way around the perimeter, inching

along it, all the time one hand brushing the scalding metal. My feet kick clouds in the dust. The sun is a constant above me, draining me. Regularly I have to stop and sit, back to the fence, gasping for my breath, sweat in my eyes. I crave water, just a drop on my tongue, on my lips. I work my way all around the three sides. My tongue is thick, my throat swollen.

About half way round my legs are too weak to continue. I allow myself to slide down the fence and rest there again, the metal hot on my back even through my clothes. My eyes drift shut and I can feel the heat on the back of my eyelids welding them shut.

My body sinks down to a horizontal and I put my hands behind my head, lie back in the dust.

I'm in the garden at home on a summer's day, the sound of the hose filling the paddling pool, somewhere in the background Harry is chuntering away. Sally is laughing, beautiful, like a waterfall. A bee buzzes over my face disturbing the hairs. I'm in the hammock. The air is disturbed by the slightest of winds, which lifts the heat from everything and I am light in the hammock, the air beneath me weighs nothing and I'm floating. I could be hundreds of feet in the air. I have the impression that if I put my feet down I would find the earth had dropped away from me. This should fill me with fear and I am touched by the ghost of vertigo, but it is only momentary and I am at peace again. The hose has been turned off and Harry is stomping with monster feet in the water. I sense Sally next to me. Her lips touch my forehead like a butterfly.

'Keep your eyes closed,' she says. So I do, then she says, 'put your hand out,' so I do. She places a bottle of beer in it and the glass is so cold I nearly drop it. When I raise the beer to my lips it tastes golden and some spills from my mouth, runs down my chin onto my neck and I leave it there, the sun drying it in seconds.

I roll my eyes under my still closed eyelids and the shadows of the trees above me are purple blotches on the inside of them. I peel my eyes open and the light is dappled though the leaves, a chessboard on my t-shirt. Harry laughs and I smile with him. Close my eyes and the summer afternoon strokes my forehead until I am half asleep.

I jerk awake to the sensation of falling. Suddenly unsure of where I am and grasped by panic. Then I see the fence and the bone white dust and know I am far from home.

Already my arms are burning red. Knowing I need to find shade I continue to follow the fence, convinced there must be a door, a gateway, another way out. Then I come back to the wall through which I climbed. The hole I came through is circled with blue spray paint, a rusty sign hanging next to it. I think the language is French. Spray paint stencils underneath, a rough approximation of a Cowboy, a Knight, a Pirate, a Soldier, a Lion and a Rhino. Then three large dots, making up a . . .

To the right of the hole is a pile of breeze blocks, sheets of corrugated iron on the top. I lift the edge of one and roll under it. The shade is such a relief. A slight wind picks the dust up and tosses it around the space. Above me the iron crinkles and moans.

The temperature begins to drop. I push my head out from under the shade and watch day descend the sky above me. The heat leaves as quickly as the light and soon I am shivering beneath stars.

At some point I make the decision to clamber back through the hole and work my way back down the blind tunnel. Now I have a destination I'm not as scared by the fact I can't see my own hands. I simply follow my shuffling feet as they drag me back to the ward, to the plastic sheet that is mercifully cool to the touch, that parts when I push it and gives birth to me into a world of fluorescent strip lights and tiles and dust and white coats, to a ward that hasn't changed, to a group of people going through the same motions at the same time and repeating the same day.

In my room I am mute. There are things I need to say now my voice is gone.

I close my door. Sit on the floor in front of The Zoo.

The skin on my arms is red and blistered. The hexagons on my hands charred black.

When I find my words they are small, cracked and pulled from the darkness inside me.

'Why did you show me that?'

The Zoo says nothing.

'What does it mean?'

The Zoo says nothing.

'Where have I been?'

The Zoo says nothing.

Frustrated, I climb onto the bed, not bothering to remove my clothing, and curl myself into a ball, hands tucked under my chin and knees against my chest. Shaking and gibbering and repeating the names of The Figurines as a mantra, while they ignore me and stare forward with their fixed gazes.

47.

The house smells of cooking and air freshener and home. Even through my cocaine-frosted nostrils it is enough to spark a cavalcade of pleasant memories. The hall lights are off, the dining room ones on, just a key line of yellow dissecting the corridor. I drop my briefcase onto the floor and hang my coat up. It immediately drops to the floor and as I stoop to pick it up I lose my balance and topple forward into the wall. Giggling to myself I hoist myself back up.

The brightness in the dining room makes me aware of how fucked I am and how much I need to hide it from my family. I need to straighten my head up. Sally and Harry are sat at the table. Harry grins a gap toothed grin at me, Sally a barely perceptible smile, just a straightening of her lips. Something at least. Even more important now that she doesn't realise I've been on the gear.

'There's a plate on the side for you, it'll probably need heating,' she says.

'Thanks,' I reply and stalk into the kitchen. The muscles in my legs are close to cramping. I am on my tiptoes. Grab a beer from the fridge and bolt it. Better if she thinks I'm drunk than high. Get another one out. I watch the blue digital seconds tick down as my lasagne heats. Taking a fork out of the drawer I join my family at the table.

'Hello mate,' I say to Harry.

'Hi D-d-d-ad, look at this,' he's holding up a teddy monkey. An ape of some sort.

'Who's that then?'

'H-H-H-ector. He's the same as the monkey we saw.'

He passes it to me. I rub the fur on my face. Again a wash of memory.

'Which one?'

'The one that s-s-s-s-spoke to me.'

'It didn't speak to you.'

Sally grimaces at me.

'You spoke to it, didn't you?' I say, conscious of softening my voice.

'Y-y-yes, but it understood me, Dad. It knew what I was saying, didn't it, Mum?'

'Yes Harry. It certainly looked like it.'

We eat in silence. Too quiet. I am aware of the sharpness of my jaw. I'm not in the least bit hungry. Every mouthful is an effort, huge in my mouth.

'I'm going to put some music on,' I say and leave the table. In the lounge I rummage about in the CDs and settle on Nick Drake, Five Leaves Left. His mournful voice follows me as I walk to the downstairs toilet. I take out the bag of coke and empty the remains of it onto the shelf above the sink. Snort it and rip the bag open, lick the residue. Wash my hands in the sink and try not to see my wild eyes in the mirror.

Harry notices I'm not eating and stops eating his food too, pushing it about the plate with his fork.

'Eat your dinner, Harry.' Sally takes his hand, tries to cajole him into eating. He squeezes his mouth shut refusing to eat. She takes the fork from him.

'Do you want me to have to feed you like when you were a baby?'

He shakes his head, puts his hand over his mouth.

'Come on, Harry, do as your mother says.'

Shakes his head again.

Sally asks for help with her eyes. I look down at my plate.

'Take your hand away from your mouth,' she says.

He shakes his head again. Mutters, 'I don't want to', from behind his finger shield.

Sally picks up his fork, the metal scraping on the plate. A banshee cry of metal on ceramic that cuts right through me. She scoops up a fork full of lasagne and aims it at his mouth. He screams *no* behind his hand and lashes out with his other hand, catching the fork and sending it bouncing off the table, leaving a jet trail of food on the tablecloth. Sally gasps and recoils. She shouts his name, grabs the fork again, gets another portion, holds his other hand and says, 'you will eat your dinner.' He shakes his head again. Before I know what I'm doing I'm around the table grabbing his head, pulling his hand away and growling in his face,

'Stop being a baby and eat your fucking dinner.'

The look on his face, the look on Sally's, makes me realise what I've done and I step back, already apologising and they're both staring at me and I'm backing away, into the lounge, slamming the door that separates the two rooms and through the wood I can hear him wailing and Sally trying to calm him down. I fall into the armchair, cover my head with my hands, but that's not enough, so I push a pillow over my face and scream into the fabric, into this thick, thick air and wonder what it would be like to suffocate. There are footsteps on the stairs, him running, Sally running after him, the bedroom door kicked shut, her muffled voice, muffled through the pillow, through the wall, through the floor, through everything that divides us.

I am remorse. I am guilt. I am too caned to know what to do. So I press the pillow tighter into my face, until it squashes my nose, fills my eye sockets and my mouth and I can taste the material, taste the dust, taste my aftershave, the air freshener, the smell of our house, our home and hold it there, hold it there, hold it there.

48.

I can't bring myself to join them, to see the aftermath, so I turn on the TV but leave the sound off, feeling sorry for myself along with Nick Drake. I hop through the channels, bouncing over a reality TV show about fat people, Gene Hackman in The Conversation, Stoke City versus Manchester City, crap, crap and more crap.

I settle on Sky News.

Visions of children with guns. A jeep on a track through jungle. Men in the back, bandanas over their faces. Another group of men firing AK47s into the sky. A journalist in front of a group of grinning and waving children. I jump up, turn off the CD player and turn the volume up on the TV. The journalist is addressing the camera.

'It is shocking how quickly the country has fallen into civil war. Always a volatile country, Nhgosa is rapidly becoming a no-go zone. The British government today warned all British citizens who don't have pressing reasons to stay to leave the country.'

I shuffle off the seat and move on my bottom towards the television, my face now inches from the screen. I reach for the connection Lou made and find enough to disturb me.

The journalist holds his hand out to the camera. Each palm holds a pile of black minerals.

I have to squeeze one eye shut so I can focus on the image on the screen. If I have both of them open the picture jumps and spins and tries to elude me.

'And it is all about this. Coltan and Cassiterite.'

He raises his left hand.

'Coltan is used in the west to manufacture electrical items. 65% of the world's supply of the mineral can be found here and is mined in small artisan mines, often dug out by hand by children and then shipped across the border and sold through intermediaries. Most of the electronic giants will deny that they buy Coltan from Nghosa, but the statistics don't support this. No matter which way we look at it, and no matter how much they deny that it came from here, there just isn't enough of it produced elsewhere to fuel the hunger that we in the West have for our electronic devices.'

He raises his right hand.

'And this is Cassiterite, again used in electronic devices, this time for soldering. This innocuous looking material is used to make the phones you speak on and the TVs you watch this report on and these two minerals are tearing this country apart.

'There are reports that the rebel army are pushing to the north of the country, to the part of Nghosa where the majority of the mines are. There is no doubt this is a civil war that is about exploiting the natural resources of this country. If you spend any time here you realise the vast fortune raised by the mining of these minerals doesn't reach the common people. It is that fortune the rebels are after. Even now they are pushing the government forces back.

'We have received unconfirmed reports of villages being burned on the way. It is impossible for foreign journalists to get near enough to the fighting to corroborate these reports and the government minders are intent on only showing us their side of the conflict, but everyone I speak to has a tale about horrific acts perpetrated by both armies. We may not have officially reached a humanitarian crisis yet, but whichever side wins it will be at a huge cost to the people of Nghosa. This is Guy Allen reporting for Sky News in Nghosa.'

I turn the sound down and listen intently for any sounds of my family upstairs, but there is none. I presume they've gone to bed. I pull myself back to the sofa, clip my bottle of beer and watch without moving as the amber liquid spreads out into the carpet.

I try to shake myself out of it, trace a ponderous and meandering path into the kitchen and take a pressed tea towel from a drawer. Halfway back into the lounge I return to the fridge and grab another beer. I can't be bothered to root around for a bottle opener so crack it open with my lighter. The lid bounces and jumps its way around the sink.

Back on the sofa I pull my legs up, lie on my side, nestle the beer against my chest, feel my eyes get heavy. I jerk awake as the beer spills onto my chest. The room spins. I prop myself up. Drape my arm off the edge of the sofa, lower it for what seems hundreds of fathoms until it touches down on the floor and barely pull my arm back again before tumbling into a drunken sleep.

In the darkness inside my head I meet the African boy. He points a gun at me. The gun is the same size as his torso. The tendons in his forearms strain with its weight. He is smiling. A grim smile belonging to someone who has seen more and knows more than he needs to. He levels the gun at my head, cocks his head and squints down the barrel. He opens his mouth and says a word I understand, 'Nghosa.'

I wake with a crick in my neck. Daylight teases me through the curtains. As I stand, my knees cracking, I realise I have pissed on the sofa.

49.

Cocooned in my room, blinds shutting off the world, door closing out the ward, I hear The Zoo talking to me. Words and ideas are all about me. It is a worm in my inner ear, tender words I don't understand, fractured and mixed up, dyslexic and confused. Amongst them my name, the names of my family, place names, times, fractions of memories, read out to me as if in a play. A harsh whisper, playing with the hairs on my neck. Then when I relax, I'm snapped out of it with static and feedback and a flow of messages that make my head spin.

I study it. Study the gap in it and strive to visualise what should be there to fill the void. I know it, I know this, it's in me, I just need to dig it out. The Zoo in my head is a radio trying to tune itself. The volume skips up and down as my subconscious plays with the dial. My focus is a red line that rolls left to right stopping at numbers and here I catch snapshots of things, then it rolls on and I am left with the chaos.

Eyes closed. Picturing The Zoo, working along its rows with my mind's eye.

Nearly there. Nearly have it.

See the shape. See the base of it. See its outline. A shadow form.

Then I have it. I know what is missing.

The Ape.

The Ape should sit beneath The Rhino. The Ape should be next and he is gone.

A mixture of fear and relief. I remember him, but he is absent. He is within me again now, even when his physical form is missing. I know him and I can remember him.

The Ape is next. The order should go: The Cowboy, The Knight, The Pirate, The Soldier, The Lion, The Rhino, then The Ape.

He is here because of his size and his power. Below The Lion and The Rhino despite his closeness to man. Perhaps because of. He is a spy in the camp of The Animals. He is one of them, but not of them. He is a surreptitious link between The Cowboy and his mindless followers in The Animals and now he is the missing link.

He is like us. But not.

He is a Chimpanzee. He squats with his knuckles down, touching the ground. He is looking up under mournful eyebrows. His eyes are just black dots, but within them is sadness and knowledge and when he looks at me I see a reflection of myself. He lived in a society that is structured like ours, then he lived in The Zoo, in a society that is structured as well, just not in the same way. From the way he is bowed, the way his head is lowered, it is obvious to me that he is not the alpha male. I could tell this even if I didn't know his position within The Zoo.

Like us he can laugh, but there are no laughter lines around his eyes. Just a smooth pink face ringed in plastic fur that doesn't move in the wind, stays frozen for all time, moulded and immobile.

He is our closest relative, regal and dignified, collected by Solomon, important to Darwin. He is dressed as Man, laughed at and pointed at and ridiculed. He is a comic sidekick. We can laugh at him because he is us, but can't complain at our jibes.

He tried to stop Charlton Heston from discovering the truth. He is Tarzan's faithful companion. He is a reminder

202

to us of our superiority and how far we can fall. He is a group of chimps drinking tea while lip-synching to northern stereotypes. He is learning to use tools in front of a black monolith. He is a character in a book that Beth is reading.

He is gone, someone else has him and I miss him.

50.

I am into the corridor before my mind can stop my legs, pushing past Asian Radio Lady so she spins like a fairground ride and her radio hits the tiles, spilling batteries. Her complaints are tracer bullets trying to find me as I storm away. I don't knock on Janet's door, I virtually kick it open; it bounces off the wall and rattles in its frame. Janet is talking to a man I don't recognise. He is dressed in a black suit, white shirt, black tie, oiled hair, pencil moustache. He looks like Howard Hughes dressed as an undertaker. They are rabbits in the headlights, wide eyes and dropped mouths, they are a freeze-frame of surprise. Then the man steps towards me, begins denouncing me for bursting in, something about manners and private but I am seeing red and his words bounce off me. Janet is holding her hand up to him, calming him, cooing at him like a pigeon and I want to hurt, hurt him, hurt her, hurt me, find it.

'James,' says Janet. Composed once more, steady, calm and in control.

I am not, I am shaking, I am anger, I am out of control.

'Who's got it?' I shout.

'Now look here,' says Howard.

I can barely see him through the red mist which coats my eyes. I point my finger at him, my arms so tense it shakes.

'No. Fucker. You look here. Where is it?'

Howard looks at Janet for support. She pats his arm. He is a dog now.

'James. You seem very upset. Is there something I can help you with?' She's doing that voice. That voice full of empathy and, even as I don't want to fall for it, I can feel it working, until I use the red to push it back down again.

'Someone has taken something that belongs to me and I want it back.'

'Okay. Well you need to calm down and tell me what it is you've lost.'

'Not lost. Stolen.'

'I'm sure no-one wants to steal any of your belongings, James.'

'Not wants to. Fucking has.'

I'll take your empathy and raise it two red mists.

She says something quietly to Howard Hughes. He edges his way around the desk and then past me, never turning his back to me, arms held as if he is surrendering. He seems so pathetic that I can't help but jerk and growl as he gets close, laugh as he flinches, whimpers and scuttles out of the room. Humour beats red mist. I swallow the laugh. It sticks in my throat.

'Now, if you're calm, please tell me what you're missing. And please remember, we have rules here, they're for everyone's good, they make the ward run as it should. You know this as well as everyone else and one of them is that you don't come bursting into my office and intimidate my guests.'

I'm not calm, nowhere near calm. I squash the anger down, bury it in my chest cavity and say, 'I'm sorry. I didn't think.'

Janet nods acceptance, so I continue.

'I am missing something from my room.'

'When did you last see it?'

I reach back, finding no definitive answer.

'I think before I moved rooms for a while,' I say.

'And now it's not there?'

'No.'

'Have you looked everywhere?'

'Yes, of course, I wouldn't have come to you if I hadn't.'
Red mist. My voice quavers.

'I'm trying to help,' Janet says, 'we can't just accuse
people of stealing. We need to be absolutely sure. If you
could describe what it was that is missing we can begin the
work of finding it.'

I find myself not wanting to tell her, while knowing that
I must. I'm unsure whether I can trust her. View her as a
suspect, whereas a minute ago I simply viewed her as a
figure of authority to report the crime to.

'Well?' she says.

'A model. A model of a chimpanzee. It was on my windowsill. I need it back. It's imperative that I have it back.
Of all of them it had to be the chimp. The only one who
understands.'

Janet realises something, I can see it on her face and at
the same time I realise I have given something away I didn't
want to, or given her an opportunity I didn't want to.

'Ah, yes,' she says, 'the toys. Are you ready to talk to me
about the toys?'

Bitch. No, I'm not ready to talk about the toys. They're
not fucking toys. I'm not ready, never will be ready. If I talk
about The Zoo it will only get angrier. We have reached an
impasse of late. It's there, but it's not hurting me or anyone
else. If I start talking about it this could all change. There's
no way I'm risking it. I think about Beth's name on a piece
of paper. I think about her telling me she's feeling better.
So I seal my lips and seal The Zoo within them like a crypt.

Instead I say, 'no, I'm not ready to talk about the toys.
I'm ready to talk about the missing piece.'

She seems disappointed.

'Okay. If you're convinced that it's been taken, of course we'll take it seriously. I will ask someone to look into it.'

'Thank you.'

'But, if it's important to you I think we do need to talk about it.'

'I don't think so.'

I try to sound determined when I say this, aware that I'm avoiding her eye and fiddling with the belt loops of my trousers. She won't leave it alone though. I should have known this before I came to her. Instead I floated in on the red mist and now I'm facing the third degree about the last thing in the world I want to talk about.

'They obviously mean something to you. These toys. They're obviously important to you and for that reason it's my opinion that it may be instrumental in your recovery that we begin to look at what they mean,' she balances her glasses on her nose, moves the mouse on her desk and the blue light of the screen reflects in her glasses' lenses.

'No,' I say, 'not now.'

I leave this breadcrumb for her and she snaps it up.

'Okay. Another time then. But being as you're here and have scared off my visitor is there anything else you'd like to talk to me about?'

I know I need to give her something. Something to take her mind off The Zoo. So I say,

'I'd like to talk about my job and the way it made me feel.'

My judgement is right, she can barely hide her delight.

'Okay, please do.'

She thinks she's winning so I make a show of composing myself. I lean back into the chair, squeeze my eyes shut and then begin in a flat voice,

'Okay Janet. This is what I do to people; you drive to the supermarket, listening to the radio and there's an advert in the break between the songs and you think you don't listen to it, but you do really. All the while stuck in the traffic jam behind a bus with a banner on the back and you take that in too, even though you think you don't. The traffic crawls along and you go past a 48-sheet poster that has a slogan on it that you recognise and a beautiful woman smiles down at you saying "everything is going to be alright". You park and the ticket is spat out of the machine, you turn it over and it has an advert on the back of it for multivitamins, so when you next cough, just a cough, maybe a dry throat, you wonder if you're coming down with something.

'As you get your trolley you idly read the message on it for holidays and then it starts raining so you have to hurry into the supermarket, and all you can think about is how you deserve a family holiday. Then this gets you thinking about your last family holiday, say Lake Garda and the hired canoes and the sun on the lake, the slap of the paddle on the water, the sound of your children playfully arguing and an idea starts to come together.

'Inside the supermarket you push your trolley along in a stupor, not really listening to the piped music and the seductive voice telling you about the manager's special, and you pass the 2-for-1's and the special offers and the discount flashes and the dump bins full of the week's bargains.

'And then when you get home you unpack your shopping and look at it all on the kitchen work surface, this consumer mountain, all this stuff you didn't want, that you're only going to throw away again and you think to yourself, "why did I buy all this crap?"

'That's what I do to people, Janet.'

'How does that make you feel?' she asks.

'How do you think it makes me feel?' I ask her because I don't know the answer anymore.

51.

I'm somewhere on New Walk on the phone to our media planners when I see the graffiti. The campaign is pretty much complete and we're in the process of booking everything.

I'm saying something like, 'We need to up the opportunity to hear. At least for the first month. We want heavy rotation initially. I want the campaign to be everywhere so everyone can get used to the change in direction.'

On the other end of the line Leary is saying, 'We might need to increase the spend then. If we want to cover as many stations as you're suggesting and get such high rotation we need to spend more money or something is going to give.'

When I see it I stop talking and it takes me a minute to compose myself and realise that Leary is waiting for me to say something.

'I'm going to have to call you back,' I say eventually.

The words: pink text, each letter about a foot high. A sensation that I'm being watched causes me to involuntarily look about, as if I've overheard my name mentioned in conversation, but not heard the context.

Your eyes are made of such fine dust.

There's no doubt that it's directed to me. That much is immediately clear. I'm not even sure that anyone else can see it.

There's no doubt that the words are mine. The urge to

ask them 'Are you for me?' is so strong that I have to clamp my hand over my mouth to stop myself from doing it.

What does it mean though? It's as if someone has left me a cryptic clue to work out and I'm missing the codex to start me on my way. I puzzle at it. The world closes in around it, like I'm looking at it down a microscope.

I take each word in my mouth and roll it around. Get the taste of it. Digest it.

Then I sit down cross-legged on the pavement in front of it and gaze at it until the words swim out of focus and I can't even see the shapes of them.

I get to the office late.

Ruth hands me a stack of mail. I put it down on the front desk with no intention of looking at it. She picks it back up, lifts my arm like a chicken wing, tucks the mail into my armpit, then drops my arm down and pats my bicep.

'There, there,' she says, 'be a good boy.'

I'm walking away when I remember I wanted to ask her to get something for Harry. Get him something to say sorry. Both him and Sally have been avoiding seeing or talking to me. When I tried to kiss him goodbye this morning he flinched, screwed his eyes up and pulled away from me.

Taking a twenty pound note out of my wallet I go back to the front desk. Just before I hand it to Ruth I spot the crust of blood along the edge of the note and swap it for a clean one.

'Are you going into town at lunch?'

Distrust skitters across her face. Then a forced smile.

'Why?' She draws the word out. Whhhhhhhyyyyyyyy?

'Can you nip by Dominos and pick something up for Harry for me?' I am sweetness and light.

'Oh yes. Of course I can. I thought you were going to ask me to do something for Hilary. Pick up a suit or something.

But I'd love to get something for Harry. Anything in particular?'

She puts the note into her purse and closes the clasp with a clunk. I consider it for a moment. I hadn't got as far as actually choosing, just knew there had to be a something.

'I dunno. Something to do with animals maybe? He loves animals at the moment.'

'Okay, no problem. Something to do with animals.'

As I head towards my office I can hear her repeating it, with animals, with animals. Changing the inflection on it each time so it becomes a question, then a statement, then a question.

My hands are shaking from withdrawal. At my desk I squeeze them shut, nails biting into my palms, trying to still them. I sit on them. Nothing works. Eventually I close the door to my office. Take the vodka from the shelf and gulp down a mouthful. It burns and I have to hold my quivering hand over my mouth to stop myself from spitting it back out. When it is gone, when I can feel it burning its insidious way down my throat I collapse into my chair and press my fingertips into my eyelids until the world is made up of explosions and stars.

Sometime later I turn on my iPad, load up the BBC news app, skim through the sports, through the local news and then stop at the international news.

Nhgosa. A video of the rebel army leader, all military bravado, medals, peaked cap and great coat, sweltering in the African heat. He's on the back of a flatbed truck, waving and leaning down to shake hands with people. A flock of children chasing after the truck, like seagulls after a fishing boat.

I press play on the video.

He talks in a deep booming voice in accented English. He is on a balcony. There are bullet marks in the wall behind him.

I'm zoning in and out. It's like someone is un-focusing the camera.

He talks about freeing the country from the yoke of capitalist imperialism, about freeing the resources of the country for the people.

The camera cuts to the crowd. Smiling faces. Cheering and clapping.

He waves at them again.

The armed guards either side of him let a volley of gunshots into the air.

The crowd disperses.

The video cuts to the mines, to the children working in mud, pulling ore out with their hands.

I click on one of the related videos. A woman faces the camera, speaking to a journalist who is just out of view of the camera. A translator talks between them. The woman holds her arms up. Both of her hands are missing, the arms ending in shiny stumps.

The journalist is saying, 'Can you explain what happened to you?'

The translator chatters. The woman nods. Big, sad eyes.

'I understand this is hard for you, but can you tell us what happened and who did this to you?' the journalist says.

She looks at the translator, who turns the question to her language. She nods and then speaks slowly, looking directly at the camera, directly at me.

'They came through our village in the early morning. I was asleep with my child. Men dressed in black, with guns and scarves over their faces. When I saw them I started to run, but I ran straight into a group of them. They cut my hands off and they raped me.'

The journalist turns to the camera, and momentarily there is confusion on his face, before he composes himself.

'They cut your hands off before they raped you?'

She waits for the translator and then nods again. 'I think so, I passed out. But I think so, yes. Then they killed my baby and burned the village.'

The voiceover says, 'this is just the tip of the iceberg. Rape and mutilation are being used as military weapons in this conflict. These things are done publicly as part of a strategy. This is public and unashamed. As the rebel army passes through the country they leave behind a trail of carnage on an unprecedented scale.'

Bile rises in my throat. I take another slug of vodka and think about an invisible boy in the middle of the road.

I spend the rest of the morning not answering emails.

52.

Now I know what is missing, and consequently what The Zoo wants, I can hold it at bay. I'm trying to suppress the idea that power has shifted, because I've thought this before and it's hurt me. If I avoid Beth, if I look for The Ape, if I show it that I'm working for it, I can play for time. I can hold it at arm's length.

In the day room daytime TV and medication are lulling me. I rock back and forth. Around me the ward is slow motion and blurs. I'm trying to focus thinking of places The Ape could be. Earlier I searched the cupboards of the kitchen. Behind the guise of tidying them I removed all the crockery then emptied the drawers. I searched the fridge, despite Beaker standing over me to ensure I wasn't stealing his food.

I feel The Zoo over me. It chides me for sitting still, for not looking for its missing component. I shake my head to clear away the drug cobwebs, squeeze my eyes shut then open one and observe the world through the fog.

Where could it be?

With soggy hands I empty the craft boxes. Shuffle them up. Crayons and paper and scissors and glue on the floor. I'm conscious of controlling myself, of not seeming manic. The task is more difficult because of the missing thumb on my left hand. Hard to grasp the pencils as they skitter around on the tabletop. I give up trying to lift things with it and instead use it as a shovel, pushing them along to my right hand.

An orderly stops, watches me and then nods in approval as I stack them tidily away again. I could even get some brownie points from Janet with this.

Not there.

Outside, as I smoke a cigarette, I root around among crisp fallen leaves, searching the dirt for disturbances where someone could have buried him.

Not there.

I'm beginning to panic now. How much is due diligence? How much effort do I need to show to placate it? Do I need to search people's rooms?

Of course I know the answer. It's not been lost, someone has taken it. No two ways about it. No doubt at all.

I stub the fag out, burning the tips of my fingers on the dregs of its heat and make my way back inside. As I cross the day room I'm conscious about not looking suspicious.

The first room I come to is The Beard. I hesitate. He's an aggressive man. I suspect even on the outside, before he went whatever type of crazy keeps him here, that he was a slave to violent tendencies.

With a shiver and a blip in my vision The Zoo reminds me why I'm here and my hesitation is gone.

A quick glance left and right shows me there's no-one in the corridor, so I push the door open and peer around the edge of it. Empty. Once inside I close the door to with a gentle click and survey the interior.

The room is the same as mine but reversed. The beauty of the layout is that there are actually very few places you could hide anything – a desk drawer, under the bed, in the wardrobe, behind the wardrobe maybe, in the pockets of clothes and that's about it.

I head for the desk drawer. Empty apart from a Bible. I have an image of prison films, of books hollowed out as hiding places. But inside there are only yellowing pages with frantic pencil notes crisscrossing the text. I push the drawer closed, aware of the sound of the runners.

Move onto the wardrobe. Nothing in the bottom apart from the omnipresent dust. He doesn't have many clothes. Two pairs of trousers. Four identical shirts. A jumper. In the pockets I find nothing apart from a dry-cleaning receipt. As I pat the collars of a shirt I sense something in my stomach. A feeling I haven't felt for a long while. Excitement. I'm enjoying this. It feels naughty, underhand, on the wrong side of the tracks. I allow myself a wry smile.I'm still smirking as I lift the bottles of shampoo, moisturiser and shaving cream in the bathroom, shake them in turn, listening for a tell-tale rattle of something inside, when the door to the room opens.

I freeze. Back myself into the bathroom even further.

There is a commotion in the corridor, the sound of people shouting. I swallow my breath. It's like a balloon inflating in my throat. It wants to burst out.

The Beard backs into the room. One arm stretched out in front of him fending off two orderlies, the other high above his head. If he turns to his right he'll see me. See me invading his privacy. I flatten against the wall. No matter how hard I press my sweaty palms against the cold plaster I will never make myself flat enough. I can never make myself invisible.

He is shouting at the orderlies. 'Stay back. Stay back. You, you, you fucks. Stay back or I smash it. I'll smash it to pieces.'

It's a radio. As he waves it above his head it tunes and untunes itself. Lou Reed's 'Heroin' fights against the static. Asian Radio Lady is trying to fight her way through the wall of orderlies, her fingers snatching at the air with increasing desperation.

'Give it back. Give it back.' Her voice is high-pitched and barely human.

My head is pounding. I have to let my breath out. I have to. My vision is a maze of spots and I'm close to passing out. The Zoo is laughing in my head. I hold my hand over my mouth and let my breath out into it, wet warmth on my skin.

Beard is hollering, his words running into a guttural monologue. His voice is changing. Deeper. Harsher.

'Not everyone who says to me, "Lord, Lord," will enter the kingdom of heaven, but only he who does the will of my Father who is in Heaven. Many will say to me on that day, "Lord, Lord, did we not prophesy in your name, and in your name drive out demons and perform many miracles?" Then I will tell them plainly, "I never knew you. Away from me, you evildoers!"'

He's waving the radio above his head, feinting as if to drop it. Every time he does, both orderlies dive in the direction the radio would fall if he did drop it. He laughs and whips it out of their reach.

All it would take is for him to turn his head and I would be discovered. One turn of the head and it would be over.

But he doesn't turn, instead he dances back on his toes, agile for a man of his size, and shouts, 'By their fruits you will know them. Do people pick grapes from thorn bushes, or figs from thistles? Just so, every good tree bears good fruit, and a rotten tree bears bad fruit. A good tree cannot bear bad fruit, nor can a rotten tree bear good fruit. Every tree that does not bear good fruit will be cut down and thrown into the fire. So by their fruits you will know them.'

I'm holding my breath again and out there in the room Beard is dancing with the orderlies, Asian Radio Lady mirroring him, following them, stabbing her hands towards her radio while Lou Reed is singing. Then the room is full of static again, The Zoo in my head, pressure, pressure, pressure.

Then Beard turns, looks right at me, right fucking at me, and in his eyes there is no recognition, only the static of the radio and at the same time he launches the radio at the wall in the corridor. I hear it explode, the rainfall of parts on the floor, before the orderlies have hold of his arms, pulling him out of the room, his body limp, while Asian Radio Lady is sobbing and pummelling his back and each hollow thump reverberates in my head.

Just as suddenly it is quiet, they're gone, and I'm escaping down the corridor, down the corridor towards the plastic sheet, towards what The Zoo shows, and I think a half thought that The Ape may be waiting for me there, the dust kicked high by my pounding feet, then I'm through the plastic, wading through the dust, stumbling over piles of wood and bricks, in the dark, with the taste of sulphur in my mouth, towards the light, as the sulphur rises, through the hole and into the burning sunshine.

53.

The heat and the fence are the same, but everything else has changed. Corrugated iron buildings lean against each other in clusters about the space. Everything shimmers with the heat.

The sky is a flat blue wasteland. I tilt my head up and rotate it, taking it all in, the sun on my face. The chaos of Beard's room is fading as the warmth takes over.

A maze of footprints is on the ground in front of me, a mess of trainer and boot prints. Then in the middle the unmistakable impression of a child's foot. I kneel and trace the outline. Inside the first print is a tracing of a cowboy hat. My knees crack when I stand, I feel dizzy, despite, or maybe because of the expanse of the sky. I feel hemmed in, trapped, the fence mocks me.

I begin to follow the footprints.

Everything is quiet as I follow them around the huts. Inside each hut there is only blackness. I follow the prints around the edge of the enclosure. Almost the same path I took on my first visit. The sun is burning my neck, crisping the hairs there. The prints take me around the perimeter once, then again in a slightly smaller circle. I swear the inner ring of prints wasn't there on the first circuit. They look fresher. I pick up my pace and complete the circuit.

The sun is lower in the sky now. Thin clouds stretch across it in delicate wisps. The orange of the sun bleeds into them, then leaches out across the blue, like watercolour on wet paper.

The prints begin the loop again. I kneel at the point they cross the first loop and look at the prints – inside the first of the second loop is a tracing of a sword. I'm getting annoyed now, starting to feel like someone is taking the piss out of me. It occurs to me that if I stay put then whoever is making them should come up behind me in a couple of minutes, so I turn around, sit on the floor and wait. Nothing happens. No child. No more footprints. Just me sitting in the dust under a massive African sky, knowing that I need to get to my feet and play out whatever it is that I'm supposed to do.

So I pull myself up and set out on another circuit. This one begins with a tracing of a skull and crossbones. I want to get this over and done with, I'm not stupid, know that I will end up doing this again, getting smaller, so I begin to trot. By the time I'm back at the beginning I can touch the nearest hut if I stretch out my arm. Getting closer. Don't need to look at the ground to know the prints begin again, but I do. Put my foot next to one of them, next to a drawing of a machine gun. The print looks so small. I can make out each toe, the light print of the heel, the heavier pressure of the front of the foot, suggesting running, so I do the same, even though I'm struggling for breath, struggling against the build-up of acid in my calves and the stabbing pains in my shins.

Sketch of a Lion.

Run around once more, as the light slides out of the day and the temperature drops, making the sweat dry cold on my back.

Sketch of a Rhino. One more circuit.

I reach the hole in the wall. The prints turn in, turn into the cluster of huts, up to a spray-painted image of a monkey on the wall, arms pointing into the seventh circle.

I follow them between the buildings, which lean into me, conspiratorial, seeming to grow in height and close in above me until the darkening sky is just visible as a sliver of blue between the iron and pallets and plastic sheets.

I'm shepherded along to a shadowy entrance at the end of an alley way.

I am held in thrall of childhood fears. I am rooted. It takes everything I have left to step into the darkness, to duck my head under the threshold and enter the hut. Inside there is just one room with wicker mats on the floor and a pile of coloured cushions against one wall. The only light is from the door behind me and a jagged hole in the ceiling and the embers of a fire in the centre. Stepping closer I see a pan of still boiling water resting on a metal grate over the fire. Something is inside it. A glimpse of bone breaks the surface of the water. I lean closer. It's a rat or a rodent of some kind. All the fur stripped from its body apart from the head and through the bubbles I can see two blank eyes staring up at me. Then one of them blinks. I scream, jump up, catching the pan as I do and the water spills out of it, into the fire, which hisses and extinguishes and all the light in the hut is gone.

I freeze. Wait for my eyes to adjust. The rat is lying on the dead coals not moving, not blinking, just a dead rat. I laugh at myself, turn to leave and walk straight into someone. Again terror washes over me, I stumble back into the hut, catch my foot on one of the mats and fall onto my back, pull myself across the floor like a crab as the figure follows me. I put both hands over my face expecting a blow. Nothing comes. I remove my hands. The boy from the road, the boy from the zoo, is sitting cross-legged at my feet.

He smiles. I smile back.

'You,' I say.

'Yes,' his voice is heavily accented, deeper than I expected it to be.

221

He is holding something out to me. A bit of paper. I don't move. He shakes it.

'Take it. It's yours.'

I lean forward and snatch it from him.

'I shouldn't have to tell you this,' he says, 'you already know.'

Then he unwinds himself and stands.

'Wait,' I say.

He looks at me, expectation in big brown eyes. I don't know what I wanted to say, so ask him his name instead.

'You already know that too.'

'I've forgotten.'

'Bamidele.'

I repeat it back. Roll it around my mouth.

'Yes. Bamidele. You know what it means too,' he says and then he is gone.

In the empty hut I look at the paper in my hand. A scrunched up bit of paper, stained with the dust of a foreign land. Half a page ripped out of a magazine. On one side a picture of a Panther and text too small for me to read in this light. I don't need light to know the words on the other side because I wrote them. Every single fucking one.

It's an advert for the bank.

54.

Ben and I are in our meeting room, the ads spread out in front of us on the table and we've just watched the commercial again for the hundredth time. I'm bored of it now and so is he. This is always the danger in launching any campaign – the client is sick of it before the public even gets to see it. It's my job to get over this inertia, to make sure they don't try to change it before it goes live or within weeks of its launch. I seem to have the same telephone conversation over and over again with various clients as they try to fiddle with campaigns just weeks into launch, about how we've got to let them run their course, explaining opportunities to see or hear, that they're only sick of them because of the processes we go through, that we've got to give Joe Public a chance to at least see it before they butcher it. Sometimes I'm more successful than others. Hilary is the best at it. His arrogance, his unwavering conviction that he's right and the client doesn't know best is only really useful in these situations. God knows he doesn't listen to what the clients want anymore. When I get the call, the inevitable call, asking for us to increase the size of the price, or add more text, or put a flash or a fucking banner on, this is the only time I really feel comfortable putting the call through to him. Otherwise it's just a recipe for disaster.We've gone over the press ads. I've got Ben's scrawl on most of them as a final sign off. There's a knock at the door and Ruth comes in with printouts of the online ads. I hand them to Ben and, as he takes them, I sense a hesitation in him. An almost imperceptible pause, and a downturn of his eyes. I hope he's not going to ask me to change something, because we're past deadline on most of them and I asked Baxter to send them to the media house this morning. But Ben doesn't. He signs the top one. Then, barely looking at them, applies his moniker to each of the remaining printouts.

He's very twitchy today. I want to write it off as the fact that he's got final say on all this, all these millions of pounds worth of media bollocks arrayed in front of us like the plan of some mad Napoleonic general, but it's something more than that. He seems worn down.

'All done?' I ask, trying to inject some enthusiasm into my voice, all too aware I sound forced.

'Yes,' he replies without looking up, 'too late to stop it now.'

I raise an eyebrow.

He gives a little shrug. Puts the lid back on his pen and tucks it inside his jacket.

'Can I go?' he asks.

'Of course. Whenever you want.'

He nods, shakes my hand without meeting my eye and leaves.

As I tidy the papers up into a pile, turn the monitor off and collect everything up, his attitude nags at me. I'd expect a sense of anti-climax at this stage, that's normal, we've been working towards this for months. I could understand it if he felt a little lost. But not this. I question myself briefly as to whether this is my ego talking, whether I was expecting a big thanks, a professional pat on the back, but no, I wouldn't have wanted it from Ben anyway. No disrespect to him, but he's just a foot soldier, my ego demands approval from up high, not from the rank and file.

I realise this bugs me enough to not let it slide, so I run out of the meeting room, through the office and down the stairs.

In the car park Ben is taking his jacket off and hanging it up in the back of the car.

'Ben, wait,' I call out to him.

He is visibly shocked to see me running like this, then he buries it behind a deadpan expression.

'Did I forget something?'

'No. No. It's not that,' I don't know how to word this. I don't know him well enough. It occurs to me again that I could be being hugely oversensitive, that my lifestyle is playing tricks on me. 'Are you okay?'

The merest hint of a smile on his lips. Then that too is stifled.

'Yes, why?'

Everything I say is going to make me sound like a neurotic girlfriend.

'You just don't seem right. There's something wrong. Look, I don't want to pry, I'm well aware I could be stepping over the client–agency boundaries here, but we've been working closely together for months now, and, well, I get the feeling that something is wrong. If it's private and I'm being invasive then please tell me to fuck off.'

The suggestion of a smile again, but the shoulders have sagged. I knew it. There is something.

'Look. I'm fine. Don't worry about me. There's nothing bad. I've not split up from my girlfriend or anything. Everything is fine.'

Despite myself I'm relieved. At least I've not put my foot in it.

'Then is it anything I can help with?' I ask.

He appears to be considering it. He closes the car door, leans his elbows on the roof and rests his chin on his fists. Takes a deep sigh and starts to say something. Stops.

'Look,' he says eventually, 'there's nothing I can do about it, nothing you can do about it, so it's not even worth talking about.'

'Talking about what?'

'Nothing. It will do no good. You'll just feel as bad as I do and that's not fair.'

'Bad about what? You're scaring me now, Ben. What's happened?'

He lowers his forehead onto his fist now. His shoulders shake. I think he's crying, but when he spins round I see that he is angry, really angry.

'Nothing has happened. It just is. There's nothing any of us can do about it, so stop asking me questions. Don't worry about it, just turn round and get on with the rest of your day.'

'Fucking hell, mate, I can't do that now. I need to know what's got you so wound up. Especially if it affects me.'

He's shouting now, flecks of his spit hit my face.

'Oh, it affects you. It affects me. It affects all of us. It's not a matter of who it affects, it's a matter of whether you notice whether it does or not. I think you'll probably be alright.' He makes a play of looking me up and down, 'Yes, I think you'll be just fine.'

'I have no idea what you're talking about. But I'm worried about you now. You can talk to me. Come on, let's go over the road and have a chat over a pint. Better than here in the car park. Come on, mate. Let's go and set the world to rights.'

He snorts with laughter. An edge of derision to it. I've never seen him like this, never thought I would.

'Too fucking late for that. Way too fucking late. We're on a path now. We've just got to follow it and see where it takes us . . .'

The shrill ring of his mobile cuts him short. He swears

226

under his breath, pulls it from his pocket. As he looks at the display his face is engulfed with sheer panic, his skin suddenly as grey as the tarmac all about us.

'I've got to go,' he says without answering.

'Wait,' I say, reaching for his arm, but he slaps my hand away.

'No. I've got to go. Forget this. Everything is fine. I'm just tired. We've been working too hard. It's done now though. We can all relax.'

He slams the car door shut behind him and guns the ignition. He looks at me once before he wheel-spins out of the car park.

I'm left with the image of his haunted face through the tinted glass etched on my mind.

55.

The order goes: The Cowboy, The Knight, The Pirate, The Soldier, The Lion, The Rhino, The Ape, The Horse, then The Zebra.

The Horse is superior to The Zebra because of his usefulness to The Cowboy. There is an image filed in my head of The Cowboy and The Horse, silhouetted against a sky that is soaked in oranges and reds and they are so small against it, so small. The world fans out about them and they are just punctuation. This is before The Zoo, or maybe never at all. He is an Andalusian, purebred and Mediterranean, you can see the passion in the flare of his nostrils and the arrogant tilt of his head. I've never seen The Cowboy ride him of course, I believe though, that if he wanted to ride him then The Horse would allow it.

He has been our friend and our mount for 3000 years. He is the outmoded transport that we keep about for nostalgia and to race for our entertainment. He used to be the car, the tractor, the train, the combine harvester, the tank, now he is there for our pleasure only.

He is the bearer of the Apocalypse, bringing righteousness, war, famine and death to us all.

He is My Little Pony, with pink bows and plastic comb for his mane.

He was Dusty, then he became Silver.

He is Red Rum, which is also murder backwards on a mirror.

He is a hollow wooden horse let into an encampment so its occupants can surprise and slaughter their enemies, so he is trust and the betrayal of that trust.

He is beloved of all teenage girls as Black Beauty, but he is also a severed head in a bed.

He has always been with us, carrying us across the Earth, but just as The Cowboy stands on his own and abandons The Horse, so too do we and he is becoming forgotten and irrelevant.

He is a beautiful accessory that is no longer tied to us by necessity.

The Zebra by contrast is squatter, his flanks broader and less elegant. Although his markings go some way to compensate for his lack of finesse, they can only go so far. In those Rorschach stripes I see moths, a crow, a rictus smile, a betrayal and the end of days.

The Zebra's back is not strong enough to hold the weight of a man. He cannot carry us like The Horse can and he tries to make up for it with pretty patterns. It doesn't work and so he is below The Horse and always will be. He is the younger brother, trying to catch up with his more successful sibling by misbehaving and drawing attention to himself. The Cowboy doesn't take any notice, so neither will I.

Beaker has gone. He's nowhere to be found. No-one mentions it for a couple of days. The ward continues on as it always has, the steady momentum towards boredom. We get up. We eat breakfast. We spend time in the day room. We talk to people. We share. We eat our medicine. No one says anything about the fact that Beaker has gone. It disarms me. How easy it is for someone to vanish and we don't even bat a collective eye. It could very easily be me and no-one would notice, no-one would say a word. One day I'd be there and the next I wouldn't. It wouldn't

229

change the ward at all. One day Beaker was there. The next he wasn't. No one so much as flinched.

I ask Mark whether he has seen him and he squints at me as if I'm speaking a foreign language, before shuffling away.

Beth sits next to me in group. Her leg is warm next to mine. I keep trying to catch her eye. She resists. I know I've hurt her, so I accept her shunning me. It has to be something I'm willing to do. I do want answers though. I want recognition from someone that Beaker was here, that someone at least remembers him. There is a pause in proceedings. Conversation breaks out between people. I nudge her and ask her whether she knows where he is.

'People come and go,' she says, 'it's just the way it is in here.'

She's right of course, the thing that bothers me though is he showed no signs of recovery at all, was just as mental as the day I got here, taking pictures with his imaginary camera right up to the moment he vanished.

Unless.

Unless he was telling the truth and he was a fake all along. I look about me. How many of the others here are faking it? To escape their lives maybe. To get a break from their everyday. Maybe to get away with a crime. It makes me feel alone. I could be the only one in here with anything wrong with me at all. The stump of my thumb throbs. Maybe there's nothing wrong with any of them at all. I glance at Mark, at the dust settling on his shoulders. He won't meet my eye. Look across at Beth, but she is gazing out of the window. The Beard alone will hold my eyes and his face is smeared with a knowing smile.

I spend the rest of the day in my room, lying on the uncomfortable bed until my back hurts, then I stand on my tiptoes and write my name into the chip paper ceiling with

230

my thumbnail and then write all the names of the people who could come and get me out of here, who would want to get me out of here and the list is so short and so fractured that I give up, bury my face in the pillow and listen to The Zoo laugh at me.

56.

On the way home I phone Lou. She doesn't answer on the first ring. Or the second. Or the third. On the fourth she picks it up and barks 'What do you want?' down the phone at me.

'Something you said at the party, Lou,' I stammer.

'Was that before or after you smashed up my work?'

My hands tighten on the steering wheel. I couldn't have expected anything else.

The city is crawling back from work. Flat light. Blind spots everywhere. I know I shouldn't be on my phone, but this is a conversation I have to have.

'Before,' I say through gritted teeth. 'Look, I'm sorry Lou, I've said I'm sorry, I mean it, I'll be sorry for ever.'

'Whatever. What do you want? What did I say?'

'About the bank. About genocide.'

She tuts down the phone. 'Still not looked into that, eh? Conscience not got the better of you yet then?'

'I think it's getting there,' I swallow it down, pride, anger, self-disgust, the whole fucking lot, 'I know you think I'm a bad man, Lou. I just need to know what you meant.'

'It's not a secret, James, everyone knows what is going on.'

'Apart from me apparently.'

A Mercedes cuts me up. I blare my horn and swerve past it, looking into the confused eyes of a tiny Asian lady as I speed past her.

'Apart from you. Get The Guardian from last week. It's all in there. How much do you know about Nghosa?'

'About the minerals. Caster something,' I say.

'Cassiterite and Coltan.'

'That's it. And about phones.'

'Not just phones, James. All electronic equipment. Everything you use on a day to day basis to peddle your bullshit is reliant on them. Everything.'

'I get that. Bad electronics. Give us cancer and exploit people. Got it.'

'You're a bastard.'

There is real hatred in her voice. If I want her to carry on I need to dial it back. I need to know.

'Sorry, I was being flippant. This isn't a joking matter. I get all that. I just need to know what it's got to do with me.'

'It always comes back to you, doesn't it? Always has. Always will.'

'Please, Lou.'

'Okay. Okay. The Dutch bank, your bank, is funding the rebel army.'

I pull off the road. Bump the car up the curb and put on my hazard warning lights. My hands are shaking.

'They're paying for it all? All the stuff I've seen on TV?'

'Allegedly, yes. I can't believe you don't know this. Don't you ever do any research into your clients before you take them on?' she asks, words thick with scorn.

'Not generally. Why would I?'

'Ethics. Morals. I don't know. Because it's the decent thing to do.'

'Is that it?'

'As far as I can tell the Rebels are pretty much solely funded by your cash cow. A couple of steps removed maybe, but it's them – no doubt. The Government was intent on pushing up the price of the minerals and the majority of the

233

bank's investment is in electronics. It doesn't take a genius to put it all together.'

'No,' I mutter, 'no, it doesn't.'

'It's not just a coup though. You say you've watched the programmes? You know about the raping, about the burning villages, yes?'

'Yes,' my voice barely a whimper.

'You know about the children in the Rebel army. That they're training children to be ruthless killers? That they're training boys that it's okay to rape women?'

My head is on the steering wheel. Reality is filling the car as if it's plunged into an ice cold lake and the water is pouring in on me.

Lou is still talking. Her voice getting higher and higher pitched as her anger increases.

'It's a no win situation. The government exploits children to mine Coltan and Cassiterite then sells them cheap to the west. The Rebels just want control of the trade. It's not like they're trying to take over to make things better for the people. They'll do exactly the same. They'll also increase the price of the minerals and they'll still use children to dig it out of the ground. The only difference is they're using children to fight their way to it. Children, James. Children younger than Harry. Is this getting through to you?'

I can't speak. I know she is telling the truth. If I'm honest with myself I've known it for a while.

'The only winners are the bank, your bank, and the electronics companies, because they control the Rebels and they control the minerals. Every time a new games console comes out, the demand for them increases and thousands of people die. Do you understand?'

Silence.

'Do you understand? That BMW you are sat in is paid for by the rape of women, murder of children and the destruction of a country. Does that make it any clearer for you?' she repeats.

'Yes,' I finally manage to say.

Cars pass by, buffeting me. I feel like I'm drowning.

'Look at the Amnesty website, James. You'll see that I'm telling the truth.'

I already know she is. There is no doubt in my mind.

'I will,' I say.

'Looking isn't enough, James. You're part of this now. Whether you like it or not. You're contributing to this. Looking isn't enough. It's what you do that counts. You've caused a lot of damage to a lot of people. And I'm not just talking about my art. You've got some making up to do.'

Something occurs to me and before I can stop myself I've blurted out, 'Have you been texting me?'

'What?' she says.

'Texts, emails and stuff.'

'Don't be fucking ridiculous, why would I do that? I don't even want to talk to you.'

'To tell me that stuff. To make me realise?'

'Fuck's sake, James. You're a grown man. Take some fucking responsibility for the things you do.'

Sometime later I realise she has hung up and I'm still on the side of the road. Rain is drumming on the roof of the car. Headlights streak past me, smears of light through the rivers running down the windows.

Then I'm alone. Really alone.

I understand now why Ben didn't want to sign off the ads.

57.

I'm through the plastic sheeting again.

I can't be in the day room. I can't be with the others. Blank faces. Denial. The lingering impression that they are fakes, actors, charlatans hasn't left me, if anything it's got stronger. As I went for a fag earlier Mark and Beth were talking and when I opened the door they stopped. I wanted to ask what they were talking about, even when I knew the answer would be a lie.

It hurts that Beth has turned on me. I can't deny it. I know I have brought this upon myself, I know I scared her, I should be pleased I am keeping The Zoo away from her and I am, but I can sense her falling away from me and it hurts. I wonder if this is what The Zoo wanted all along. That it planned an endgame of divide and conquer to keep me away from the others, to let me think that I'm winning by holding it at bay, while all along it's laughing at me.

Bamidele is waiting for me just inside the plastic sheet. We walk together in companionable silence towards the light and the warmth. In the dark I reach for his hand and it's rough and cold to my grip.

Through the hole in the plastic.

Into a world of ash and smoke and screams.

Bamidele's hand is in mine. I can feel his tension through my fingers. Around us the town is burning, plumes of smoke reaching up into the sky to escape the carnage. I can barely see a few feet in front of me. The air is full of noise, the crackle of burning wood, the crack as a hut nearby collapses, the whump as the ceiling hits the floor, people crying all around us. The darkness is tainted with the red and yellow and orange of fire, people bursting out of the darkness, their faces grey with ash, eyes stapled open by terror. As we stumble forward the smoke fills my lungs, I cough and splutter, unable to catch my breath, the heat scorching my tear filled eyes. I trip over something and lose Bamidele's hand, look down and see a woman cradling a bloody child, limp in her arms. Everywhere is so chaotic it's hard to focus on anything. The world flickers and shimmers, dances in flames. I cast about in panic, try to find Bamidele, but he is gone and I am alone in the burning confusion. I stagger deeper into the village, past shattered homes, treading on mounds of burning wood, wood that used to hold up walls, roofs, contain families. I trip and fall face first into the dirt, my hand on a pile of embers, instantly searing my palm. A dog trots past me, something in its mouth. As it gets closer I realise it is a hand, severed at the wrist and I gag and heave, nothing coming out apart from smoke. Panic now. Panic seared with a desire to return to the ward, to find my way back through the hole. I try in vain to get my bearings. Walk, then run, to my right, attempting to find my way to the fence, to work my way back round. Instead there is only a maze of burning buildings, of choking smoke. I bump into a man, his chest crossed in blood, and he flinches and pulls his hands up over his face, I splutter reassuring words, want him to understand I mean no harm, but my words are alien to him and he backs away from me into the crackling darkness. The world is just heat and smoke, I can see nothing, feel nothing, I wander, blind, disorientated, terrified until I collapse in the dark and the heat drops a suffocating blanket over me.

58.

I wake quickly, as if from a bad dream, but there is only a blank space. I don't know how I got here. The last thing I remember was being in my car on the side of the road. I am wet with sweat. Unaware of the time I go to the blinds and pull them open onto a flat grey day. Midmorning? Early afternoon? Hard to tell. From the main office I can hear the thump of someone's stereo, so it's got to be in work hours. I fumble about on the desk for my phone, find it lying against the far wall. I turn it on. Ignore the cavalcade of emails that pour out of it. Phone my home number. Sally answers. As soon as she hears my voice she hangs up. When I ring back it's engaged. I ring her mobile. She rejects it. Again. Again. Again. I slam it down on the desk, it bounces near my foot, so I hoof it against the wall.

My desk is covered in a maze of post-it notes. A mass of scrawled capitals, some of them backwards, childlike, spidery, mocking and chiding. As I read them I curl up and clasp my knees against my chest.

Traitor.
Murderer.
Spineless.
Fucking Killer.
Lie.
Joke.
Charlatan.
Killed them.

Kill him too.

I sweep them up, bundle them together. Muttering, 'Fuck you, fuck you, fuck you, you don't know what you're talking about, fuck you, fuck you', when I catch sight of my desktop, at the screensaver of a pile of dead children, flies on their faces, flies crawling into their mouths, black eyes staring at me saying murderer, charlatan and killer. So I grab the mouse and maximise my email client and there too, every email the same, every one of them from me to me, saying murderer and killer and charlatan. I scramble the power off and fall away from it, smash into my bookcase, knock the award from Campaign magazine so it hits the side of the desk and the glass explodes across the room. A second later Ruth smashes the door open, her hand over her mouth and I can see the horror in her face. I say something about an accident and push past her, out of the office, into the corridor. Bamidele's there in the doorway, blocking my way. As I push him he's solid and real, he pushes me back, pushes me back with stumps, holds them up in front of me, the arms stopping in bloody stumps, behind them his manic grin, wide and white mouth as he laughs. The blood is in my mouth and my eyes, I taste the iron, as he pushes them into my chest. The sharpness of the bone, the warm wetness of the blood and he's laughing and pushing. I'm screaming, 'Fuck you, you're not real, you're not real', even as I feel the bone piercing my clothes and the blood warm on my skin and in my mouth, 'You're not real'. Then I'm past him too and he catches me with a glancing blow which unbalances me at the top of the stairs, then there is air. As I fall I look back at him, with his smile and the gaps where his hands should be, then I hit the concrete, the wind forced from me. I am up again, running now, stabbing pain in my side with every footstep and breath. I am away, in the street, away from him and his laughing, into a world of

239

staring faces and flat grey light. I am panicking, running, a blood covered maniac. People step aside in horror as I gibber and stumble and trample them, until I turn into an alley and collapse to my knees and sobbing and sobbing and sobbing, throw up until there is only acid and bile and nothing left.

Sometime later I find myself outside the bank. The sweat is dry on me. I can smell myself. I've stopped shaking and I'm calm now. Everything is clear. I know what I must do.

Through the automatic revolving doors, the interior stretched by the glass, ugly, contorted. I'm in the foyer and there is a wall of warmth, stifling, and I loosen my scarf, gulp, then I'm through it, at the huge curved desk. The mahogany is cold on my palms, I'm looking into the smiling face and cold dead eyes of the beautiful girl and she is saying 'Can I help you?'

I tell her my name and she's on the phone, saying my name, looking at me under worried eyelids, her hand covering her mouth. She's smiling at me again, but I can tell it's false and a lie.

She's asking me to take a seat, pointing at a sofa.

I sit and wait.

Music in the air, smell of perfume.

I try to work out the music, no vocals, just guitar, but I can't place it. I can taste his blood.

A man comes in, leans over the desk, talks to the receptionist, only his toes touching the floor, and they look at me, talk again, huddled and conspiratorial.

Then the man is standing in front of me, saying, 'How can I help you?'

My voice is taut, calm, I know what I must do.

'I'd like to see Ben Jones please.'

He surveys me, makes a decision, says, 'Wait here please,'

returns to the desk, to the phone and makes another hidden call. When he comes back his demeanour has changed. He is ruthless efficiency.

'I'm sorry sir, but there isn't a Ben Jones here.'

'When will he be back?' I ask.

'No sir, I don't think you understand. There isn't anyone of that name here.'

'Has he left?'

Stay calm.

'No sir. There is no-one of that name that works here.'

'I think you must be mistaken, I spoke to him the other day. Ben Jones. He works in the marketing department.'

'Sorry sir. I think it's you that is mistaken. There is no-one called Ben Jones who works here.'

My anger is rising. I'm barely strong enough to hold it back as I say, 'Can you check again please? I work for your advertising agency. He's my contact. I need to speak to him. It's important.'

His look is incredulous. I glance down at my chest. The blood is gone. The tears have gone. There is dirt on the knee of my trousers where I fell, but the rest is gone. He isn't writing me off as a mental tramp, he just doesn't believe me.

'It's really important that I speak to him,' I repeat, 'or Mr Berkshire, can I speak to Mr Berkshire?'

'No sir. That isn't going to happen. Now I'm very busy, so I'm going to have to ask you to leave.'

His hand is on my shoulder. I shrug it off. It finds its way back. Harder, more insistent, I am turned. I grasp his knuckles, try to move them. Nothing. Iron. Solid. As he turns me to the door I twist and turn, break away, run back towards the lifts, shouting 'Ben, Ben Jones.'

The receptionist reaches out a manicured hand towards me, but I bat it aside, press all the buttons on the lift, the

241

numbers impossibly high and I'm still shouting 'Ben' as I'm hauled out of the doors, my arm high behind my back. He punches me hard in the kidney so I drop to my knees, then he kicks me in the back of the head, it meets concrete and as I fade away I feel him lifting me, dragging me across the car park and dumping me on the pavement, where I lie listening to the thrum of cars as they pass me, huge spots of rain drumming unhindered on my upturned face.

59.

The order goes: The Cowboy, The Knight, The Pirate, The Soldier, The Lion, The Rhino, The Ape, The Horse, The Zebra, then The Dog.

It is true that dog is man's best friend. However, the cold authority of The Cowboy has pushed him down to a lowlier position. In a time of war The Cowboy has no time for The Dog. He has no time for friends, only the order of The Zoo. Maybe if The Dog was a Collie or a Husky then he would be higher, but he is a mongrel, the sort seen scavenging on the streets of a South American city, the sort seen trotting behind malnourished teenage gang members, being chased away from bins with a stick, only to return when the humans have left.

He came from the wolves, but he is tamed, broken and beaten. He runs alongside us, docile, friendly and not as intelligent as we like to think.

We train him to walk us when we are blind, but we also dress him in human clothes and carry him around in handbags as trophies to our ego, reducing him to fashion.

He is Lassie telling us a relative has fallen down a well.

With three heads he guards the gates to the underworld.

He is Greyfriars Bobby standing guard over his deceased master for 14 wasted years.

He is Toto following Dorothy into the unknown.

He carries a barrel of brandy to stricken climbers, pulls a sledge across the tundra.

He is doting and mindless, and this weakness means he sits at the bottom while The Cowboy ignores him.

The only Animal below The Dog is The Chicken and he has no worth other than fodder. They are the last of The Plastics. They are well thumbed. Like The Rhino's horn The Dog's tail has been chewed and flattened with teeth marks. Without the rule of The Cowboy they would simply be wild and aimless. They are after all the beasts and this is what they do. They are the brainless, the followers, the masses.

Without the structure of The Zoo I would have found them concerning. There seems to be a propensity to violence under their plastic shells, an implicit threat which, through the taming and structure put in place by The Cowboy, The Knight and The Pirate, has been suppressed. Their primal instincts have been calmed into something altogether more settled and subservient. They needed to be contained. This, I have learned, is the nature of The Zoo.

The order goes: The Cowboy, The Knight, The Pirate, The Soldier, The Lion, The Rhino, The Ape, The Horse, The Zebra, The Dog, then The Chicken.

And that is the totality: The Zoo.

After lunch I traipse back to my room. Lethargy slows my legs, dragging them through weary treacle. No-one is really talking to me. It's amazing how much I miss them now I'm on my own, when I thought of them as irritating and wearisome. I tried to begin a conversation with Beard at lunch, but he simply raised a hairy finger to his lips and ssssh-ed at me. I reached out to Mark for conversation but he turned a shy face away from me.

In the corridor the orderlies brush past me, Beth is a back turned on me. I long for my meeting with Janet, even though I know it'll be probing and prying more than a conversation.

In my room I sit next to Bamidele on the bed and sigh.

'You're here now then?' I ask.

He nods towards The Zoo.

'It asked me to come.' His accent is less thick here and easier to understand.

'You're not going to hurt me? It didn't ask that?'

He shakes his head. 'We're past all that. I'm here to help you.'

'The Zoo wants to help me?'

'Why wouldn't it?'

He puts his arm around my shoulder. It weighs nothing at all, it may as well not be there.

It always tries to hurt me, that's what it does. The Zoo is there to hurt me, I know that. I try to tell him. He stops me talking by squeezing my shoulder.

'It's time you understood. It wants you to understand.'

'Understand what?'

I am aware I sound like a child.

'You know what it all means. You've just forgotten. It's time for you to remember.'

In my memory there is nothing apart from pain and confusion. I shake my head.

'I can't,' I say.

'You can. You have to. There's no need to be afraid anymore. I told you, we're past all that. Things are different now you know what The Zoo is and what it means. You just need to work out your position in it and the rest will fall into place.'

He gets to his feet. Bare feet on cold tiles. He is taller than I expect. He towers over me. I want to know more. He needs to tell me more. I open my mouth to ask him questions, lots of questions, but he is already padding away from me. At the door he turns and nods at me, then he is gone. After a pause I jump to my feet and run to the door, open it and glance up and down an empty corridor.

He is just fading footprints in the dust.

I face The Zoo.

It shivers, seems to pulsate, the room is filled with a low hum that permeates my skin and bones, the hair stands up on the back of neck, on the back of my hands, my arms alive with electricity.

'What do you want me to do?' I ask and I swear it smiles back at me. It wants answers. I need to go back to get them.

60.

I'm in a bar in the centre of the city, nursing my bruises. My face is swollen where it struck the pavement. There's a mountain range of lumps on the back of my head, a head coated in hair matted with blood. I am surprised they served me. Guess they were scared not to. A pint is going flat on the table in front of me. I spin my phone on the wood, take a gulp of my flat pint. Scroll through the names on the phone until I reach Leary and click dial. It rings and rings long enough for me to assume he's not going to answer, then as I'm putting it back down onto the table I hear him say, 'Wotcha.'

I consider hanging up. But I know what I must do. I am calm and rational. I am on a path.

'Leary,' I say.

'Hello mate. How's it going?'

'Good,' I say, even though I couldn't mean anything less. I am definitely not good.

'How can I be of assistance, sir?'

I take another gulp of my pint. Then another. The penultimate one in the glass. I wave a hand at the barman, point at my drink. He tuts, but begins to pour another anyway.

'Have all the ads gone?'

'Yes mate. All gone. TV, digital, radio and press. All of them sent out and ready to air. All done and all on time. An excellent job on both parts even if I say so myself sir,' he says, his voice full of pride.

The barman places my pint on the table. I rummage in my inside pocket and pass him a fiver.

'Is it too late to pull them all?'

Silence on the other end of the line. My hands shake. I take another drink.

'You're kidding, right?'

'No. Afraid not. I need to pull them.'

Silence again. I can almost hear his mind working on the other end of the phone, trying to work out why I would want to do this, whether he's done something wrong.

'Something wrong with the ads?' he asks.

'No. The ads themselves are fine. I mean, they're fine.'

'Something wrong with the schedule?'

'No. The schedule was fine. More than fine. You did a really good job.'

There is palpable relief on the other end of the phone. He knows he hasn't made a mistake with a multi-million pound campaign. Even while I can understand it annoys me that he is more concerned with covering his own arse.

'I just need to pull all the ads,' I say, 'every single one of them.'

Silence again while he considers it. A group of middle aged woman at the table to my right bursts into laughter.

'Want or need?' Leary says eventually.

'What difference does it make?' I ask.

'A huge one. The deadline has passed for pretty much all of them. We may be able to pull some but it's going to cost and there's a fair chance they'll have to run blank space instead, it's going to be too late to resell the slots. They won't be happy if we pull. It won't make either one of us look very good.'

'Need then,' I say, 'I need you to stop them all.'

'James. We've worked together for a long time. I have to trust your judgement.'

I mutter thanks through my pint even while I sense a *but*.

'I've got to ask you why? I'll do my best to pull them, but it may help me if I know why. Is it something to do with the Advertising Standards Authority? I can work with that.'

'No. I'm afraid not. They just need to be pulled. And I'm asking you to do it. I can't give you any more than that. Can you do it?'

Silence again. My hands shake around my pint glass. The phone is getting hot against my ear.

'I'll see what I can do. I'll give you a bell later.'

He hangs up and I am left with an empty phone. I drop it back on the table and spin it with my forefinger again. It has barely made a revolution before it rings again.

Hilary.

I answer, holding it away from my head.

'What the fuck are you doing?' He's screaming at me, his voice oscillating with anger.

'How do you mean, Hilary?' I ask. I have to swallow a sardonic smile. It turns into a thin-lipped sneer.

'Don't play dumb with me, you little prick. You know exactly what I mean. What the hell are you playing at? Is this some kind of sick joke?'

Of course I know what he means. You'd have to be an idiot not to. And I'm not an idiot. I am clear. I am calm. I know exactly what I must do.

'No, Hilary. I'm deadly serious.'

'Then explain to me, please. Because it seems to me that you're trying to pull the biggest campaign we've worked on for years.'

I can literally hear the spit leaving his voice as he talks. I am getting a perverse pleasure from upsetting him this much. I have to remind myself what I am doing. And why.

'It needs to be done. It needs to be stopped.'

'What the fuck are you talking about? It doesn't need to

249

be stopped. It definitely needs to *not* be stopped. Are you trying to wind me up? Tell me you and Leary are playing some sort of prank on me? Fucking with an old man? It's sick, especially as my marriage lies in tatters, but I'd rather have that than you trying to sabotage our campaign.'

'It's all a lie.'

I know this won't cut it, that he'll never understand, not even if I explained the whole thing. That's it's so far beyond his understanding that even if I held the body of a dead child in front of him he would raise an eyebrow as if waiting for the punchline.

'What's a lie?' he asks me, the words thick with scorn.

'The campaign. It's all a lie.'

He laughs. Empty. Callous.

'Of course it's a bloody lie. It's an advertising campaign.'

Laughs again. Like he's cracked a hilarious joke. Normally I would feel like I should laugh. I want to smash the phone on the table until the glass breaks. Get in the car. Drive round to his house and stick the shards in his smarmy fucking face.

Instead I try to tell him about Nhgosa. About the mines and the rebels and the children and the rape and the murder. But the words are jumbled and confused and I know I sound like I'm ranting and desperate and mad. All the while he laughs over me. In the end I peter out. Hilary is laughing so much he snorts.

'Listen,' he says, when he manages to control himself, 'you've been working hard recently, probably too hard. Burning the proverbial candle. You know it's true. You're not thinking straight. God knows you're not speaking straight. Here's what I want you to do, and I'm not going to take no for an answer, I want you to go home. I want you to take a shower. I want you to drink a big coffee, a pint of water, then I want you to sleep it off. You'll feel

250

better tomorrow. I promise. Then I want you to spend the day with your wife and child. When was the last time you spent some serious time with Sally and Harry?'

My wife. My son. A lump in my throat. Everything else fades away, replaced by my son, with my wife.

'I don't . . .'

'Okay. It's okay. I'll sort everything out. Go home. Sober up. Mend things. Take a couple of days off. I do not want to see you near the office. And while I mean that out of concern, I mean it literally too. I do not want to see you near the office.'

He hangs up.

My wife. My son.

Fighting against the rest of it.

I dial Leary's number. It's engaged. On a hunch I ring Hilary again, ready to hang up if he answers, but he's engaged too.

My wife. My son.

I force a soggy hand into my pocket, fish out my car keys, focus on the door through four empty pint glasses, then stagger to my feet, back to my car and drive home drunk.

61.

The whole way Bamidele is seated next to me in the passenger seat, gibbering and shouting, half African, half English, so loud I have to play the stereo at full volume to drown him out. All the while waving his arms in front of me, blood on the dashboard, on the steering wheel making it slick, on the inside of the windscreen so I have to repeatedly wipe it clean with my sleeve.

The car lurches to a stop. Stalls as I leave it in gear, lift the clutch, bump into the garden wall. I drop the keys as I get out, smack my head against the doorframe and watch them skitter underneath the car. Leave them there for now, concentrate instead on getting to the door. I realise now how pissed I am. I make it to the door, half expecting the lock to have changed, fumble the key into the chamber, hear the click, push the door open, where it snags on the security chain. I put my weight against the door, lean into the world spin. The hall light is on. I lean out of the door again. The lounge curtains are closed, a chink of light between them. Back to the door. Squeeze my hand into the gap, attempt to unlatch the security chain. Snag my nail on it, bend it back painfully. Curse and sway about. Grasp the door for balance. Steady myself. Level. Movement from inside the house.

'Sally?' I call out, more slur than words, 'Sally. Are you in there?'

Light across the hallway. Outline of a body in shadow.

'Sally,' I holler again.

A noise behind me. Look over my shoulder at Bamidele's

252

grinning face. He gesticulates with his stump, a sign I read as encouragement.

'Sally. Is that you?'

'Leave us alone,' she says, staying out of view.

'Let me in, darling.'

'No way.'

She says something I can't hear to someone behind her.

'Harry, Harry, it's me, son. Daddy's home.'

'No, go back into the lounge, wait for Mummy there. I need to talk to your father. No, it's adult talk, baby.'

His blond head, her arm around him. My heart shatters, the pieces only held together by booze.

'Come on, Sally, let me in,' I whine, face squashed inbetween the door and frame, air forced from my cheeks.

'Fuck off, James. Leave us alone.'

'No. Don't say that. Let me in. It's my home too.'

'Well, if it's your home, where the fuck have you been the last few days? Where have you been when my mother has had to look after Harry? Where have you been when he's been crying for his Dad at night? Where the fuck have you been?' Her voice is high-pitched, stretched, hissing out through her teeth.

'Let me in and I'll tell you. I've had things to sort out. You told me to sort myself out. I needed some time. I had some things to do.'

'You're drunk. I can hear it. You disappear. Abandon your family. Abandon me. Then come back here, drunk and shouting.'

'I'm not shouting. I'm not drunk. I just want to come home. Please, Sally. Let me come home.'

'Too late, James. Way too late.'

'Please?' I plead.

'Go away. I don't want to see you. I couldn't hate you any more than I do now. You should go. If you stay I'm going to say something you don't want to hear.'

253

'Sally.'

'Go away.'

The hiss raised. Sharper, cutting me open.

The door to the lounge closes. The light gone. The shadow gone. My wife gone and with her my son.

The curtain flickers again, spitting light across the lawn. At the window. Press my face against the glass. Searching for a gap in the curtains. Searching for my family.

Back to the door, kicking the base of it, shaking it on its hinges, screaming for my family, screaming for my wife and child, banging on the wood with numb hands. Lights come on in the next door house. Disapproving faces at windows mouthing words of reproach. Me responding, 'Mind your own fucking business. Fucking busybody. Mind your own business. Go on. Fuck off back inside.'

Scrabbling about on the floor I find the keys, then I'm back in the car with my foot to the floor. Reversing onto the road, the door flapping like loose skin, ripping tyre marks into the tarmac as I career away. Bamidele is in the passenger seat and we're weaving down the road howling out of the window. Tears of rage and anger and despair and emptiness freezing on my face. Cold lips mouthing missing names.

Hotel.

Dropping credit cards onto the reception desk. Scrawling a messy signature. Empty room. Starchy bed. Neat vodka in a plastic glass. Another. Another. Another.

Falling.

So far so . . .

Falling.

So far so . . .

Falling.

So far so . . .

Fallen.

62.

Time passes. Minutes are hours long and hours fly by so quickly I can't hold onto them. I can't sleep, stare instead at a pockmarked ceiling. Then I can't wake. I burrow myself into spiky dreams, then wake in a screaming sweat. The room gets smaller, compressing about me, then expanding so rapidly that I shake with agoraphobia.

Images scroll around the wall – burning villages, a child scrabbling at the dirt with bleeding fingernails, a hail of gunfire across a fire-orange sky, convoy of trucks, berets and grimaces and the cowering public. Over the top run the words from the adverts like a telecaster, the words I wrote, the lies I wrote.

I order bottle after bottle from the hotel bar and ask them to be left outside my door. Bolt them back neat as I write texts to Sally I never send.

Days in. Could be days in. May only be a few hours. There's a knock at the door. I ignore it. Another knock, more insistent this time. I yank myself from the floor, skin peeling away from the carpet. I realise I'm naked, my torso is covered in welts and bruises, some old, some brand new, a lattice work of tiny cuts on my forearm, beads of blood caught in my arm hairs.

Another knock.

The door is so far away, so far, like a reverse dolly zoom from a Hitchcock film. I reach out for it with overlong arms and tiny spindly fingers. Then I am there smack up to it. My face is against the wood and I am massive, Alice massive, tottering over the tiny room, so far down, so far down, that the room spins with vertigo. I clutch my head in my hands, squeeze my eyes shut until the carousel slows then squint through the spyglass and see the shiny bald head of my dealer. Runner. Thank God. Though I don't remember calling him. Opening the door a fraction I scope the corridor out, then let him in.

'Easy, bruv,' he says.

I nod at him then, remembering my nakedness, scuttle into the bathroom, ignoring the debris in there, and pull on the complementary dressing gown.

Back in the room he's sitting on the chair at the desk, legs crossed tightly, camply, mocking me.

'What's going down, Howard Hughes?'

I just hold my hand out and say, 'Please sir, I want some more.'

He's examining me. Like he's questioning me. Like he doesn't want to give me any.

'I'm good for it,' I say.

'Oh I don't doubt that, my friend. I don't doubt that at all. But, look at the state of this place. I'm the last one to do myself out of business. Are you sure you need it?'

'Fuck me. Are you a drug dealer or a drug counsellor?' I pull a wodge of notes from a stained wallet, wave them in front of him. 'Now, I want a quarter, here's the money. Are you going to sell it to me or are you going to fuck off?'

After he's gone I'm searching in my pockets for something to chop it up on when I find an invite with a charcoal drawing of my wife on it. Checking the date against my phone I realise it's today.

I rack out a massive line and offer one to Bamidele who is seated on the end of the bed. He refuses, so I do his too.

I question myself the whole time I am in the shower,

256

scrubbing off days of detritus, scrubbing away at the pain until my skin is raw and bleeding and my eyes are stinging with the soap.

I continue to question myself as I dry myself with crispy hotel towels. Pulling on dirty underwear I notice someone has written in the steam on the mirror, *you're only lying to yourself*. As I smear it away with the back of my hand I catch a glimpse of my red-rimmed eyes and shudder.

I order a clean shirt from the hotel reception and, while I wait for it to arrive, light a cigarette and watch the smoke curl around the ceiling fan.

My juddering fingers are only just capable of phoning a taxi and, in the time it takes for it to arrive, I inhale three sweeping lines of chop and drink two miniatures from the mini bar.

As the cab slides through the city I watch the world through a sheet of glass and am full of panic and loss, everything running away from me like the rivulets of rain chasing each other across the windows.

63.

The party is at a champagne bar tucked away in one of the side streets of the cultural quarter. It's the sort of place with a tiny sign that lives by the idea that it only wants you as a customer if you know it's there. The sort of place that doesn't think it needs to advertise. The sort of place that makes people like me redundant and paradoxically the sort of place people like me gravitate to.

I hover outside, smoke a cigarette, letting fine rain drum on my head, trying to let the cold water clear it.

'Can I come in with you?' asks Bamidele, suddenly at my side, blood running into his eyes.

'No fucking way,' I say quickly.

He seems sad, but doesn't follow me.

Inside it's low-lighters and little booths with leather seats and people leaning in to talk over mahogany tables. Exposed brickwork, low archways – it's self-conscious, stylish, quickly dating. Bamidele is at the window, face against the glass, big eyes following me around. I wave a hand at him, tell him to go away. He lowers his head and disappears into the night.

I find the others downstairs milling around the bar, all scarves and jackets and jeans and smiles. They looked shocked to see me, bury it quickly and there is a round of pats on the backs and kissing on the cheeks. Hilary clasps me tight on the shoulder, tells me he's pleased to see me, tells me that everything is alright, that the bank is fine and everything is going well. Bile rises in my throat. Alan tells me I look like shit and laughs a warm, beery laugh in my ear. Despite myself I'm pleased to see them all.

Baxter makes his way over to me. I shake his hand and tell him as sincerely as I can, congratulations. He's glowing. A beautiful woman is at his side. A happy, beautiful woman.

'Melissa?' I ask.

Baxter nods. She holds out a delicate hand. I ignore it and kiss her on the cheek.

'Congratulations to you both. I'm sure you will be very happy. Would you like a drink?'

'That would be very kind of you,' she says and her voice is like crystal.

At the bar I order a bottle of Dom Perignon and ask the barman to take it over to them. I slink away to the toilet and do another line off the toilet roll dispenser. It burns on the way down the back of my throat.

Back at the bar I order a Jaeger bomb. Collins is next to me, so I order another two and insist he chugs it down with me. He does and then fades away into the gloom. I order another beer which doesn't taste of anything. Find myself wandering around and through the booze and the drugs I'm thinking, *things will be all right, things will be fine, just like they always were, everything will go back to the way it was, this will all wash away.* And at least on face value I'm right, with every drink it washes away. With these people about and this booze inside me it all seems okay, Nghosa is a country far away and nothing at all to do with me. I'm feeling better, feeling much better, calmer, orderly, back on top of things.

Jessica appears at my side. She glides out of the darkness into a pool of light, lit perfectly from above, she is all cheekbones and kohl eyes, like a movie star.

'I've missed you at work,' she purrs and some of the strength goes from my legs. She's emboldened by drink and I'm weakened by it.

'You have?' I say, smothering the hint of desperation with a sip of my drink. 'You want one?'

'How could I refuse you?'

Big moist eyes gaze at me from under perfectly curled eyelashes.

I order two glasses of champagne. We chink them together. Our fingertips touch.

'So,' I say, bubbles filling my mouth and nose, 'how are you enjoying the job?'

'Great. It's very stimulating. And I've met such great people.'

She looks at me when she says this. I force myself to look away, when really I want to be swallowed by those eyes. To plunge right into them, to dive deep and not come up for air.

'Yes. They're a great bunch.'

Great bunch? Great bunch? I don't even sound like myself.

'Some more so than others.'

A pearly white smile. Perfect lips over perfect teeth.

My head swims in alcohol.

'You staying around for the duration?' she asks.

'Was planning to,' I reply.

'Good.'

Then she's swaying away, my head following her arse like a metronome.

My phone beeps for a text message from an unknown number. *Selfish Cunt.* I delete it.

Sometime later I'm in a booth with Baxter, hedged in by glasses, a White Russian in my hand. I hold it cold to my cheek, the rattle of ice cubes against glass. Take a sip, crack one of the cubes between my teeth. I'm speaking earnestly, rolling each word out between my lips, saying, 'Why did you get into advertising, Baxter?'

'I don't know. I just fell into it, I guess. I wanted to do something creative. But I wanted to have enough money to live on.'

'And you can't live on poetry.'

'Too true.'

He holds his glass up and I smash mine into it, spilling White Russian onto the tabletop. I'm drunk now. Really drunk now. Baxter is too. I can see it in the roll of his head, the weight of his eyelids.

'I didn't have enough skill to be a designer,' he slurs.

'Don't do it,' I blurt out.

'Do what?'

I wave my arms above my head, taking in everything, a demented helicopter.

'All this. All this bullshit.'

A look of horror on his face. It takes a second to register in my soggy head, then I get what I think he means.

'Shit, no, sorry, not your marriage. Do that. Definitely do that. Probably the best thing you'll ever do. Was the greatest day of my life. Before all this turned it to shit. The muck spreading we do for a living, Baxter. We're a disease. A parasite. We play on people's weaknesses. We're disgusting. You're a good guy. You don't deserve it. Get out now while you still can. You're young. You can find a new trade. Don't let it screw you up. Because I promise you it will. It ruined my life and I don't want you to ruin yours.'

I tap out the last sentence with my glass on the table.

Baxter is gawping at me mouth wide open, half full glass halfway up to it.

And then I am swallowed up by an empty space. Fall right into it.

261

When I surface I'm in a cupboard. Coats surrounding me. Coat hanger banging off the top of my head. Hand on flesh. On warm flesh. My mouth on Jessica's. Pressing hard against it. And she tastes so good. So warm. How the fuck did I get here? She's pushing back against me, the heat of her groin against mine, hands around my neck, nails against my skin, moaning in my ear. My other hand is on my back, pulling my shirt out, forcing her hand down the back. I'm fumbling up the back of her shirt, finding the clasp of her bra, undoing it, easier than I thought, all the time thinking, she doesn't smell like Sally, she doesn't taste like Sally, kissing her hard, our teeth clacking together. My hands back round to the front, pulling her breasts out from the cups of the bra, fingers finding her nipples, twisting them hard. She shudders, pulls away from me, so I loose them, hands back down to her trousers, undo the buttons at the front, push my hand down the front, feel the lace of her pants, then inside them smooth skin, then her wet warmth. She's moaning again and I'm pulling her trousers down, saying to myself 'I want this, I want this, I want this.' Pushing down thoughts of my wife. Jessica's trousers are on the floor, she's stepping out of them. I yank my belt off, rip my flies open and she pulls my boxers down. Before I can stop myself I'm inside her and she screams out, so I put my hand over her mouth and I'm slamming into her really hard, her feet locked around my back and I'm so close, trying to stop myself as she's bucking against me and then something flashes behind me. The cupboard is lit up by a flashbulb. Then it is dark again. I pull out of her, spin round, reaching for my trousers with one hand, the door with the other. Horribly aware now of what I've done. My cock is already shrivelling as I bolt out into the corridor. No-one is there. Mutter apologies over my shoulder. Out of the bar, pushing past Alan, past Collins into the cold street and it hits me, the horror of it, of what I have just done. I raise my face up to the sky and beg the rain-filled sky for forgiveness. It laughs down at me and offers me nothing.

64.

I knock on the door to Janet's office and wait. After a minute or so she asks me to come in.

'Good morning,' she says, bursting with professional courtesy.

'Good Morning, Janet.'

She gesticulates at the empty chair opposite her. I slump into it. Even though I have rehearsed this moment in my room, even though I know exactly what I want to say, I am struggling to get it out. I suddenly feel naked and tiny.

'How can I help?'

'I think I'm ready.'

'Ready?' she asks.

'To talk about the toys. I'm ready to talk to you about the toys.'

She smiles, then immediately hides it behind a manicured hand and by clearing her throat.

'Good. That's really good news. How do you want to start?'

'Can I go and fetch them?'

'If you think that would help.'

I nod.

'Go and get them then.'

Even as I am walking down the corridor I'm questioning whether this is the right thing to do. Whether this is what it wants me to do.

In my room I face it and ask, 'Is this what you want?'

I'm not surprised when nothing happens. I didn't expect it to. I am on my own now. It is inert and empty.

The Zoo.

For now it's just toys, so I scoop them up.

The Cowboy, The Knight, The Pirate, The Soldier, The Lion, The Horse, The Zebra, The Dog, The Chicken.

Scoop them all up and run back down the corridor, before I can change my mind. Back in Janet's office I sit down and drop The Zoo onto her desk. She looks up from my file. When she sees me she tries to slam it shut, but I catch words here and there, words that aren't a surprise to me, but words I would never want to see associated with me: sectioned, cocaine psychosis and a photo of me looking wild and shamed. She pushes it aside, says, 'Okay, where do you want to begin?'

My mouth is dry.

I arrange them in chronological order, then look up at her and say, 'I want you to help me find out what they all mean.'

'The first step is to confront it and you've done that. Now we have to acknowledge each of them.'

She picks up The Cowboy.

'Tell me what he means to you.'

I am all panic and full of betrayal. I am frozen and dumb.

'It's okay,' she says, putting him back down, 'take your time. Whenever you are ready.'

My vision blurs. I swallow hard, lick my lips and then say:

'At the very top sits The Cowboy. He is crafted from metal, although his base is plastic. This seems to be the wrong way round. The metal is heavier and yet it is the plastic that does the supporting. In the past this has bothered me, I have tried to understand why he would be crafted this way, when the opposite is more logical, but the train of thought leads nowhere so I have buried it.'

65.

I'm halfway home before I remember Sally won't let me in. She has barred me from the house. She hates me and now I've given her reason to. I'm crying. I hate myself. I'm scratching at my arms, punching myself in the head. Screaming out 'no, no, no, no' until it becomes a wordless howl.

My wife.

My son.

I need them. More than anything.

I scrabble around in my pockets for my phone. Find only lint and receipts. It's gone. I must have left it in the bar. I had it when I bought drinks for Baxter. I search through them again. Not there.

Now I can't get hold of them and I can't go home.

A loneliness stronger than I could ever have imagined poleaxes me, forcing me to my knees, my face against the tarmac, pleading, begging.

Then I'm up and moving again, the world mixing with tears until it is a montage of blurred light and smears of pattern and I don't know where I'm going, just pushing on, one foot, then the other, staggering forward, perpetual motion.

Through the night, wild and incoherent. Words pouring from my mouth, speaking in tongues, spilling out into the night as it steals them away from me.

And then.

Everything pulls into focus.

I am standing in front of a billboard.

A 48-sheet poster site for a make-up company.

A perfect photoshopped face. Flawless. Smooth skin. Irridescent blue eyes. Diamond white teeth. The lie of perfection. A facsimile of feminine beauty. This false beauty we have forced on everyone. This is all you want to be, this is what we want you to be. The only way you can ever dream of attaining this is to buy these products. This skin cream. This make-up. This anti-ageing face mask. This moisturiser. This exfoliator. Buy all of this. All of this crap and even then you will fall short. Only photoshop can help you.

My eyes are filling up again. As I wipe them clear the image on the billboard changes. The features on the model change and become something I recognise. The woman in the advert is Sally.

It all hits home again and I'm telling her I'm sorry, shouting it up at her. Sorry for the drink and the drugs and abandoning our child and the way I treat her and the way I treat our friends and what I've just done about the job and the bank and the child soldiers. God. What I've just done. I'm climbing onto the roof of a car, jumping up to catch the bottom of the billboard, just my fingertips getting purchase, then the rest of my hands, managing to take my weight, pulling me up until my upper body is clear, then my knee on it, then the other and I'm standing and from here I can see the whole city. I can see it all and it's so big and so bright and I'm so small. I kiss the billboard, telling her I'm so, so sorry. I feel my balance going, arms flailing too late, then I'm in the air, falling backwards and for the time that I'm falling everything is lifted from my shoulders, until I hit the ground and the world is pain. Absolutely full of it. Then I pass out.

66.

I wake up in hospital. White. Bright white. Lilies in front of a window through which I can see a stark bright day outside. Hilary is sitting in a plastic chair at the end of the bed, reading a newspaper over the top of his glasses. He notices I'm awake.

'Fuck me,' he says, 'look what the cat dragged in.'

I laugh. Something stabs me on the inside of my ribs and makes me cough, which hurts even more.

'Easy there,' he says.

He drags his chair up to the head of the bed, pats me on the shoulder almost with tenderness.

'What happened?' I ask.

'Was kind of hoping you could tell me that. They found you in the road. Looks like you fell. God only knows what you were doing up there. Could have been a lot worse, they tell me. Should count yourself lucky.'

I try and raise myself up on my elbows, to look down at my body. Before I collapse back onto the bed I take in a bandaged torso and a plaster on my right arm.

'Broken arm. A couple of broken ribs and a bloody massive lump on the back of your head. As I said, it could have been a hell of a lot worse.'

There's pain. Lots of it.

'Have I got to stay in here?'

'No. Apparently you can leave today.'

He must see my face change.

'You're staying with me of course. Won't take no for an answer. We can look after each other. Lord knows I need the company.'

I am loose and ragged and can't say no.

Later I'm in Hilary's big car being driven to his big house, feeling every bump, being helped up his big drive to his big lounge and then helped into a big chair as he places a big glass of brandy in front of me.

'That should work nicely with your painkillers,' he says.

And all I can say is, 'Sally?'

'Not just yet, old boy. I've spoken to her. She's very angry with you.'

I feel shame. Shame I've made her feel that way. Shame that she's spoken to my friend about it.

'Harry?'

'He's okay as far as I know. She certainly didn't say otherwise. Look. Things aren't irreparable. Let's get you cleaned up. Focused on what you need to do. Let's get you back to work and firing on all cylinders and then we'll go and see her. Believe me, if you go and see her now, it's all over. Not to put too fine a point on it, you're a fucking mess. Now drink up and get some rest. We've got lots of work to do.'

The following Monday he drives me into the office, papering over the cracks and wheeling me out. Ruth fusses over me, brings me coffee into my office and pats my plaster.

'You can write on it if you want.'

She takes a pen from my desk and draws a big pair of lips.

'Ruth, I've got a confession.'

'Oh no,' she says, 'what have you done?'

I consider being playful, but it's just not in me.

'I think I've lost my phone.'

269

She is visibly relieved. It makes me wonder, not for the first time, what she thinks of me. For a long time I thought she considered me as a bit of a friendly scoundrel, but I'm not so sure any more.

'Oh, is that all? I'll get onto them. Can you do without it for a while?'

I nod and say, 'Be a bit of a relief to be honest.'

She smiles at me. A smile laced with pity and concern. I have to turn away. In my office I curl up under the desk and laugh with my fist in my mouth until I gag. Tiny feet dance on the desk above my head and the air is filled with the sound of gunfire. I stick both my fingers in my ears and hum 'Long way to Tipperary' and when I take them out the air is thick with sulphur and the room thankfully quiet. At my desk my attention wanders and when it returns I find that I've filled my pad with skull and crossbones. I start to laugh again. My skin itches under the plaster as insects crawl up and down my arm. I bite on my knuckle until it bleeds and swallow the hysteria. I can't stay in here on my own anymore, so go and talk about the weather at Ruth's desk. Over her shoulder her screensaver shows a pile of severed hands.

I'm grateful Jessica avoids me. If I think about what happened I am engulfed with a heavy wave of shameguiltregretselfdisgust. We caught eyes once and she couldn't maintain it. It occurs to me that aside from being extremely unprofessional, me running off like that probably humiliated her too.

At 2pm I tap Collins on the shoulder. He silently rises and follows me out of the office. Neither of us sign out. Surprisingly no-one seems to notice us go. Or care. On the stairs I ask him, 'You got everything?' and he pats his briefcase.

'Laptop, mini-projector, printouts, set of business cards. All there.'

'Good work,' I say.

We drive there in silence, listening to the news on the radio. The whole world is rotten with war and swimming with natural disasters. Inside I'm screaming, barely holding it together. Craving cocaine.

A couple of hours later I've pulled in at a shitty chain pub and we're at the bar with a bottle of cheap shit champagne. Collins is all smiles. Literally shining. I can see the pride through the seams on his cheap shit suit. Despite myself I am pleased. Pleased with him. He seems to have opened up to me again. I know I'm going to regret it, will look back to the days of frosty silence with fondness, but for now I'm trying to enjoy the moment. He tops my glass up. Fills his own until the bubbles fizz on the laminated bar top. I tap my plaster on the bar and it sounds hollow.

'I can't believe she said yes there and then,' he says.

'Unusual, for sure.'

'Unusual? It's fucking brilliant isn't it?'

I consider raining on his parade, but not now, not today, so I let him have his moment.

'Yes, yes it is fucking brilliant,' I say, and then with gritted teeth add, 'you did well in there.'

Ear to ear smile.

'I did? Thanks. You were brilliant. They were eating out of your hand. Don't know how you do it.'

'Practice. Years of practice. Knowing what buttons to push. And, believe it or not, there aren't that many. People are pretty simple things.'

I'm sweating. I need something. The grip of cramp on my calf and a pain lancing through my chest. I grit my teeth. The cramp is bearable. I can get through this.

271

I wave the empty bottle in front of Collins' face, water running down my forearm, say, 'this is shit, let's celebrate properly.'

His face is built around a cheesy smile, all the surliness gone, he is compliant acceptance.

Weaving into town I text Alan and Hilary, tell them to meet us in our local Italian restaurant.

Hours later, in the fog of booze and food and cigarette smoke, Hilary is leaning in close, brandy and cigar on his breath. Telling me that he was right about Collins and that he needed to do it for himself, that if we'd have given him the bank he wouldn't have appreciated it, would have coasted. I don't want to agree. Stubbornness and pride make me want to deny it. Hilary spits on my face when he talks. Alan and Collins are together at the bar. Collins looks over his shoulder, beams at me and it occurs to me that I can't deny Hilary was right to not put him on the bank. Anger flares up in me. Anger at his arrogance. I excuse myself, go to the toilet. My face is stark in the mirror. White with dark rings under my eyes. Eyes which stare right through the mirror, right through the reflection. Veteran eyes with a thousand yard stare. Bamidele is behind me, hand on my shoulder, muttering words I don't understand into my ear. His stomach cut open, the purple of his intestines visible underneath the peeled back skin of his torso. He sees me looking at them and pulls at them, unravelling them and looping them about my neck like a scarf.

Back in the restaurant I remember the chop in my inside pocket and then it is as good as over again.

67.

Janet is trying not to judge me. She's trying to keep her face neutral. I can see that she's overflowing with questions.

I am naked and shamed.

Everything is in the open. I've worked my way through the whole Zoo, she knows who they all are now.

'I would like to try something,' she says.

She's waiting for me to reply, so I say, 'Okay.'

She takes a packet of post-it notes and places it on the desk before me, then adds a marker pen.

'This is a just a hunch, so I want you to just go with it and trust me. But I think you're ready now.'

The sentence rises at the end in a question, so I nod at her, my eyes on the post-its.

'If you feel uncomfortable at any point just let me know and we'll stop. I think this will help. Okay?'

Again I nod.

'Right. I want you to take the post-its and I want you to write the name of everyone who is important to you. Everybody who means something to you. Is that okay?'

I nod and reach out for the pad. Hold it in my hand and strum the edge of it like a flick book.

'When you're ready,' she says, soft and reassuring.

I grasp the pen and place the end in my mouth. Search. Choose where to start. Glance at The Zoo.

'Do I have to like them?'

'How do you mean?'

'Do you want to me to choose the people who are most important to me because I like them?'

She considers it.

'No. People can be important because they are a negative influence as well as positive. Go with the people who have had the most impact on you. Who have driven the direction of your life. For better or worse.'

It's my turn to consider. Chew the end of the pen.

'In here or out there?' I say eventually.

'Up to you. But I think it should for the most part be people from before you began your stay with us.'

I chew the pen again. Then write HILARY in block capitals on the first post-it.

'Good,' says Janet. She tears it off and sticks it on the far left of the desk in front of me. 'Who's next?'

I write SALLY. Janet examines me over her glasses as if to say *interesting*. I scrawl HARRY on the next post-it, my hand shaking as I do so. Then ALAN on the one below. I hand them all to Janet who lays them out. I'm struggling now.

'Go on,' she says.

Write BAXTER. Hand it to her. COLLINS on another.

'Good. Any more?'

I think of the bank. Think of the effect it has had on my life. The damage it has caused. Momentarily consider writing Bamidele, before I realise I could never explain it, so instead scribble BEN. Push the pad back to Janet. Then grab it back. Write BERKSHIRE, then JESSICA, sit back and fold my arms. Lean back in the chair.

Lou? Should I include Lou? Yes. Write her name. What about Dan? No. Dan is always there, but not important. I feel a flash of guilt even as I think this, but know it's true. Good old Dan. Dependable Dan. Ineffectual Dan. An appendage to a stronger personality. No, he doesn't need to be there.

They're all there.

'Now what?' I ask her.

She takes the post-its, writes my name in an elegant hand and sticks it to the desk, then lines The Zoo up above the post-its.

'Now we choose which is which,' she says.

68.

I'm cowering in my office when I hear the smash of glass and something heavy hit the floor.

I've been looking over the creative we've produced for an energy company we work for. The words and images swim before my tired eyes, out of focus and then reforming into something threatening and hostile. Rub my eyes and pull them back to the images of wind farms and sunsets and warm reassuring copy. Then, as soon as I allow myself to drift, they twist and turn, becoming fire and skulls and the words tell me things I don't want to know.

When I hear the furore it comes as a relief.

I open my door to a room full of scared faces. Ruth points towards Hilary's office. I mouth, 'What's happening?' and she shrugs.

Another smash. Something hits the inside of the door of Hilary's office, which shudders in the frame. I knock and Hilary shouts 'fuck off' from inside. Open the door a fraction. He growls at me and launches a book at the gap. It hits the wall instead.

'What's going on?' I ask and he tells me to fuck off again.

'I'm coming in,' I say, ease myself into the room, close the door and press my back against it. Hilary's eyes are cold as he weighs up a picture frame in his right hand.

'Don't,' I say, trying to sound firm.

Hilary looks at the picture as if it's the first time he's seen it and replaces it on the desk.

276

'Sorry, old boy,' he says.

The office is a mess. The glass top of his desk is crazed with cracks, the bookcase tipped over, folders and text-books spilled from it, the tide nearly reaching my feet. Pictures have been pulled from the wall and shredded into confetti. The glass in the picture frame Hilary was holding is shattered. It's his wedding photo.

'What happened?' I ask him, although I already know.

He takes an envelope from the desk and holds it out to me.

I know what is inside before I open it. Before I read the words.

'I'm really sorry,' I say and it has more than one meaning.

'Irreconcilable differences. What does that mean any-way?'

I shrug. But I know. Even now I can see my family falling away into blackness.

'I always treated her well,' his voice choked, 'she never wanted for anything. Fair enough, we argued, but who doesn't?'

'I'm not really in any position to talk.'

Hilary pulls a bottle of whisky from under his desk, takes a huge swig from it, winces, then passes it to me. The liquid is a razor on its way down.

'I've tried talking to the old biddy, but she won't have it. She won't take my calls. I'm too old for this.'

'You don't need to be here. Let's take you home.'

I hold my unbroken arm out to him. Help him clamber over the wreck of his office. He clutches the bottle to his chest.

In the car on the way to his house, as I struggle to change gear with the weight of my plaster, he drinks continuously, chuntering about how he loves Angie, how he'd never hurt her, how she knows that, and I agree with him, nod and

277

smile, all the while thinking about condoms in a pocket and hoping against hope this isn't my fault, my heart plummeting with every mile unravelling beneath the car.

'I think I'm losing my mind,' I say, 'I'm seeing things, things that aren't there.'

Hilary doesn't acknowledge me, carries on talking.

'I know I'm a man and I shouldn't be worried about this, but I haven't been on my own for my entire adult life. I just don't have the skills that she does, never thought I'd need them. Pathetic, isn't it?'

'Violent things. Awful things. I don't know how to tell anyone. I'm going insane and I can't stop it.'

Hilary sighs and drums his fingers on the dashboard.

'I think I might hurt someone,' I say, 'I nearly hurt my son. I don't trust myself anymore. I think I'm dangerous.'

Hilary shows no sign of having heard me. He turns the radio on. The car is full of classical music. It should calm me; instead it's like blades over my skin.

'Don't let this happen to you, old boy. It's not too late for you. We'll go home. Get you cleaned up and then you need to go and see them. Beg and plead. Do whatever it takes to get them back.'

'It's possible I'll hurt them.'

Hilary nods sagely. 'Yes, it's too late for me, but we can save your marriage before it all goes to shit. I'm going to make it my mission to put things right. It's time for you to give it a whirl. Last chance saloon, old fellow.'

I trace the vein on the inside of my wrist with a numb fingertip.

69.

Sitting in my car outside my house I'm so cold my hands are numb. My neck is sore where I scraped at it with one of Hilary's blunt razors.

There's movement inside the lounge.

Swallowing my nerves I get out of the car and creep up the drive, open the gate at the side of the house and shimmy down the alleyway. In the back garden winter has taken hold of the grass, all the green has leached from it and it looks like a monochrome photograph. Framed by the window the kitchen is an oasis of warmth. It looks like the archetypal home in the tripe I pump out to sell stuff. Half expecting it to be locked, I try the back door and am shocked when it swings open. I slide my shoes off at the door. The sound of the TV wafts into the kitchen, welcome as the smell of freshly baked bread. The lounge door is slightly open. Through it I can see the back of Harry's head, bobbing along with the theme tune of a kids' programme.

I step into the lounge.

Sandra jumps up from the sofa.

'What the f- . James. What happened to you? What are you doing here?' Her plummy accent is sharpened by hysteria.

'I've come to see my son.' I say.

'D-d-d-d-dad,' says Harry, moving towards Sandra, who puts her arm across his chest.

I kneel, so I am at his head height.

'I missed you, Harry. I love you. I wanted to see you. Don't worry about this,' I say, waving my arm in front of him, 'Daddy had a little accident.'

He looks up at Sandra and then me, confusion on his face.

'Sandra, don't try and stop my son from coming to me.' Attempting to keep my voice calm, to stop it being threatening. I'm not succeeding. I know she's scared of me and despite myself I get a thrill from this.

'Okay,' she says and lets go of Harry.

'Harry, come and give me a cuddle, I've missed you.'

He's thinking about it. I can see the turmoil in his little head, see it register in flickers of his eyes, from his Gran to his Father.

'Come on, Harry,' my arms reach out. He leaves me hanging there.

Sandra kneels too. Looks right in his face. Right in my son's face and says, 'Harry darling, would you mind going into your room for a minute, Nanna and Daddy need some adult time.'

He looks at me, his eyes a question and right there I know I haven't lost him, that it's not too late, so I nod and he shuffles out of the room.

The minute the door is closed I turn on Sandra. 'How fucking dare you try and stop my son coming to me. My fucking son.'

She's rattled. Her gaze rests on my clenched fists.

'You did this. Don't try and turn the blame on me, young man.'

'Fuck you,' I say, 'you meddling old witch. You've never liked me. And now you see your chance. I won't let you though, I won't let you use my son as a wedge between Sally and me.'

'She doesn't want you here. And she doesn't want you near Harry. Not at the moment.'

The red mist is descending, filling the lounge, I can hardly see through it. This is not what I wanted. This is not what I planned. Anger and hatred are coiled up in my stomach.

'Do not think that you can speak for my wife and child.'

'I'm only repeating what she has told me. I think you need to leave now. You're scaring me and you're scaring Harry.'

I slam myself down in the sofa, kick off my shoes.

'You can't tell me to leave my own home. Now, why don't you fuck off and meddle in someone else's family and leave mine alone.'

Sandra is white. Her hands are shaking as she pulls her mobile phone out of her trouser pocket and goes out into the hall. I can catch odd words. Assume she is talking to Sally.

I want to speak to Harry. To calm him down, to tell him everything is going to be alright. In the hall Sandra is sitting on the bottom step of the stairs. I try to step over her but she stands and puts her arm across the stairs. I can't believe she's doing this, didn't think she'd have the balls. I peel her fingers off the bannister and lift her arm. She immediately puts the other one down. I peel that one away. The first one replaces it. Anger boils over. I raise my hand, anger encouraging me to backhand her across the face. The look on her face, horror, disgust, fear, pity, stops me.

As I make my way into the lounge she says, 'Sally is on her way back to deal with this.'

'Good,' I say and sit down on the sofa, my hands shaking so hard that I can't light an illicit cigarette.

70.

The Zoo is lined up in front of me. In front of the line of yellow post-its. Above them both is Janet's face, expectant and eager.

Inside I am confused and terrified. Feel like this is a test, one orchestrated through the collusion of The Zoo and Janet. One that I don't want to fail.

Is this what The Zoo wants? Has it pushed me here? There certainly feels an inevitability about this. I've been hiding from it for so long, maybe it is time to confront it? But what if doing this angers it? What if by trying to define it like this I awaken it again? The damage it could inflict in here is terrible, it's already shown that, and I can't help thinking about the piece of paper with Beth's name on it. But then Bamidele pushed me this way too and he seems to know what it wants.

And there is Janet. She seems to have been wanting me to get to this moment too.

'Shall I help you?' she asks.

My eyes pass over The Zoo.

The Cowboy.

The Knight.

The Pirate.

The Soldier.

The Lion.

The Rhino.

I push them aside to make a gap where The Ape should sit.

The Horse.
The Zebra.
The Dog.
The Chicken.
Then I look at the names.
JAMES.
BEN.
BAXTER.
COLLINS.
JESSICA.
SALLY.
LOU.
ALAN.
HILARY.
BERKSHIRE.
HARRY.

I can't. I can't equate my son with all this violence. I shake my head vigorously and mouth no.

She can sense my anguish. Pats my hand, says, 'it's okay, don't worry. We can stop whenever you want. You can change it any time. Just try putting a name next to one of the toys. It doesn't matter if any are left over. It's just an exercise.'

I snatch up HILARY. Run through The Zoo. There is only one place he could sit.

He is at the top. He is the principal and takes his place as a leader of men with a stoic acceptance I respect. He knows this is his position, he expects it, but doesn't seek it, and this is why it is his.

I stick the HILARY post-it to the desk underneath The Cowboy.

Next I pick up BAXTER. This is harder. Much harder. I dial through the story of The Zoo. A flash of warm feeling that surprises me. I am genuinely fond of the boy. I am worried for him.

He is an Andalusian, purebred and Mediterranean, you can see the passion in the flare of his nostrils and the arrogant tilt of his head. I've never seen The Cowboy ride him of course, I believe though, that if he wanted to ride him then the horse would allow it.

I position BAXTER under The Horse.

'Good,' says Janet, 'you're doing great.'

'More?'

'Yes please,' she says. My hand hovers over the next post-it.

71.

In the empty lounge I huddle around a small fire of photographs on a plate and my mind projects images of murder onto the wall. I light a cigarette from the flames and it burns until the ash falls onto my carpet.

Sally is gone.

Harry is gone.

My family leaking away from me like heat from a bleeding radiator.

Sometime in the night Bamidele appears on the other side of the flames.

'The first time I went into the mine it was so hot that I could not breathe.' He sounds older. 'It was like climbing down into hell. Now it takes me so long to get down there I stay for a week. Hundreds of us in there. Hot. Torches strapped to our heads. The bang of our tools against rock,' his voice drifts away, his face distorting in the flickering candlelight. Changing. Hints of Hilary. Skin turning white. Eyes sinking into black pits.

Thinking back about Sally, her arm around Harry. Pulling him away from me. Screaming in my face. Stopping herself from swearing, but full of venom. Sheer hatred. Refusing to allow me to speak. Screaming infidelity. Screaming cheater and I understand that she knows. She knows.

Denial and feigned hurt, my mind scurrying underneath, looking for excuses, for a way out.

Bamidele passes me a magazine. A finger on the advert.

He hands me a pair of scissors. I hack it out, hack it and tear it. He points at the wall. Gesticulates at my hand, I hold it out. He takes the scissors from me and draws the blade across my palm. Presses the advert onto the wound and then crosses the room, sticks it to the wallpaper with the blood. I watch crimson seep through the image. Watch it stain the smiling face of the happy couple. He leaves the room. I can hear him clattering about in the kitchen. I pick up the bottle of red wine, push the cork through with my thumb and take a deep, bitter slug.

Thinking back.

Sally holding her phone out, stabbing at the screen. Taking it from her, knowing even then what it was. Looking at the text, seeing the image. Remembering the flash, remembering the chase. Seeing my number attached to it. Denial. Complete denial. All the while I'm scrabbling to unravel it. To understand it, how the text came from me. Her palm stinging my face. The tears on her face.

Bamidele is back with a pile of papers and magazines. He slams them down in front of me, then the scissors on top. He turns the TV on, and the images spill out of the screen onto the walls and fill the lounge. We are amongst them – figures and words about us, threatening us from the corners of the room. Then it is there. The advert. The smiling faces, the bone white teeth. Instinctively I reach for the remote. He snatches it away. I grab for it again. He skips away, too agile for me, I stumble to the TV, turn it off, but the images are still there on his face, dancing across his dark skin. He's laughing. I take another slug of the wine and squeeze my eyes shut.

Thinking back.

Sally shouting at me demanding that I leave. Me refusing. My home. My home. Our home. And her screaming no, no, this is no longer a home, you killed it. She's slapping me, stinging blows on my face and I take them, each one jolting my neck. Taking them, wanting them, welcoming each jarring blow.

Sally throwing the toys at me. The gifts I asked Ruth to buy. Shouting, 'You can't buy him, you can't buy us.'

It's over.

Sally is gone.

Harry is gone.

And I am alone with Bamidele.

I pick up the scissors and take a magazine from the top of the pile. Flicking through, it doesn't take long to find the first advert.

The images dance across Bamidele's teeth as he laughs at me.

72.

The name on the post-it is ALAN. I scroll through The Zoo and try them all for size, all along knowing where he should go.

The Pirate is the first of The Plastics and the last of The Figurines. His sheen and gloss is peerless amongst them. This is the reason that he is first, because he is quite child-like in his rendering, certainly nowhere near as delicately drawn as The Knight. It is his sheen that saves him. As Head of The Plastics he has his own subjects to lead, but answers to The Metallics.

Tipping up the base of The Pirate I slide ALAN'S name underneath. My fingers burn as I remember dropping him and I want to apologise.

Janet is all encouragement. All professional smile.

Next.

COLLINS.

The Zebra by contrast is squatter, his flanks broader and less elegant. Although his markings go some way to compensate for his lack of finesse, they can only go so far. In those Rorschach stripes I see moths, a crow, a rictus smile, a betrayal and the end of days.

The Zebra's back is not strong enough to hold the weight of a man. He cannot carry us like the Horse can and he tries to make up for it with pretty patterns.

Collins through and through. No hesitation. Collins is The Zebra.

Janet taps her finger in the gap.

'What is this for?' she asks.

She knows. I told her. I fucking told her.

'I told you,' holding it down. Biting it back. The Ape will have to wait, so I scan the remaining names.

Mine. SALLY. LOU. JESSICA. BEN. HARRY. BERK-SHIRE.

The Knight. The Ape. The Dog. The Chicken. The Soldier. The Rhino. The Lion.

I take the easy option and pick up BEN.

Put him straight under The Dog.

Maybe if The Dog was a Collie or a Husky then he would be higher, but he is a mongrel, the sort seen scavenging on the streets of a South American city. The sort seen trotting behind malnourished teenage gang members, being chased away from bins with a stick, only to return when the humans have left.

He came from the wolves, but he is tamed, broken and beaten. He runs alongside us, docile, friendly and not as intelligent as we like to think.

We train him to walk us when we are blind, but we also dress him in human clothes and carry him around in handbags as trophies to our ego. He is fashion and as such is utterly ridiculous.

Poor Ben. He knew and he tried to warn me. He gave me the opportunity to stop it.

Something smashes in the hallway. The sound of raised voices and running feet. I swivel my head round. When I look back at Janet she hasn't moved. She's used to it, immune to the noises of the ward.

'Don't worry about it,' she says, 'someone else will sort it. We don't need to worry about it. This time here is just for me and you. Carry on when you're ready.'

The Knight.

He is about fighting for an ideal, for a belief even if that means committing wrong in the process. He is the muscle behind a cause. The horrific violence that only unthinking loyalty can deliver.

LOU?

The Knight has a sword as his peacemaker, a long sword. And he leans nonchalantly on it as he looks off into the distance, the wind whipping his dark shoulder-length hair up around his face. It is this alertness that makes him The Cowboy's lieutenant; he is surveying the horizon, protecting The Cowboy's domain. But you have to ask whether he is happy with this position, whether that alertness is something more sinister.

SALLY?

It could be either. He could be either.

'Can I put two names to this one and come back to it?'

'Of course,' she says, 'whatever feels right.'

I want to tell her that none of this feels right. That this could anger The Zoo.

73.

The TV is off. The phone is off. Still, I am drowning in the messages. They fill my lungs and my throat until I am gasping and gagging and struggling for air, my broken ribs stabbing at me.My words makes up a blood stained montage on the wall of the lounge.

Days have gone by.

Time means nothing.

Bamidele brings me magazines and newspapers and fliers. I cut them out and stick them in my gallery with my own blood. He tells me of the success of the campaign. How my poisonous words have increased sales, the public impression of the bank has improved. I have been successful in my work. I can just imagine the smiles and the congratulations. In the past I would have been pleased with what I have done.

Instead I scream at a wall of print.

As I piss thick yellow urine into a stained bowl I catch a glimpse of myself in the mirror. I am a ghost. Newspaper print spells out reversed threats on my white cheeks.

I search the house and find all the transmitting devices, pile them up, full of horror at the amount of them. At the ways that the insidious little words and slogans and propaganda seep into our lives. At the drip, drip, drip of all this poison. Even there, in the mound, I can hear them whispering to me, telling me secrets and making me promises. From the garden shed I get a crowbar and an axe and set about them. Even when they are reduced to an electronic graveyard the words are there.

Once there are no transmitters left, Bamidele tells me to go outside. I'd forgotten there was such a thing. We stand on the threshold and wait for the world to slow down before stepping out onto it. The pavement is cold to my bare feet. The wind stings as I breathe it in.

The sound is almost unbearable. The air crackles with it. The hum of electricity in the overhead wires. The voices coursing down the phone lines. The megabytes screaming through the cables under my feet. I spread my fingers wide and force them through the viscous mobile conversations about me. I can see the traces left by my hand amongst the words. Amongst the breakups and the arguments and the laughter and teasing and emotional confessions, through the day to day chatter, through the confusion and collusion, through the monotone and through the diatribe.

I stumble past a string of 6-sheets, each one with my face on them. Each one taunting me. My face. Grimacing at me. Saying, you know. You know.

As I get nearer to the city centre it's worse. People walk around me, avoid my gaze and there is always the noise of the messages. They increase, and I'm washed along in them. My feet no longer need to move. I am swept along in the river of messages. It washes me up in front of an electronics shop, where I press lacerated palms against the glass.

An ambulance tears past me, the siren rattling me, the screech scraping my bones, blue light throwing dancing shadows about me.

A stray dog stands next to me, baleful and shy. I shoo it, shove it with my leg. It doesn't move, just pushes itself against my leg, showing no sign of hearing me, understanding or caring.

On the TV screens are repeated images of an ape sucking its multitude of teeth at me.

My reflection in the glass as I look into dark chimp eyes. A foot hanging over the edge of a hammock. The swirl of fingerprints, calloused and grey. A lip curled over human teeth. It picks at its nose and the gesture is so familiar. The blink of an eye and in it I can see recognition, understanding, empathy.

Harry showed me the sign language for chimp.

I call at the chimp, call its name at the glass and the chimp turns, looks at me and I am screaming, 'it heard me, it heard me, it knows its name'.

I look at its hand on the screen then my own pressed against the glass and I see the comparison, grasp the link between us. I look down at the dog, blissfully unaware of the noise all around it and then up at the chimp, see how the chimp understands, again the link between us, and I wiggle my thumb and the ape wiggles its thumb too, back again at the dog, at its stationary paw.

In that moment I understand, understand the difference between us and the animals, how the chimp understands it all too, but the dog doesn't. Then in an explosion of clarity I know absolutely know how I can make the noise stop, what I must do and where I must do it.

74.

JESSICA.

The only Animal below The Dog is The Chicken and he has no worth other than fodder. They are the last of The Plastics. They are well thumbed. Like The Rhino's horn The Dog's tail has been chewed, flattened with teeth marks. Without the rule of The Cowboy they would simply be wild and aimless. They are after all the beasts and this is what they do. They are the mongs, the spackers, the retards. They are the brainless, the followers, the masses.

I push Jessica underneath The Chicken. There is no doubt. I look at the gap where The Ape should be.

He is a spy in the camp of The Animals. He is one of them, but not of them. He is a surreptitious link between The Cowboy and his mindless followers in The Animals. And now he is the missing link.

He is like us. But not.

He is a Chimpanzee. He squats with his knuckles down, touching the ground. He is looking up under sad eyebrows. His eyes are just black dots, but within them is sadness and knowledge and when he looks at me I see a reflection of myself. He lived in a society that is structured like ours, then he lived in The Zoo, in a society that is also structured, just not in the same way. From the way he is bowed, the way his head is lowered, eyes looking up, it is obvious to me that he is not the alpha male. I could tell this even if I didn't know his position within The Zoo.

Like us he can laugh, but there are no laughter lines around his eyes. Just a smooth pink face ringed in plastic fur that doesn't move in the wind, stays frozen for all time, moulded and immobile.

He is our closest relative, regal and dignified, collected by Solomon, important to Darwin. He is dressed as Man, laughed at and pointed at and ridiculed. He is a comic sidekick. We can laugh at him because he is us, but can't complain at our jibes.

He tried to stop Charlton Heston from discovering the truth. He is Tarzan's faithful companion. He is a reminder to us of our superiority and how far we can fall. He is a group of chimps drinking tea while lip-synching to northern stereotypes. He is learning to use tools in front of a black monolith. He is a character in a book that Beth is reading.

I put my name under the gap.

And for now it is done.

I collapse back in the seat, exhausted, exposed. Afraid of what The Zoo might do.

'Well done,' Janet says, 'Really well done.'

I nod. Squeeze out a flat smile.

'I'm proud of you, I think we've made real progress.'

In that moment I realise it's been a very, very long time since anyone said that to me and it is a struggle to stop myself being overcome with emotion.

'I think that's enough for today.' She waves a hand over The Zoo. 'We'll leave this here for now, okay?'

I surprise myself by agreeing and return to my room hollowed out and rattling.

75.

Back home I ignore Bamidele, force myself to imagine he is not there, as I shower and watch weeks of disgust spiral away down the plughole.

I am determined now. Lucid.

I take out pen and paper. My hand has to remember how to write.

Dear Baxter, I write at the top of the paper, *you are too good for this business. It will eat you up and spit you out. Take this, use it to marry your girl, and get out. Go somewhere else and do something else.*

I write him a cheque. Worry about how many zeros to put on it. Stick it in the envelope and seal it before I can change my mind.

On another sheet of paper I write the name of Hilary's wife at the top and then tell her the truth.

Next I call Sally. Her phone goes straight to answerphone, so I tell her the truth too. All of it. Every last little bit.

I pull a shirt from the wash basket, press it flat with a lukewarm iron and force myself into a suit. All the time I'm pushing Bamidele away, brushing aside his pleas, his questions about what I am doing. I cannot be stopped now. I must not be stopped.

Outside the world spins.

Behind the wheel of the car I remember how to start it and roll it out into the street.

When I enter the office Ruth smiles warmly, squeezes my arm and tells me she is glad to see me. Baxter isn't in yet, so I push the envelope under his keyboard until just the corner is showing. As I cross the open space I see Collins, who says, 'Sorry to hear about your wife.'

I try to decipher what his smirk/smile means, wonder about the phone, assume it must have been him, he must have taken my phone, my temper threatens but then remember why I am here and what I must do, so lock myself in the office.

Then I wait until it's the monthly board meeting.

I've got a pad in front of me and I've written *fuck you, fuck you, fuck you, fuck you* next to the names of the other Directors. There's all these words floating around us: Hilary is looking at me with his veiny face and bulbous drink nose, he is saying something about forward-loading and I think I'm supposed to reply so I pretend to check something on my pad and say something back about Media Spend Analysis and Return On Investment, about Tangible Measurable Results that will lead us into the Next Quarter, and from the way they are all looking at me I realise it wasn't a sentence so I excuse myself and go to the kitchen. I splash water onto my face. I try and breathe, but the same thought keeps coming back to me – now is the time, do not stray.

I open the drawer under the sink to get some painkillers and find the cleaver. I take it out, hold the cold metal to my forehead and everything feels a little better. I tuck it into the back of my suit trousers and go back into the meeting,

They look up at me briefly as I enter, the conversation continues, but I don't want to understand the words, I want it to be somewhere between the fuzz of the un-tuned television and animals. And it's clear.

A chimp's hand on the glass. How the chimp understood,

the link between us, the opposable thumb and the dog, its paw, and the difference between us and the animals and how the chimp understands too. It's all about the opposable thumb. The animals don't have it, so they are separate and they don't hear or have to understand the noise.

No going back.

I have to give up my humanity. I have to lose the understanding. Become an animal. So I take the cleaver out and watch them recoil, scuttle about the room like cockroaches, trying to flatten themselves against the skirting boards. I lay my left hand flat on the glass table and swing the blade down onto the joint of my left thumb, struggling to hold the cleaver even as the bulk of my plaster gives the arc weight , and it goes about halfway through, so I drop the blade again, but this time it goes all the way, severing it, hitting the glass underneath, shattering the table. I look at Hilary, his face speckled with my blood, he is speaking and already I can only just understand him. The words are going. Thankfully, they're all going. So I swop the cleaver, clenching it with difficulty in my remaining fingers, shove my other thumb out of the plaster, my blood pumping onto the table as I try to raise the cleaver but Alan has hold of my arm, then Hilary is up too and they're wrestling me down, my face flat against the frame of the table and one of them smashes my hand against the table leg, my grip loosening, smashes it again, the handle of the cleaver impossible to hold in my blood-slick fingers, and it's now that the pain hits me, searing pain, shooting up and down my arm. Someone is screaming, Me. I am screaming. Someone else is hollering for help. More people now. My arm is behind my back and I'm forced onto the ground. All the fight gone from me. The harsh carpet against my face. Then there are medics and police and painkillers and I drift away.

76.

Back in the office. Janet is waiting for me. Waiting for The Zoo. So I address it again. Grab The Lion and put it in place.

He sits like the Sphinx and there seems to be a trace of a smile on his face.

He is the endangered species that is also the top of the food chain. He is losing his fight with Man the species and paradoxically is individually more powerful, more instinctual and more deadly.

I take SALLY from where I left her and slide her under The Lion. Feels right. Feels perfect.

Two more names. BERKSHIRE and HARRY. Sitting opposite The Soldier and The Rhino.

The Rhino.

He is an automaton. A tank. He is bullish and instinctual. He is prehistoric. The past in the present.

He is thick skin.

He is point and go. A machine. Trampling. Squashing. Barging.

Berkshire. No doubt about it.

That just leaves . . .

HARRY and The Soldier.

He doesn't stand, he can't stand, he leans and rocks on his ridge like a weeble and for this reason, despite the sensory pleasure I derive from him, he is lower in the ranking than you would immediately think he should be.

Harry the boy soldier. Seeing things he shouldn't. A pawn in other people's games. Lower in the ranking than he should be. It is so pertinent I nearly cry. He should always have been number one.

When I can bring myself to look at Janet the horror on my face is reflected in her eyes.

'Well done,' she says, 'well done.'

Later my room seems empty. I stare at the lumps in the ceiling, at the indentations I made with my thumbnail and I wait.

Eventually I fall asleep.

I dream I am in the corridor, the floor is chequered and I am walking the hall using the moves of a Knight and I can't make it back to my room, I keep missing the door because making his move doesn't allow me to reach it and I can feel a scream growing inside me, growing and growing until it's too big. I'm trying to keep it in, but I can't, then it's out there and hands are on my shoulders and they find my room, because they don't need to use his move. The door is slammed shut after me. There are childlike words scrawled on it, *the truth*.

Then it is morning and I am lying in a noose of the sheet. It's rapped tight around my body and it looks like sinew. I feel calmer but the sheets are wet and they cling to me and I thrash about trying to get free as they tighten and tighten. When I am free I perch on the edge of the bed, shaking, my knee twitching up and down with the exertion and I think of The Zoo and I remember the way a Knight moves.

The move.

I run through it in my head. It is important to remember it, so I run through it.

Two squares horizontally and one square vertically.

Or two squares vertically and one square horizontally. Think. Think, Think. Two and one. One and Two.

The move means The Knight can jump over other pieces. The Knight is not stopped by a bank of other pieces. The move means that The Knight is at its most powerful in closed positions. I realise that's fucking it and I'm through the door, hitting it hard, so it slams back against the wall, the noise fills the corridor and an orderly looks up from the desk with a face full of contempt, so I gently close it to and raise my hands in apology and surrender. I mouth 'sorry' and she shakes her head and goes back to her magazine. I think of the ad space in between the pages and think 'I fucking own you' and I feel a bit better about her.

I make my way to Janet's office and knock on the door. From inside I hear her ask me to come in. I want to confront The Zoo. I don't want to appear nervous, but I don't want to be too cocky either, so I sit in the chair, casual and then quickly, before I lose my nerve, lift The Knight, remove LOU, take my name from under The Ape and swop them over. I lean back, afraid of the response, but nothing happens so I know I'm right. Janet smiles at me. Minutes pass.

LOU is under The Ape. She knew. She was the only one who knew, the only one who understood all along. It crosses my mind again that she could have been sending me the messages. Then realise it doesn't matter.

'Is that right?' Janet asks, 'Are you done?'

'Yes,' I say, 'definitely.'

She leans into a drawer under her desk and takes out a copy of the Times.

'Then you're ready for this.'

She leafs through it, finds the page she was looking for and folds it open on the desk between us.

A full page advert. White text on a black background. I read through it. Raise my head, a questioning eyebrow at Janet. She smiles encouragement. It's all there. About the mines and the children. About the bank and the blood

301

minerals. About what they are doing and about how they lie. About the lies I was peddling for them. At the bottom is my signature.

'You did this,' she says, 'Before you went into the board meeting for the last time.'

'I did this?'

'Yes, for one day you changed all the adverts in all of the major papers.'

And I remember. I remember the surreptitious emails. I remember writing this. Writing this and sending it off. Sending it on the same reference numbers, then calling the papers to tell them the ads had been updated, knowing they wouldn't check them.

I smile and say, 'What happened?'

'What do you think happened?'

'I imagine they were pretty fucked off.'

'That would be an understatement. I'll let you find out the rest, but it's not ignored anymore. People everywhere are aware of what is happening in Nghosa and they want things to change. You should be very proud of yourself.'

I want to be. I really do.

'I've done some terrible things,' I say.

'And one great thing. Are you ready to tell me all about where these came from now?' An elegant hand takes in all of The Zoo.

I think of my son. Already his face is fading in my memory. I feel his little hand in mine, and the softness of his blond hair as I place my palm protectively on his head, but there is a gap and then only the moment when he is taken from me in a hospital room, just as he hands me the string bag with The Zoo in it. The toys I asked Ruth to buy him to apologise for my behaviour: The Cowboy, The Knight, The Pirate, The Soldier, The Lion, The Rhino, The Ape, The Horse, The Zebra, The Dog, The Chicken. Then he is pulled away, mouthing 'Daddy' and they are turning him away from me. I can't see him amongst the adults. I am left holding a yellow string bag. My son is gone and I have only The Zoo.

'Can I give them back to him?' I ask.

'I'll see what I can do, but I can't promise anything.'

I'll take that for now.

I get my cigarettes out of my pocket and go to leave. I can't resist it though and tap the paper, where it says 'James' and lean in, whisper to The Knight.

'I fucking know you.'

I take his silence as acceptance.

77.

Waiting. I'm in the garden, smoking a cigarette. I'm nervous. First day of school nervous. The sun is warm on my face. I close my eyes, the inside of my eyelids purple. Bask in the heat. I'm drifting off when I sense someone next to me. I open my eyes. Beth. She's holding two cups of tea.

I start to apologise. Struggle for the words. Stop. Take another swig. Start again, but I can't find the way to say it. Not without explaining The Zoo and that would mean explaining everything.

Instead I say nothing. She puts the tea down on the bench and leaves me there.

Sometime later I return to the day room and watch facile daytime television and try not to fidget too much.

Just before they are due to arrive I return to my room and shower, put on a fresh shirt and pace.

A knock on the door. I open it to Janet. She leads me down the corridor, waits for the outer door to buzz, presses the string bag into my hand and gestures for me go through. I momentarily pause, then step over the threshold.

In a small room on the ground floor. I sit drumming my fingers on the table and tapping my feet on the lino. The door opens and they are there. My family. Sally and Harry. My everything. I rise shakily to my feet. Sally sits without saying anything. Harry holds his hand out formally and I shake it, tiny in my palm.

I push the string bag across the table to him. He reaches

into his pocket and shows me The Ape, then puts it in the bag and gives the whole thing to Sally.

As we sit in silence the camera begins to track away from us and from where I'm sitting I can see the plywood backing to everything. The orange make-up of the actors under the lights, the plastic whiteness of their teeth and perfect hair. I look at the darkness behind the dome made by the studio lights and I can't see the ceiling, can't see the back wall, just black extending back and back and back, and my eyes un-focus, a softness around the edge of things, still falling away from me, so far so good, so far so good, so far so good.